Created, as a humble gift,
for a beautiful Creator.

The Sawdust Festival

By: Jordan Robertson

Preface

It was the finest of times, it was the foulest of times, it was the era of perception, it was the era of folly, it was the period of certainty, it was the period of calamity, it was the spell of light, it was the spell of darkness, it was the spring of promise, it was the winter of misery, all was before us, all had passed us, we were all heading to a good place, we were all heading to somewhere of torture, -shortly, our place was like so many other places, the sawdust festival ruled, the loudest authorities insisted on it being received without an excellent degree of judgment on our parts, for good or for evil, the sawdust festival reigned supreme!

And because of this, they said the mill was the best place to work in town, they still say it is in other places; but I'm not so sure? Why didn't I think my job at the mill was a great one? Very simply because other than the pay being rather minimal, as they felt your primary reward was from the ostensible enjoyment derived from the sawdust you helped produce, it was a very tiresome job. Long hours, little rest, and sawdust, constant sawdust, everywhere all-the-time, it was maddening!

The mill as it were, is where all the sawdust for our region was produced, so it was a highly desirable place to work, at least from an outsider's perspective. I have always thought perspective to be an interesting thing; because you see something, and it makes sense to you in

1

a unique way. The way I see something is different than the way you see something, though we may observe this thing very similarly, it is not identical. Kind of like a snowflake, formed and shaped by its individual weather conditions, scientists, or mathematicians, will tell you 'there will never be another like it': is that true? I'm not sure about that either, but I think you understand what I'm trying to communicate.

So what is it that forms our perspectives? Though I don't pretend to have the most insightful, or text book answer, I have thought about the question, and feel for our purposes, I can draw some parameters. Experience being in the for-front, we all endeavor to reconcile how we think, feel, and behave, with a generalized norm from our environment. That is to clarify: when I taste something sweet, something I like, like ice cream, I have a natural response, especially when I see others like it also, to say that is good. And when I stub my toe, it hurts, I say that is bad. Each incident revolves around my mind with certain force, influencing my future choices, and thus, depending very much so on that initial experience, my perspective on ice cream, and stubbing my toe are formed.

I will elucidate on perspective as we continue our journey through my story. What is my story? Well, that is a good question, but reading further will answer that. A better question for us now is, why do I tell you my story? I can answer that in a rather simple way, so I will do that now: it's so I may inform you of places you would rather not go, and if you find yourself already in one of the places I have been, I shall expound on how I found my way out.

This being mentioned; as I was saying, I work at the mill, or rather I used to work at the mill, it burnt down a couple months ago, and for that I am quite grateful! Gratitude is a strange beast, for it is rarely seen until some travesty happens, and then we acknowledge its pertinent existence. As if a giant grizzly bear were sitting in your living room eating honey, but not noticing it until you go to make toast; grizzly gratitude roams about waiting to be observed and shown respect. Why do I have all this gratitude? My hope is that, that is the picture I will paint for you with my words, as we push forward.

To make some clarification as we trod, the writers treading; the mill is the name of 'the mill'. For whatever reason, although every place that mills wood is a mill, they never gave ours a special name. I suspect when they build another one, as they most surely will, that one will get a special name, as it should.

I shall humbly ask for your forgiveness ahead of time for my digressions. They are sure to be had, and although I would say with apt reason; as to inform the reader of necessary qualities surrounding a given situation, to make what I'm saying clear and unabridged, they can make one weary. I will do my utmost to keep these diatribes to a minimum, and make them strictly pertain-able to the story at hand. Or that is to say, of a pithy nature. If you can't tell, I enjoy writing, so I will do my best to tell my story in an interesting way.

The country I live in, which I shall not name, as to protect the egos of those who live therein, is a country that loves sawdust! Twice a year, in the spring and the fall, we have a festival. Much-ado is made about these times, and one might even observe that all the time in-between each festival is only growing anticipation of the one to come.

The festival is held at a central location in the region, to make participation fair and accessible for all. The central location, as deemed by the authorities, is called the beacon-of-hope. I suspect this very misleading name, came about as a result of some clever marketer who wished to quiet naysayers of the festival, and promote a feeling of goodness by all those who participate. Needless to recognize, after much pomp, and several laws passed by the government, the name stuck.

That's a good place to stop: I think enough detail has been espoused by myself thus far, and further telling would become redundant, as you will see much of this explains itself while my story unfolds. So without further ado, bear with me, keep an open mind, think keenly, or as my violin instructor used to say, 'listen carefully', and let the story begin:

1

It was an early morning, as all mornings on your first day of work tend to be. The spring sawdust festival had just concluded, and the people were reveling in a feeling of goodness and kindness towards all. I having participated in the festival myself, enjoyed what had occurred at the beacon-of-hope, and longed for another time, a time when I would never have to leave. I woke up that morning thinking grand romantic dreams of my days to come at the mill, and how, on a daily basis, I could steal a bit of happiness from that place.

My friend Nathan, being an engineer who worked on designing some of the equipment for the milling process, had the ear of management at the mill. And calling in several favors, management being filled with generosity from the festival themselves, gave me a job. I paced my living room floor in anticipation of this beginning!

It was Monday, another day like any other. The sun was up early, enjoying a cup of cedar infused coffee; I fantasized about the day to come. Not just any fantasies, but the anxious fantasies of something new, and indulgent. Like the first time you get to cuddle with a girl other than your mother: if I draw her close, will she pull away? What if I accidently touch a place I'm not supposed to? It was torturous thinking, very tortuous indeed!

Then pacing, watching the rising sun, I began to ask myself other questions. Like, I wonder if we are allowed to take home the rejected sawdust? If they cannot use it for the festival or sell it, why not? That was a pleasant thought, free sawdust.

Sawdust was expensive, and the rarest ground-woods could cost you a small fortune. It was costly for a few reasons, one being everyone indulged in it in some way or another, and I mean everyone! From the most educated, to the dull; from the most pleasant disposition, to the most cantankerous; for rich or for poor, for sickness or in health, it permeated all of society. And it was in everything: from drinks like cedar flavored coffee, to oak scented perfumes, even sawdust textured paint, you couldn't escape it!

But as I was saying, I was pacing my porch, butterflies abounding in my stomach. My muscles were tense, and sweat would form on my upper lip at the thought I might mess something up on my first day on-the-job.

The weather was warm and the air smelled of freshly cut grass. The mill sat on the Hoio River, by far the largest river in the region, and one that connected itself to a continental water shed. Part of the mill, the old part, was water powered. This was very cost effective, and it was great to be environmentally conscious while you ground up every tree you could get your hands on. Because when nature provided part of your energy need unsolicited; you could at least, in this way, not feel so bad about what you were doing.

My house sat on the edge of town, not in the bustling city, but not in the complete staleness of the country either. It was nice, I liked it, and it provided a healthy morning walk to work. On my first walk to work, I walked more swiftly than I planned. I had noticed myself crossing streets more quickly than usual, and I slowed my pace. But every time I did this my mind would soon wander to the day before me, or my reviling memories of the festival past. Such was life in this land, never ending thoughts of tree molestation!

Peaking one of the large hills in town, I could see the giant smoke stacks by the river. Part of the expansion done on the mill ten years prior, it was a grand sight. The stacks billowing smoke with intensity; the intensity of an angry dragon spewing forth steam from his nostrils. It left the red brick columns looming with imposition. And just as every other time, goose bumps formed on my arms, staying longer than normal, at the thought, I would be entering those hallowed grounds very soon. "I forgot my lunch" I said to myself, my wandering mind had left more at home than just my sense. Well, they are sure to have something to eat there, I told myself. So I continued my walk, skylarking with pleasure, nothing able to deter me from my feeling of optimism.

Security was tight around the mill. There was an honor system in place a century ago that had kept the mill protected, but deforestation had caused people to lose their honor, I'm guessing. Cement barriers now stood near the roads and the entrance, razor wire fence was next, and last but not least armed men with dogs; very mean looking dogs. I've always wondered where they got those ferocious looking canines?

As I walked up to the security booth, I pulled a pint of oak aged whiskey from my pocket and took a swig. It was a grand way to prove my allegiance to the powers-at-be, as a tree lover trying to infiltrate the grounds to sabotage equipment, would never so flagrantly show their love for this wood infused nectar. I passed through security unhindered. Taking the job acceptance letter from my pocket, I read the building number one Mack Avenue, and began looking for the address.

The large white building sat in the shade of several old growth yellow pines. I stopped before the trees and touched the bark. It was amazing, I had never seen trees this big before and they were beautiful. The shade felt pleasant, I smelled the fresh pine needles and was overcome with the thought of what an entire forest, enveloped in the aroma of these magnificent trees would be like. "Hey you, get away from that tree before I take you to confinement!" Someone yelled; looking back, I saw it was one of the armed men with the angry dogs. "Yes sir, I apologize, it's just; I've never seen a tree like this before." I offered in my defense, stepping back into the hot sun. "I know, that's what they all say… Are you here for new employee indoctrination?" The burly guard asked. I looked at him then his dog. The dog had his tongue out. Not in the I'm tired on a hot day sort of way most dogs do, but in the I'm hungry and you look like you would be good to eat sort of way. "I am sir." I replied, my eyes darting for the nearest place of refuge, if in fact, the handler should lose control of his canine and I should be his next meal. "Head through those double doors over there, get registered and get your identification badges. They are to be worn at all times, I could have taken you for a conservator and shot you on the spot." "Yes sir, I apologize again, I'm sorry for any trouble I caused. I'm definitely not a conservator." I responded quickly, taking my pint of nectar from my pocket and taking another swig. The drink was more helpful in what it did, than just providing certainty of my membership into this society. The drink relaxed my nerves, and boy were they ever writhing; what a day I had to come! The guard said nothing, just turned and walked away muttering to himself, "Stupid new guys, always think they can touch the tree, one of these days I am going to shoot one and you can have him for dinner bubba, doesn't that sound good man, a conservator for dinner?" His furry friend glancing back at me in sorrow at a meal lost, seemed to agree with his burley owner on many more things, than just shooting conservators.

As the guard made his rounds, quickly I followed his directions, made my way to the white building, and walked up the grand porch opening the double doors. Walking through, I enjoyed a long hallway with paintings and flowers in the most ornate vases. As I approached the end of the hallway, I observed a pretty woman around my age sitting at a table that blocked the entrance to the next corridor. Approaching the table stacked full of papers I said, "Hi my name is Benjamin Silversin, I'm here for orientation class. I'm a new employee." Glancing at a piece of paper in front of her, "ah yes Benjamin here you are, my name is Miss Rachel, I'll be getting you settled in today, if you have any questions don't hesitate to ask. Let me mark you down and you can sign in. Do you have your job acceptance letter and birth certificate with you?" "I do, but may I ask why you guys need my birth certificate, I always thought a picture ID would be much more helpful?" I asked, very naively I might add. Looking up over the top of her glasses, she answered. "That's a very silly question, to help make sure you're not a conservator of course. Not that being born here prevents one from being a

9

conservator, but it's just very unlikely." "Oh, I see." I muttered, embarrassed at my ignorance, seeing they take being a conservator much more seriously than I had imagined. I mean, in my mind, what's the worst one has ever done, jammed up a wood chipper, maybe? "Here I need you to read through these papers and sign them, then I will take you to get your picture taken. Any questions?" She acknowledged, presenting me with my needed items for the day. "No ma'am, well, actually, now that I think about it, just one. Who are all the guys in those paintings I passed in the hallway?" "Here sign these, we have to walk that way, I can explain the importance behind the paintings as we go."

Signing the papers, I was excited to receive a history lesson, I love history! Walking together, rather strolling, I observed Miss Rachel moved in a special way, with special attributes. And falling behind I began to admire her for this movement. Rising and dropping suppleness, alluring my eyes, taking my mind to a lustful place, what a beautiful view. But realizing she was on to me, and that such looks were unbecoming of a man in my new position, of woodchip laborer, I turned my mind to sawdust. Oh sawdust, always thoughts of sawdust, how foolish I had been.

We stopped at the first set of paintings, all done with vivid color, and attention to detail, they provided the viewer with very romantic scenes. "Benjamin." Miss Rachel began, then paused, pointing to the first painting, one with a scantily clad muscular man, holding a half-eaten apple in his hand. "Of course you know Mr. Adams, everyone knows him, because he is the founder of the Sawdust Festival. Here he is pictured, in probably his most famous scene, eating an apple and holding it

10

to the heavens… Now, if you look to the next painting, we have Mr. Ham. As you can see he is looking out over a field of newly planted trees. He is the one who invented tree farming. He's a very special person to us here at the mill." We stood at each painting for several minutes, letting the important imagery stain our minds. "Next we have Miss. Eves, she is probably my favorite. They say she was the most beautiful person to ever live. What do you think?" Rachel asked, turning towards me, looking at me in a very brooding way. "Well, she certainly is very beautiful in this picture, very beautiful. But I'm not too sure about the painting. How come she doesn't have on any clothes?" I inquired, hoping she could provide me with the historically significant answer I sought. "That's an interesting question, I'm thinking that's because she represents life to us, and not just life, but life in a rich and full way, a way for us to glimpse our humanity as it was meant to be. I will tell you, as much as I love the festival and the fun I have there. Do you see the woman who they use to promote it, very beautiful woman, and ones with seemingly no flaws…? Well, those woman, they can kind of make you feel bad about yourself, you know? Not just because they have something you don't have, but because they seem to offer something you can't. And, what they offer a lot of times is no more than just fun, sensual pleasure without commitment, not my idea of real beauty. I think Mrs. Eves offers something different when she is portrayed. Maybe I'm just naïve, but I think there is something to the innocence she has in this painting, that's why I like it." My eyes opening large, significantly impressed with this answer, not being the answer I expected. I thought I might have been told a lot of other things like: beauty is important, or she is expressing her individual freedom, and comfort-ability with her sexuality. But that was not the answer I received, a weighty and fresh answer, I wasn't able to look at Miss Rachel the same way again.

"Let me take you to the orientation room, you have a long day, you even get to meet Mr. McNabb today. He is the owner of the mill, so it is very rare you will make his personal acquaintance. But he feels meeting the new employees is important."

The room she took me to was big and impressive. Carpet or tile, the only flooring with which I was familiar with, was nowhere to be seen. The only time I had seen pictures of it was in textbooks. Long and smooth, shiny and clean, board after board of oak flooring, stripping out before me; like a placid lake on a cloudless night, the only reflection to be seen was of the stars above. I watched the way the chandelier glittered off its surface, and in awe, standing at the threshold, Miss Rachel smiled at me. Probably knowing what was on my mind, she came and grabbed my hand to waken me from my trance. "Come on Benjamin this is nothing, just wait, if you ever get a chance to see Mr. McNabb's house you'll never look at the world the same again." Rachel commented, pulling me by the hand to my seat. I really came to adore her, and if she only knew what an ominous premonition that had been.

Patiently sitting, I watched the room begin to fill. It was interesting to see others who had been chosen for jobs at the mill. Because at this time, I had always thought quite highly of myself, one might even suggest I was a bit pompous. But here, watching the room fill, hearing the chatter of the new employees; I discovered the room was packed with of all sorts of thinking people, people who could even challenge a man such as myself on an intellectual level. Doctors, engineers, teachers innumerable, had all left respected carrier fields to join this prestigious class of wood-refinement. And this is where I met my dear friend, the beloved Stephan.

"Hey, is anyone sitting here?" Someone asked, looking up from my orientation paperwork, I saw a gentle being. Olive toned skin, a thin mustache plastered on a roundish face, and a large white smile. What a dear smile that was, one I will never forget. If I could bleed to you the nature of this man, as I had come to know him, I would; for what a man that he was, one which defies description. Tears come to my eyes at the thought of him, and a hope, that one day we will be together as friends should: unhindered in our time together, conversations, reminiscences, a meandering of love that is kind and patient, that we shall never have to part life's parting; this thought brings a happiness to my heart like few things do.

"No, it's all you." I said, but before sitting, he offered his hand. "My name is Stephan, starting a new job at the mill, exciting!" "Yeah, but a lot of hum drum, all this paperwork and orientation is, I was really hoping to get right to work, you know? By the may my name is Benjamin." I replied, meeting his hand, and eyeing Miss Rachel make her way around the outside of the room to a podium that stood in front with a microphone.

"Your attention please?" She said, trying to overcome the chattering room. "Your attention please?" She repeated, the talking growing gently less bothersome with the second attempt to bring order.

13

"We'll talk later, nice to meet you Benjamin." Stephan whispered, turning toward the voice, which was Miss Rachel.

"Now, you will have time to socialize later, and if you are still signing forms please put them aside. All your attention should be drawn to the front for your first indoctrination teacher Professor DuckÄtape. He is our safety philosopher here at the mill, and probably has the most important job, outside of Mr. McNabb's of-course. So without further ado, let's give a warm welcome to the man of the hour." Concluding, and stepping aside, Miss. Rachel made way for a tall skinny man, well dressed and in a nice suit.

But something was off, squinting from the back of the room where I sat, what was wrong with his jacket? I asked myself. Knowing the question was on all our minds, he began to speak.

"Hello everyone, welcome to the mill, congratulations on making it through our strict hiring process. My name is Professor DuckÄtape, I have a long list of credentials, several doctorates in varies areas of safety philosophy, along with relative safety instruction, applied modern well-being, employee feeling welfare, and comparative hope. I hope having said this, you will listen to me more closely, as what I'm going to teach you could save your life, or the life of your friend!" Slamming his fist on the podium, a loud bang echoed through the speakers and off the walls. Startled at the loud noise, and seeing this guy meant business, I sat up in my chair to listen closely. "First, before I begin, let's get this out of the way." Holding up his arm, or rather the limp sleeves of his jacket, he said. "All of you get a good laugh now because this is the only opportunity I will allow for such childish wrangling. As you can see,

I am missing one arm. I lost it many years ago in a terrible mill accident during my undergraduate research project." Letting his limp sleeve drop from his hand, the room filled with snickering, and covered whispering mouths. Although he permitted this, there was no doubt much irritation to be endured on his part. And I suspect the muttered talk, and quiet laughter was more bothersome to him than if the whole room would have erupted in merriment. "Alright very good, now that, that is out of your system. I shall begin… Knowledge, knowledge is the key: for although I enjoy bread and billiards, satire and truth, the asylum and the church, water and the desire to thirst, a place of rest and work, many things play in to what I will say. Well, what is a thing, is it something I see? Do I really see it? How do I know if what I see is proper, giving me an accurate account of the reality before me? The bread of which I for-mentioned, and formally ate, was tasty bread. It is said to have nourished my body, and my salivating tongue and masticating jaw, and peristaltic stomach would agree, along with my replenished Krebs cycle, and amino acid renewal. But time, what is time? Does the fact that all these things, qualities of the bread that were so agreeable to the secret processes of my body, should yield any bread that follows, to be enjoyed in this same way? Does this inference exist? What is the axiom, the chain of reasoning you will show me to provide me with the appearance of some similitude? I say it is not there, a vaporous intransitive of the mind that passes comprehension!" Throwing his arm into the air, and his sleeve blowing in the breeze created by his animated lecture, I turned towards Stephan.

Leaning over, and holding up my orientation paperwork in front of my face, I whispered to him. "What the heck is this guy talking about?" "I'm not sure exactly, I don't think he really knows either." Stephan concluded, looking back towards Professor DuckÄtape. "Excuse me gentlemen in the back, I am open to instruction if you have anything to add to this discussion on safety ethics?" Professor DuckÄtape admonished, staring at us. Observing his dangling sleeve, I thought of many things I wanted to say, but felt it prudent, at that time, to keep my mouth shut. "No sir, I apologize, please continue." I offered instead, placing my papers back on the table in front of me.

"Ok, where was I? Oh, yes, safety ethics. Having the knowledge of the saw blade, or the planer, and the good it will produce in sawdust accumulation: do I have the responsibility to tell you of the potential danger entangling yourself in one of these contraptions will pose to your well-being? That is hard to say, because is not all our experience with the blade different? Shall I withhold the lessons the blade can teach each of you in a unique way, by forbidding you your own experimentation with it? That is not for me to answer either, each of you must answer that for yourself. All the learned through the ages have wrestled with these questions. And myself not wishing to deprive anyone of you from being among that class, shall not hold over your heads, any consequence of learning that came before you. This is here, your opportunity at the mill, to discover what safety means to you! I shall applaud you only from the background, as each of you undertakes this journey for yourselves..." Professor DuckÄtape concluded, I looked at Stephan and he looked at me, giving me a gentle smirk and shrugging his shoulders, as if he could read my mind.

16

"Next I would like to introduce Dr. StrusselCööK, she is from our human responsibility department here at the mill, and is a very wise woman, one you should listen to very carefully. So if I may step aside and introduce you to her, let's give her a warm welcome." Professor DuckÄtape said, tapping his hand on the microphone and stepping back from the podium.

Dr. StrusselCööK looked to be quite the opposite of her co-worker, frazzled hair, baggy clothing, and a coffee stained blouse, left you thinking this woman was either some tortured genius unable to communicate her brilliance to the world around her, or well, for lack of better words, had just been pulled from a homeless shelter.

"Good morning all, what a pleasure this is, to be able to address the newest employees of the mill, my name is Dr. StrusselCööK, or for any of you single men out there you can call me Miss. StrusselCööK." She offered, giving a giant over-exaggerated wink to the audience and curtseying. A few snickers could be herd, and when I glanced at my new friend, I could see his face was buried in his hands in laughter. I still couldn't take my mind off the coffee stain on her shirt. "Let me start off with my credentials and then we can get into what I do here at the mill. My undergraduate degree is in post-pre-travesty-non-consequential-contemporary-counseling, I know that's a mouthful so don't feel obliged to remember it. And my doctoral degree is in human-sawdust relations with an emphasis on thinking-rational behind sawdust addictions. I know this is a topic many of you don't wish to speak about, but it's very serious one, and one that should not be taken lightly. You must realize we act out all sorts of unhealthy behaviors from the sub-conscious, and sometimes unbeknownst to us, our inner child is calling from our dreams to be nurtured and loved. Many of you, if not all of you, while you are working here, are going to be tempted to put some sawdust in your pocket to take home with you, or maybe to place a woodchip in your lip to suck on while you work. I'm telling you right now, it's not worth the trouble it will cause you. That's why I'm here. Come talk to me before these things happen and I can help you avoid the shame and embarrassment this will cause you and your family. I have developed a pre-cognition external-analytic-deep-massage-therapy along with talk-analysis that helps relieve stress, overcome urges, and allows you to transcend your work environment. These things along with a proper diet will allow you to function normally here at the mill, and enjoy the sawdust festival in the same responsible way everyone else does. Are there any questions?"

The only hand that was raised was Stephan's. "Yes Stephan." Dr. StrusselCööK said, gesturing her hand towards him. I tilted my head and sat sideways in my chair, full of curiosity that she already knew his name. "What would you suggest to someone who is in sawdust recovery? And what should they do in moments where they are overcome with the compulsion to indulge?" Stephan asked sincerely, keeping his eyes on the doctor. What a peculiar question, I thought. "Ah, yes what a terrific question, as no-doubt some of you in here fit that description. Much research has been done on this topic, and after years of experience, and working with hundreds of people; I think I have come to a most satisfactory answer. In those moments, like you have just described, I would say first start by jumping up and down twice, no-more, and no-less. This will get your blood flowing and allow the dopamine receptors in your brain more access to this needed chemical. Second I would say begin talking to yourself, not just in your mind, but out-loud, the conversation needs to feel real, and talking out-loud helps accomplish that. Tell yourself all the bad things that happened the last time you gave into the urge. Like they found me face down in the sawdust storage area after operation hours, and I had to spend a month in confinement. I hope that answers your question, we can always talk later. Ok lads and lasses, thanks for hanging in there, we are going to have lunch now, and then after lunch you will get to hear from Mr. McNabb, he is such a brilliant man, I'm sure all of you will enjoy the speech he gives to the new employees."

Standing and stretching, I looked to Stephan, a small roar of conversation happening at the moment I began to speak. "Well, that was interesting." "Yeah, definitely interesting, we got the abbreviated version today so be thankful. I've heard it all once before and I still get a chuckle out of it." Stephan replied, leaning back in his chair and extending his legs. "We have to go through another one of these?" I asked, hoping that this was the only day of lecture I would be forced to endure. "No, I guess I should explain myself… I got caught stealing sawdust about a three months ago, but I had just joined the union not even a week before they confined me. So while I was sitting in my cell waiting for sentencing my union attorney came to see me. He said, he had talked to the judge, and that I was going to get time served as long as I agreed to re-education classes, and seeing Dr. StrusselCööK. I asked about my job, and he told me you have to get caught stealing at least three times before they can fire you. I was pretty excited, so as long as I complete my court ordered classes, I'm good"

"That's cool… But let me ask you something. Was Professor DuckÄtape, saying what I think he was saying?" I inquired of Stephan, hoping his experience at the mill could shine some light on this peculiar man. "What do you think he was saying?" Stephan asked back, his eyes intent, with a smile that left me wondering even more what he thought. "So, it sounded to me like he was saying, safety here at the mill was a matter of perspective? And that we could, or rather we needed to interpret safety rules for ourselves if we are going to be real thinkers? I must say that is kind of funny coming from a guy with one arm!" I responded, and Stephan became a rolling ball of laughter, holding back tears to answer. But after several long moments, and deep breaths, he was finally able to respond. "Yeah… that's basically what he was saying. I must say you're pretty perceptive, most people don't catch that. They are usually so enthralled with his big words, or his ornate reasoning that they don't see the harm in that view. Not until they have lost a finger, or have been impaled by a branch, anyways."

"Your attention, your attention please." Miss Rachel called from the front of the room. "I just spoke with Mr. McNabb, he is not feeling inspired today, so we are going to have to reconvene tomorrow. I want all of you to know attending his speech is necessary for employment here at the mill. I know you were all looking forward to hearing from him, so I'm sorry about your disappointment. But he assures me the stars will be properly aligned tonight, and he will receive the inspiration he needs from this cosmic order. You will be paid for the rest of the afternoon. Have a great rest of the day, feel free to stay here and eat, the food is in the other room along with refreshments. See you guys tomorrow."

"That kind of sucks, I was hoping to get to work tomorrow." I commented, turning towards Stephan. "You are definitely in for a treat meeting Mr. McNabb, I think I'm going to take off though. It was nice meeting you Benjamin." "Nice to meet you too." I replied, watching Stephan leave.

Grabbing my belongings, and the unfinished paperwork, I started my journey home; the first questions, questioning the mill, and what it was all about, rolling around in my mind.

2

Before I knew it, like no time had passed at all, I was back in the grand ball room, the one with the oak flooring and chandelier. Obtaining a cup of coffee for myself, I added my own special flavoring, a splash of mahogany brandy. When all you could do was think of sawdust, I mean: dream, ponder, muse, skylark sawdust, all day long, you needed something to help keep your wandering mind in check. And the contents of my silver flask, smooth and dark, brought a serenity to my soul, rarely attained in any other way.

I sat in the same spot as I did the day prior, hoping my friend Stephan would choose to do the same. And sure enough, after grabbing himself a cup of coffee, he made my acquaintance from the neighboring chair. "Good morning, what's up?" I asked, watching his tired eyes move about the room. "Oh, not much, just had a long night, didn't get much sleep." He replied, falling lax into his chair. Pulling my flask from my pocket, I responded. "Sorry to hear that, if you need a little splash of this, you're more than welcome to take the edge off." "No man, can't do that, you remember that story Dr. StrusselCööK told yesterday about the guy passing out in the sawdust pile, well that was me. So any sawdust infused drinks are off limits for me."

"Ehchm, may I have your attention please, Mr. McNabb will be making his appearance soon, we are getting the red carpet rolled out now… you will see the lights dim and hear music begin to play when he is nearing the ball room, so if you could please take that as your cue to refrain from talking, it would be much appreciated on my part. Thank you." Everyone regarding the front of the room, Miss. Rachel had spoken. And adjusting the microphone far a taller speaker, she walked away from the podium.

"A special carpet, music, dimmed lights, this is kind of strange." I commented, looking to Stephan, who was staring out the window, something obviously on his mind. "Yes, well, he is a special man, or so they say, I prefer to call him interesting, that is to be kind anyways. Last time I spoke out against him, when I was in confinement, they took away my good-time. I had to spend an extra week in jail for that joker!" "Oh, I'm sorry to hear that, but thanks for warning me, I will be careful what I say about him." I answered back, curious to hear more of Stephan's story, confinement, jail; a man who was brilliant beyond description, had gotten himself into quite a mess, and I wondered how?

And as promised, not a moment too soon, as my mind began to wander once more, the lights dimmed and a piano began to play. This was very interesting to me, I had always indulged endlessly in the spectacles of sawdust, marooned myself in incessant drinking, never giving the man behind the mill a single thought. How strange that is, to spend one's life serving an ideal without trying to quantify the philosophy behind it? But this was my time to come face-to-face with something much bigger than myself. And so I did, finding a nuance in between the notes of that piano;

how unsettling it was, which left me uncomfortable, moving about in my chair, asking myself, why should all of this be for this? And as the progression of the music gently picked up, several people trickled in through the archway on the far side of the room, watching behind them.

"Which one is Mr. McNabb?" I whispered to Stephan, in a barely audible voice, not wanting to be admonished again the way I had been with Professor DuckÄtape. "He hasn't walked in yet, that is his entourage." Stephan whispered back, apparently not as enthralled with the show as I was. Then, in a stunning purple suit, cane of some sort in his hand, hat on his head with a giant woodchip sticking out, and a very peculiar exaggerated strut, I recognized who could be no one else, but the man himself.

This quite pretentions character made his way to the podium, his following dropping behind, melting into the backdrop to take nothing away from their superior. The room fell silent, and I could barely see the face of the man we all wanted to be. As if waiting for something, I looked about the room, and sure enough a moment later, a short portly fellow came walking in: carrying a red velvet pillow, looking hurried, and with what appeared to be a clear plastic box on top. The man stopped before the podium, and placing the pillow on the stand where one would normally keep his written speech and glass of water for speaking, he drew his arm across his forehead, bowed and departed. A spotlight clicked on, and a voice boomed from the front of the room.

"Given that I am unhappy, I have a right to your help… What is this you see Mr. Zooty? Ah yes, I agree, a bunch of worthless good-for-nothing scoundrels who wish for nothing more than to get their hands on some free sawdust, yes I couldn't agree more, very worthless indeed. We are here today Mr. Zooty to inspect something, something of which they call workers. We have been known to intermingle with them periodically, but not for too long lest they should rub off on us. These slugs, as you like to call them Mr. Zooty, have not been endowed with the beauty you and I have. We are very fortunate creatures, or rather special individuals, beings who subsist on nothing more than ourselves. For what is greater than to need no one else but your own being for happiness. And I suspect that if we were to look for equals to sharpen us, and extol us, we would not find one suitable for the task. Shall we walk the room Mr. Zooty and see with what putty we are being forced to work with, or slugs as you like to call them? Yes, I couldn't agree more that is beneath us, far beneath us, but as great and special leaders, as you and I are, we are forced into this unbecoming task. What, what is that Mr. Zooty?" Mr. McNabb spoke and then asked, leaning over, tilting his head, and placing his ear on the clear box. Glancing at Stephan from the corner of my eye, he was already looking at me with a small grin on his face, the type of grin that is being withheld from full-laughter. Waiting and watching for my response, I looked to him, then the front of the room, then back to him again, unsure of what to think?

      "I know you're upset, but I told you this was something we had to do today. Yesterday you said you didn't want to do it either and we postponed. We can't postpone again, plus we are already down here. What, what did you say? Yes, get on with it, I couldn't agree more, but what? You would like some special French radish leaves for dinner, well ok, that can probably be arranged. So you are happy now? No, I know you're not happy, but mollified, is that a more precise word choice. Ok, good, get on with it, I'm trying too but you keep talking, I don't want to be rude. Ok, I'm getting on with it!" Mr. McNabb soliloquized, picking up the clear plastic case from the pillow, and beginning to walk the room. I sat in my chair, my brows furrowed together, scratching my chin, uncertain of what to think of the spectacle before me.

Stopping before the outside table, two rows back from the front, Mr. Zooty inquired. "Mr. Zooty would like to know your name beautiful lady?" A young lady in a light green summer dress, watched sheepishly the clear box that was questioning her. "My name is Stacey." "Oh, ok, wait give me a second, ok. Well, Mr. Zooty doesn't like that name." The lady turned, looking at her friend, and then back to Mr. Zooty and said. "I'm sorry, but that is my name." "WHAT, WHAT, HOW DARE YOU TALK BACK TO MR. ZOOTY! YOU UGLY WRETCH WHAT IS WRONG WITH YOU! THE ONLY REASON WE STOPPED IS BECAUSE WE FELT BAD FOR YOU BECAUSE YOU ARE UGLY AND PROBBABLY DON'T HAVE ANY FRIENDS!" Mr. McNabb yelled in a screeching voice, which cracked under the strain of the forced octaves. Young Stacey stood, and holding her face in her hands, ran from the room, tears and sniffles following her the whole way.

I went to stand, to do something, to see how Stacey was doing, but Stephan placed his hand on my shoulder, and glanced at me, shaking his head from side-to-side mouthing the word no. Mr. McNabb watched her run from the room, and a crooked grin formed on his face. Oh that grin, how I have come to despise that grin, and the fact that this man and his box seemed to be deriving joy in such a ruthless manner. I could have strangled him!

All I could think of was, if he said that to me: I was going to take that cane of his from his hand, and smash Mr. Zooty with it, whoever Mr. Zooty was. I poured a bit more Mahogany brandy into my cup and took another drink, hoping to relive the building tension. And then, no worse scenario presenting itself to my mind, he walked my way. At that instant, a conjuring of happy places, alone and far from Mr. McNabb raced through my head. No, no, no, please no, I don't want to speak with this man and his box, I thought. But all the hoping, and asking, and wishing to be somewhere else, did nothing. For whatever reason, I could not be relived of this burden, and he stopped at our table.

"Mr. Zooty would like to know your name, young fellow?" Mr. Zooty spoke, and taking a drink to moisten my sticky mouth, I answered. "My name is Benjamin." "Oh, ok, what did you say Mr. Zooty, you like that name, it is a fine name, I do agree. Tell me what is something you do with your free time? We would like to know." Mr. Zooty and Mr. McNabb asked, tilting my head sideways I saw the clear box was lined with leaves. Turning my eyes back to Mr. McNabb, I thought of what I should say. "There are a lot of things I like to do… but I really enjoy playing my violin." Answering as best I could, I moved in my chair trying to get a better look into the clear plastic box in Mr. McNabb's hands. "Ah, very nice, very nice, undeniably nice. We may have hope for our workers yet Mr. Zooty; for a man who confesses to play the violin cannot be a slug." They said, and looking, observing the box to see who 'they were': what I saw was the strangest sight I have ever seen, two antenna came poking over the edge of a leaf, vacillating back and forth, I could feel the intelligent eyes behind them. Squinting, trying my utmost to focus on the image before my eyes, what I saw was a snail, Mr. Zooty the orange snail!

This critter, as I have come to know him, is well, a snail. Where does that leave us? Well, more appropriately analyzing Mr. McNabb; if he was a forerunner to the saint-ship of knowledge; sailing and raising his own flag of significance, then Mr. Zooty would be his warrior; a soldier called to the battle of self-reflection; how long shall we be looking into the pool? Will we stand there until we perish?

If to be good is pretty, and to be pretty is loveable, then most of us are pretty loveable; but if this is true, let us love-less ourselves, but rather love-more those around us. Oh, how I wish this man who loved himself, beautiful above all the world less, would have headed this saying more. And how I long, if I could, to spare you the diatribes of Mr. Zooty and himself; but this was the condition of his heart and though unpleasant to consider even for myself, there is much to be learned from him. And no doubt some of you have had those in your lives who resemble this man, perhaps yourselves at some point unmentioned. A terribly pitiful sight a person like this is, one who we struggle to feel any pity at all for, but is not his torturous thinking and uneasy mind worse than the most excruciating hunger pangs, and how much more difficult to alleviate? For how inseparably dark are the thoughts of those, who must find everything they need within themselves?

As we dare return to the conversation, Mr. Zooty spoke again vicariously through his owner. "Mr. Zooty would like to invite you to our home, at some future opportunity, for you to enjoy a meal with us, and all we would ask is that you bring your violin with you to play us a few notes. How does that sound?" I was asked, pulling my head back like a bird, and looking from the corner of my eye to Stephan, I wondered if this was some kind of joke. Observing the expressions of my summoner, I discerned this was not a ploy. Though I was wishing to never attend any more time with this individual than I must, as you will probably appreciate, I was not in much of a position to decline, so I answered. "Sure, I'd love that, I love to play the violin for people." The first half of what I said was a lie, though some hidden process of my mind compensated, weighing out my lie with truth. And so playing the violin for others is most assuredly a passion I hold close to my heart, and if I could do it for you through my words I would surely try. For how I would love to compensate your own misfortunes in reading about some of the characters in this book with some beautiful music. But for now we must read on: and for that, all I could think of was the day, the day at Mr. McNabb's, now standing tall and dark, holding, rather gluing itself inseparably to my future; like a drowning man and his rope in the open sea.

With some gratification on his face at the culmination of our conversation, and snail in hand, he returned to the podium to deliver parting wisdom. "New employees of the mill, be thankful I will not treat you as you deserve!" The piano began to play on cue, and myself guessing, this was probably a line he gave to all new trainees, I watched as the procession exited the room.

Pointing my head towards the floor to meet my hand, I began rubbing at my eyes with my fingers, thinking for the first time, that maybe I had bitten off more than I could chew, with my new job at the mill.

"Hey do you want to grab some food, and go down by the river to eat lunch? I looked at our itinerary, we have over an hour before we have to be back." Stephan inquired suggestively, awakening me from my musing. I thought about his suggestion, and after considering that some fresh air would do me some good, I consented. "Sure that sounds good, let me go turn in some of this paperwork to Miss Rachel, and I'll meet you outside after I grab my lunch."

We parted with an agreement to meet in fifteen minutes. I began walking the halls looking for Miss Rachel, only to find her sitting at her desk drawing a picture of some sort. Though interested in what she was doing, I felt the conversation to be had about her art, was best left for another time. Turning in my paperwork, I couldn't help but feel a pleasantness about her person, a truly charming woman she was, one who will do that thing to you; leaving you delighting in her presence. All I could hope for was a few moments of her time to explore my curious inquiries of her mind, searching her for insights into the workings of the mill and Mr. McNabb. But this must wait.

Meeting Stephan outside, the day was warm and sunny. The cedar logs from the north must have just come in because the air smelled of their sweetness. I thought of the great cedars of Lebanon, and how in those stories, something grand and significant was seen in those trees. A picture of might unobservable, the noise they must have made when they fell them; a quaking that left the earth moving with the toughness of pudding. Though the tree itself, unlike in the land of the plenty, didn't seem to be the object of worship, but something beyond it did. A reflective adherence to a powerful force who could take chaos and bring it into order. A tree that was magnificent in its ability to inspire awe, but was barely a single thought for him who made it.

How hindsight leads us to a place of dogmatic bickering with ourselves, if I had done this here, if this had been that there, where would I be? So strongly are these opinions of ourselves and others held, that they refuse to bend, even when under the greatest weight of truth. And as I write this to you now, I must acknowledge there is still a part of me, though weak and barely audible, that can still be heard calling for that sawdust. I shall only subdue this urge, presently, by relating to you the dangers it possess; not just to yourself, but to all those you love, those who you come into contact with, and even many you do not.

And as the memory of that cedar aroma fills my mind now, I see the day clearly, a day of warnings unheeded, compassion refused, but grace given to change. "What are you thinking about?" Stephan asked, as we made it to the single person trail that cut through the tall brush and long grasses that led to the river.

"Oh, nothing, just smelling the fresh trees they brought in… You know; I've never been down to the river this way before?" "Oh man, you have been missing out, this is probably one of the nicest spots to watch the log barges go by." He said, looking back at me as he pushed overgrown bushes out of his way. The trail turned parallel to the river, and as we began to descend a hill, I could just see the water beginning to go by.

I love sitting by the water, hearing it slosh against the shore, and the warm sun hitting my face; always allowing me to put my day, and Mr. McNabb far behind me. Nearing the bank, I was able to see grass that had been matted down, were others had sat before. But gaining on this small savannah, I could see a post and sign of some sort ahead. I figured this to be a sign posting prohibiting fishing, or swimming alone, but as I neared and the words came into focus, this is what I read: Here rests my Ebenezer, though I sought to enlighten, I found I was too heavy to float: Jean RowBăck.

Stephan sat first on the grass, and began pulling his lunch from his plastic sack. "Hey Stephan, what is that sign over there for?" I asked, pointing to the post, and finding a spot next to my friend, letting the warm grass tickle the back of my legs. "Oh, you've never heard of Jean RowBăck before?" "No, should I have?" "No, not exactly, people don't talk about him much anymore, but there is a legend... the legend of Jean RowBăck!" Stephan's voice lowered in the ominous way of campfire story telling. And sitting up, watching me intently, he began to tell. "As the story goes, many, many years ago, when thick elms and willows still lined the banks of the Hoio River. Mr. RowBăck had been coming to this very spot every day to think and write, probably just about where you are sitting." Chills rolled up my arms at this proclamation, and I stopped chewing my food, listening to every word Stephan uttered closely. "Sometimes people in town wouldn't see him for days because he would never leave the riverbank. He was a tinker by trade, and made his living selling his ideas. One day after looking and watching, his eyes longing into the depths of the river for many days and nights, he is said to have

32

been struck by a moment of inspired genius. The next day he ran through town screaming like a mad man ranting and raving unintelligible things; but exclaiming he had found truth within the waters themselves, of course nobody paid much attention to him, because everyone knows thinkers can be a bit eccentric, and well, as you will see a lot of their ideas are not as brilliant as they might appear. But none-the-less, he was able to talk his friend out of a few shillings, and he bought a canoe from a native. What he told his friend to get him lend him a few quid is all speculation, of course, but rumor has it, it is said, he had a dream, and in that dream, a beautiful man named Cato, with wings like an angel came to him and said, 'now you are your master, as now I am my master…' Why he listened to that guy in his dream I don't know? But he did, and he started writing, well, not just writing, but obsessing over self-killing as they used to call it. You see that stone over there? The letters SK were scratched into it by Jean RowBăck himself." Stephan Promised, pointing to the largest rock on the shore by us.

　　　"No way… this story is getting a little ridiculous Stephan!" "No I'm serious, go and look for yourself." Watching my friend doubtfully for the first hint of joshing, his expression remained as straight as an arrow; so getting up, though very skeptical, I walked to the rock. "No way, those aren't real, you scratched those letters in yourself just so you could tell me this story." I answered Stephan, at the sight of the letters SK scratched in the rock. Stooping down, I ran my fingers over the etchings and noticed the grooves were deep, probably not the product of a practical joke.

"I promise, I didn't do that Benjamin" "Ok, whatever, just get on with the story, I want to know what happened to Jean RowBăck." I replied, returning to my spot next to Stephan, and picking up my sandwich. "Anyways, as I was saying, this guy had great ideas, he had written many books, and was writing one now on the benefits of self-harm. And in his moment of brilliance, he said let me show them this, they will never read another word of mine the same. So he went on with this great experiment, calling all the towns' people to the river, promising them insight that they had never had before. He pinned a copy of his unfinished treatise, or whatever they're called to a tree, and rowed to the center of the river waiting for the people to gather. His friend, first to the side of the river, took the papers that were pinned to the tree and began to read. Realizing Jean was going to commit some self-harm to himself to bring attention to his work. His friend called from the shore as loud as he could, Jean row back, please row back. And the crowd that had gathered in the mean-time began to yell the same, Jean row back, please row back, he thought the chant to be encouragement for the ultimate deed, and so Jean RowBăck plunged head long into the river, never be seen again, and his ghost still haunts these banks to this very day!"

Beginning to snicker, Stephan barely finished his story. I thought the joke so far, was moderately funny, but not wanting to give Stephan the satisfaction of my laughter, I kept my mouth held tightly shut. He only grew in merriment as I tried to avoid laughing with him: finally to try and coax Stephan out of the rolling ball of laughter he had become, I started by saying. "Very funny, very funny, you had me going there for a second… the sign, the letters in the rock; that is all kind-of elaborate for a practical joke though; don't you think?"

Pulling himself together by biting his knuckles, he thought he was quite hilarious, but then Stephan began to speak. "That was pretty funny, but not all of it was a joke, the guy really did kill himself after philosophizing about life and death, but really, he is more of just a philosophical joke, more than anything. Not that I think people killing themselves is funny, it's not by any stretch of the imagination. And I am one to speak from experience, I have been there myself, in that dark place, ready to end it all. But there is a way out, and that's what I like to tell people. I just think it's funny a guy like that thinks he has something to offer humanity. I' am sorry if that offended you, but sometimes making light of serious issues is the only way to get anyone to talk about them."

I didn't know what to say, Stephan kept dropping these hints about his life, and I wanted to know more. There was no doubt that this man had some wisdom in him, a wisdom that few people at the mill had shown so far.

"You know, we have got to get back soon to hear our last orientation speaker; Ohm Matzo, I think his name is." I reminded Stephan, crumbling up my bag and wrappers from lunch. "What do you know about this guy, you said you have been through orientation once already?"

"Ohm Matzo is new working here, so I didn't hear him speak last time I did orientation. From what I've herd though, they hired him as the spiritual leader hear at the mill. I guess a lot of people were getting burned out, there was a couple retirement suicides, along with some very strange things going on with sawdust, and new personal applications of it; so they thought people would benefit from some guidance of a transcendent nature, a motivational guy if you will. But I'm not actually sure what he does? I'll be interested to see…"

"Ok, well, this will be new for the both of us then. Let's go." I encouraged, placing my hand before Stephan; grabbing my hand almost immediately, I nearly fell over, but regaining my balance, I helped him rise from the warm grass to his feet. Making our way back to the white house, following the single-person path from where we came, I felt encouraged from our brief respite. Heading to the place where all the important administration of the mill is conducted, the air-conditioned interior, was welcoming air indeed. After a few moments enjoying this cool atmosphere, we found our table, and made our seats.

Looking at our table, then glancing at all the others, I observed most of them holding several blue pamphlets. At a second glance about me, near the front of the room, I saw a very strange looking individual. This peacock if you will, was adorned with long colorful linens, some wrapped loosely, some tightly around his body, giving him the appearance of, well, a perplexed peacock during his mating dance. Several pieces of petrified wood, carved and polished, within the custom of our sawdust nation, were strung around his neck. Small movements, made large noises, as the petrified wood clanked together, and short observation of this man, would lead one to conclude, he greatly enjoyed the disruptions he caused.

Picking up one of these pamphlets, I read its title, 'why are we here?' But as I began to open my pamphlet, to begin my enquiry, a strange humming interrupted my efforts.

"Humm-diddy-humm-humm-humm…" Lifting my head and turning my eyes to the front of the room, I saw this man, for-mentioned, close the drapes and lite some incense of some sort. Continuing to hum as he made his arrangements, finally he began to address, well, something, I'm still not exactly sure what?

"I am so self-reflective, that sometimes in the mirror, I reflect myself. This image which is before me, come hither Ohm Matzo. For you reflect all and nothing in singularity, and the things you say are very profound; profoundness, oneness; a singularity of profundity, how clever you are Ohm Matzo… Now hip-pity hop-pity! Let us begin, as rabbits down the bunny trail: and as we close our eyes together and move down the path, let us first hip, and then hop, smell the gardener's greens, imagine carrots, a rainbow of carrots:

red, and orange, and white:

as we stop to take a bite;

they make a crunching sound between our teeth,

but that is not all the goodness we wish our farmer to bequeath;

to devour, on our journey to the gardener's garden; who is he to look down from his high tower?

But in the end, he was forced to relinquish, his high power.

Never mind, sweet beets, that's the treat we seek,

but oh my goodness, into our garden-of-self, someone has tried to sneak a leek;

for although we are proud rabbits, they say he was lowly and meek.

Our solution, well, let us nail him to some teak!

Cabbage, and radish, and rhubarb, are things we also like,

but to ensure the death of death, I will strike him with my pike.

For as we hip, and then we hop;

my hope, is your pity.

And what is my hope, that I will kill him with my mind,

and it will not be the truth, you will come to find,

telling a rabbits own proud story instead,

where in my story god is truly dead!

And I will make it have a hoppy-end!

Thus speaks Ohm Matzo."

Wow, what do you say to that? I mean, if you can even decipher what it is he is trying to say, it leaves you feeling kind of strange. There is definitely some animosity, some internal contention going on, that makes it difficult to separate anything he says, from some deeper resentment within. And as I consider this man, if we were to agree Mr. Zooty is a snail who hates slugs, then Ohm Matzo would be a caterpillar who hates butterflies. But for now I was intrigued by his words, and kept these enquiries of mine, questions concerning spirituality, pushed to the back of my mind. Because, well, who knows when you could use some spiritual advice of some sort?

Ohm Matzo looked up from the front of the room, from behind his hair, and through the thick smoke of the incenses, his eyes seemed to pierce something beyond the temporal. But the ever inquisitive, and plain spoken naivety of Stacey was waiting for him the moment he finished.

And Stacey raised her hand, a lady of gentle manors, she had returned to the ballroom after Mr. McNabb and Mr. Zooty had left, unbeknownst to me.

"Yes ma'am, there in the green dress." Ohm Matzo acknowledged, pointing to Stacey in slow careful movements. "Ok, I'm still kind of confused, so why are we here?" Stacey enquired, brushing her hair behind her ear with her fingers, and sitting up for an answer. Good question I thought, we are wasting the day, I would much rather be by the river talking with my friend Stephan.

"Well, to answer your question, I will stop speaking in witty prose; for your simple minds roll in pity repose. But first I shall say, read the pamphlet, for spirituality as complex as that which is held close unto me, can hardly in the uttered word be so simply set free."

"Uhm, I did read the pamphlet?" Stacey assured, interrupting Ohm Matzo, and holding the limp blue paper into the air to prove her point, she waved it a few times for good measure. As if no one had spoken at all, Ohm Matzo continued his funny rhyming. Personally, I think this came so natural to him, to speak this way; that he didn't even realize he was doing it.

"As we hop forward and ascertain what is meant,
first from the pamphlet, a quote shall I rent.
As I shall show what it is to seek true ascension,
let us not squabble over words to hip into dissention.
Relationships and people, in our question, we shall not consider;
for to define what is spiritual will only embitter.
Now what I shall suggest, is hop unto the self, and hip into the –ish:

then you will truly see what is meant by teaching a man to fish.

Love and long no one else but that which is me,

and then you will know what it is to be truly set free.

Seek the pain and minimize the pleasure,

and at the end of the struggle you will find your special treasure.

Because what you see when I help only me,

is I will become the cosmos number one payee..."

Leaning over and lifting the pamphlet in front of my face, like I was reading, I said. "Wow Stephan, this guy seems pretty disillusioned about something, what do you think it is?" "That's a good question, I'm not really sure, I'm going to have to think about that one myself." He responded politely, obviously mulling over the question in his mind. Turning back to watch Stacey, she looked about the room trying to see if anyone else was as confused as she was.

"Humm-diddy-humm-humm-humm... thus speaks Ohm Matzo!" He professed of himself, and the spiritual lesson for now, was over. And Ohm Matzo left the front of the room loudly, jingling pieces of petrified wood clanking like broken symbols, following him as he left. Miss Rachel replaced him at the front of the room, and boy was I glad to see a face of reason. Waving her hand in front of her face to remove the lingering smoke from Ohm Matzo, she spoke. "Well guys, thanks for hanging in there. I know it has been a long couple days, but now that indoctrination is over, we will be able to celebrate why all of you are really here. Tomorrow will be your first day as official employees of the mill. So get a good night's sleep, and don't forget to return any unfinished paperwork. You are dismissed! Have a great day!"

Yoo-hoo! I was as happy as a clam in a clam bed of sand! The day was finally over, and soon, very soon, I would be rolling in all the sawdust I could imagine! What a grand day I had to look forward to!

3

The arrow of love has pierced me in the back, a joyful, painful, stinging to my soul with lust; lascivious sawdust: you ravenous, unappeasable, unquenchable desire and thirst, flee from me. You rip a hole within your victims too large to mend, you are ripping a hole within me now. You come with the ferociousness of a starving lion, and the stubbornness of a pack of flies. You sawdust, never at a loss for yourself, leave me be. Feel for yourself, why must I feel for you; you parasites who cannot love for yourself, I swat you away. You steal love; that you should not love us back, and only desire us for more of what we cannot give. Giving everything in us to be nearer our true love, which is you. How torturous is this paradox, you diametrically opposed opposition, you, the anti-thesis to all goodness; turn and leave me to myself. How we have fallen like Apollo? Daphne my beautiful, my beloved, where have you gone? Who has been so cruel to inflict me with this desire, or rather this burden of wantonness upon me; too heavy for any man to carry? That I should need you so close to my heart, that any separation vexes my soul. How I hate this need to rebel into my swimming pool of sawdust. I am bending under the weight of dispensations untold, for where shall I go for rest? And now my dear Daphne, that I have fought this fight for you, with all my might, to hold you close; who is so cruel to turn you into a laurel bush, to keep us apart for eternity? Now, for, I have nothing else, so I must have as you, which I should stand to worship the laurel leaves, waiting for your flowers to bloom again? Let me cast the world's greatest curse on him, the one who has such a fowl, and detestable imagination; who has dreamt this dream, this crime?

A criminal above all criminals, is this man, who must head the call to retreat to the sanctuary of absolution. For it is only in entreating the great founders of Rome, begging for their merciful protection, that the one who fired the arrow will find peace. In no other place will he rest, but in this city of refuge. Yet like the barbarians, I will storm its walls, as no grater anger and hate falls upon me, raining drops of disdain and contempt, you contemptible rain, find this man and get him drunk with your drops of malice! Ice him into the corner of the temple, so I may strike him with my sword, and I may take his inebriated imagination and pierce it with some sober truth. This demon, a demon above all demons, has set me chasing my tail for sawdust, and now the new day: the day of sawdust infinite, has fallen from my dreams into reality.

But what you have not counted on archer, you who are shooting arrows of lust, piercing those with love for sawdust, what you have not counted on, is hope. Hope for a new day, hope for a new beginning, definitions of self, left undefined by your cruel dictionaries. Because in me, there is that which remains in me, a hidden spring of enlightenment. And a day has been set to spring fourth, a set aside day, where I can choose for myself, who I choose to worship in spirit, and in sober truth.

And I only write these emotional dialects to you now, in memory of the past, thinking of places, of past self-accusations, where I wish I had never been. Being accused, by the accuser, I shall tell you of those early days at the mill. And how hindsight has altered a warped mind, to true perception. This being said: nothing gets me so emotionally stirred as remembrance of the lies I believed, the lies I be-lived. So how this first day, lives in my mind vividly, unaccountable to reality as it is now!

What a splendid day, I thought, walking onto my porch. And if you can imagine the sun creeping over the horizon, illuminating a hazy humid summer sky, the morning that is still cool enough to be pleasant, but holds the stickiness of heavy air, this was my morning, a special morning to remember. My cedar infused coffee in one hand, a black walnut bourbon in the other, a happier man, you would be hard pressed to find. Allowing those sweet drinks to fill my soul, all pleasantness and contentment was mine to enjoy. And as I sat in my old wooden rocking chair, letting the boards of my porch squeak as I moved, I thought; and a wonderful way to increase the happiness of this morning came to mind.

Retrieving my violin from its case, I brought it to the porch and set it on my chair. Rosin up the bow, think of a special tune, one that causes pause for reflection and harmony in your heart, and that was the melody my violin began to sing. Pulling that bow across the strings with care, tasty notes wafted into the air. The flutes of summer birds, and the base of morning frogs, accompanied myself in this ensemble of serenity. And how I thought, at this time, that life could get no better than it was at that moment.

But what is greater than my violin, and some happy drinks to be my friends? Ah, yes, a day of sawdust inconceivable, all that waited beyond those fences, more sawdust than you could shake a stick at! (And because all the sticks had been ground for sawdust, a stick to shake would be difficult to find.) So unable to tame racing thoughts, even with my emollients for the mind, the violin did what my strong drink could not, and even though it was but for a short time; I was able to stave off the desire to be waiting for the opening of the gates.

Yet, the time came, and as we recount, I made my way through the town, crowning the hill to see the giant smoke stacks; and my heart raced and stomach fluttered at their sight, once more. Making my way through security, I had quickly found dropping a shot of my special nectar into the guard's coffee, gave them a pleasant disposition towards myself, and allowed me to gain quick entrance to the mill; so this became a regular practice of mine.

Walking about, I found my dear friend Stephan in the break-room, filing a bottle of water for himself to take to the line. And in my ignorance I might preface, I noticed I was a bit repulsed at the idea of drinking water without some sort of wood additive, and wondered how he did it? "Good morning, it's supposed to be a hot one out today! Where does the schedule have us starting?" I asked, hoping Stephan could provide me with some direction, on my first day. "Good morning Benjamin, well, first thing we have to do, is go out and stand for morning colors, and wait for a small motivational endorsement from Mr. McNabb. Then after that's done, Miss Rachel will post the assignments for the new employees."

"Oh, ok, I didn't realize Mr. McNabb addressed us again after orientation, Miss Rachel said we don't usually make his acquaintance." I appealed, wishing my own desire to stay away from this man, might somehow alter the reality Stephan was setting out before me. "Yeah, I kind of wish that myself… that would be nice if we wouldn't have to hear from him again, but it's just a PA announcement given over the loud speakers of the mill, nothing to personal. You might want to grab yourself some water, like you said it's supposed to be a hot one out." Stephan suggested, walking away from the water cooler, and tipping his newly filled water bottle towards the suggested drink.

"No, I'm good, I've got something to drink." I replied, with the measure of assurance of a man who detested drinks not lined with wood sugars. "Alright man, whatever you say. Let's get outside, I just herd the five-minute bugle warning call." Stephan proposed, walking towards the door, and pulling it open for me to exit the break-room.

Exiting the break-room, we made our way towards the north side of the mill, passing the white house, and security headquarters, we climbed a hill to stand before a grand structure. The house of Mr. McNabb himself, held high, looming over the courtyard, I stood gazing mouth agape. We found ourselves with several hundred of our co-laborers, waiting for the morning pep-talk. A tall black wrought iron fence, held us just out of stone's throw from the residence. A sculpted water fall, equipped with retention ponds, and roaming guard dogs, left one feeling impotent and unworthy. But as fancy as the three-story mansion was, with its ornately detailed exterior, that was not what caught my eyes. Weeping willows, blooming Magnolia's, towering pines, if I

46

had been impressed with the trees in front of the white house, this left me awestruck. I can still recall the sound those willows made as they swayed in the breeze, and the aroma of the magnolia flowers as they wafted our way. What beauty those trees held, something I could see and feel, but never quite identify and make real in my heart.

Taking my eyes from the trees, I saw movement from within the mansion. High on the third story, behind several white pillars, a pane of glass, about the size of a school-bus, gave Mr. McNabb full-view of his empire. And I watched as he moved about inside, standing before, what appeared from my vantage point, like a mirror; saying something into it, and moving with the same over-animated aggressive gestures he used at orientation. How peculiar, I thought.

"I wonder what he's doing up there Stephan?" I said, wiping small beads of sweat from my forehead that had begun to accumulate in the warming air. "Yeah, me too, that's been something a lot of us have been wondering about for a long time. Every day before his speech, he's up there talking to himself, for probably like ten-minutes. I'm not exactly sure what he's saying, but it would be cool to find out." Stephan concluded, taking a drink of water.

And then, startled by the trumpet blowing, chills rose up my neck at the long piercing sound. Finally subsiding, the trumpets call faded into the expanses, and I heard an electric crackling as the speakers on top of metal poles spread about the grounds, came to life. And then following, I heard the voice of Mr. McNabb and Mr. Zooty:

"On this day, many, many years ago Mr. Zooty, our great sawdust nation, though but a babe, separated itself from its mother land,

and today the fourth of many fourths of July's since, we celebrate freedom, Mr. Zooty. But what they do not know, these vile creatures that work for us, is that they don't even know what freedom is, they celebrate what they do not know! Don't you find that curious and comical, my beautiful friend? But how fortunate for us, for how else could we have fresh French radish leaves flown in for you daily from the Burgundy region of France, and how else could we sleep on our sawdust filled mattresses? It is the sawdust we create, that they take such pleasure in, which makes this possible. Our great founders said everyone has an equal opportunity to the pursuit of woodchips, and so let it be, my petty detestable workers, indulge yourself until you fall over. Now, what, what was that, Mr. Zooty? You said, you think, they are enjoying my history lesson to much, because they get to avoid working while they listen to it. So you are saying they are only pretending to listen, to avoid their duties? THOSE WRECHED SCOUNDRALS, WE SEND YOU TO WORK, WE ORDER YOU TO WORK NOW, BE THANKFUL WE HAVE ALLOWED YOU TO LIVE; that is all."

And as the speech had started with a crackling static, so it ended, the speakers shut-off, and the motivational speech of Mr. McNabb hung in the past with all the other memories of him, dripping with contempt. Looking to my friend, he had a serious look of disgust plastered on his face. "I really don't like that guy Benjamin, but I was thinking about your question during his rant, and I got an idea... You know what I think would be funny?" Stephan inquired, with a mischievous grin, replacing the expression of disdain.

"Hey man, whatever I asked you, forget about it! I don't want an answer to my question… plus didn't you say, you just got out of confinement not too long ago?" I quickly reminded him, and as the crowd began to head to their work posts. Stephan grabbed me by the back of the arm, turning me to usher us away from the remaining stragglers, whispering. "You wanted to know what Mr. McNabb was saying in the mirror, well, so do I. I propose we sneak into work early tomorrow and turn on the PA system before his speech, so everyone hears him talking to himself, I'll get a kick out of it, plus I think it would serve that arrogant scalawag very nicely. That is, to make his private thoughts public, no one will get hurt. What's the big deal?"

What could I say, I was revolted at the idea of getting caught sneaking into Mr. McNabb's mansion, plus I saw no feasible way of accomplishing his proposed task. For a while, I said nothing, but as a friend looks at you, placing you in a position, which leaves you feeling like you are the only person in the world who can accomplish what is being asked, and death will befall him without your consent, so I felt, and finally, after his longing exasperated looks, I declared. "I'm in!" And that was how I fell into that special trap, set by my friend, with skill.

"Great! After work, I'll meet you down by the river where we had lunch the other day, and we can make our final preparations." Stephan said with an evil laugh, as his speaking continued with a sinister satisfaction in his voice, presumably from my easy concession to take part in mischief, "Come on; let's go see where Miss Rachel placed us today."

Before the white house administration building was a giant cork board, but it wasn't cork, it was some composite, our sawdust nation had claimed all the real cork many years past. This is where the assignments had been posted, we approached, and placing my finger on the paper to follow the tiny print, I searched for our names. "Hey Stephan, it looks like you are in quality control, it says I'm working in the inventory department. Do you know where I have to go?" I communicated, asking for some help to find my way around this maze of a mill.

"Yeah, it's actually not too far from where we were just at." Stephan replied, bending over and writing in the sand. "If this is Mr. McNabb's house here, and we are right here, this is where you have to go." Stephan pointed, showing me the route to take to begin my work assignment. "I have to get going so I'm not late, but don't forget to meet me down by the river after work." Stephan ordered, directing his index finger my way, to ensure I was paying attention to his command. "Ok, gotcha, see you then." I responded, making my way back up the hill, wondering what he had in mind for our efforts of sabotage at the McNabb residence?

The inventory department, was right where Stephan had promised, though he neglected to mention there was additional security precautions in place to enter this restricted area. "Sir, I need your mill identification card, please…" I handed this very serious looking man my card, and he began flipping through some papers on a clipboard. The sun glasses, the uniform, and posture, were all very intimidating, and seeing his coffee, I wondered if I should advance my normal friend making procedure on this buttoned up fellow? Considering the benefits a good relationship with the law could provide, I went for it. And in a very nonchalant, but thought out fashion, I pulled my silver flask from my pocket and took a swig. Next, leaning into the security booth to block the prying eyes of any onlookers, I let a handsome drought fall into the man's mug. He continued with his very busy looking paper shuffling, and for a moment, I wondered if he had seen me do it, but he had. Taking a drink, and smiling, he continued with, what he had to continue with, but I could see the façade beginning to fall. "Here you are Benjamin, by the way my name is Berry, I have to tell all the new guys this, but just please also know, you must declare any sawdust you have on your person before entering. If you do not declare it, and you try to leave with it at the end of your shift, we will assume the sawdust you are possessing is property of the mill and it will be subject to confiscation, and you may face legal prosecution for receiving and concealing stolen sawdust. Is that understood?"

"Yes, got it." I responded, and Berry, probably feeling a little lonely and disconnected from those around him, began to talk. And though I suspect this was because he was forced to enforce rules, rules he probably wanted to break himself, and no one liked to follow: now, my drink taking effect, so he began to share the way people do when life's detour signs are removed; how so many things had built up inside him, and I listened as he drained his sink of mixed emotions. "Sorry, Benjamin, I didn't mean to come off like a prickly pear, but it's just I deal with so many people who have lost all control when it comes to sawdust indulgence, it leaves you a little jaded and cynical you know?"

"I didn't think you came off that way, you came off more like a guy, well, just doing your job." I submitted, hoping to encourage this discouraged man. And I thought about the people he was forced to deal

51

with, and how they all wanted him to look the other way while they committed themselves to vulgar woodchip spoilage. I imagine, it would be easy, to always see the bad in people, when you were forced always, to deal with bad people. And though I couldn't count myself out of that class, I had an open ear, and that was all this man seemed to need, so I poured another shot into his coffee.

"I just don't understand people sometimes, I got this low key job as a security officer here at the mill, hoping I could escape the chaos of the street enforcements and sawdust gang control. You know Benjamin, I saw people hurt each other in the most terrible ways imaginable, and I'm not just talking about physical harm. I mean physical harm is bad, but it was this entire culture of carelessness that had really discouraged me more than anything else, ladies selling themselves for sawdust, men who weren't really men because they had never grown up, treating woman and children like objects to be had…"

And at these proclamations, a man's heart beginning to soften with my emollient for the soul and an open ear, his eyes became wet. I could tell there was some real pain behind the things this man had seen, and I became sad myself at the thought of what they might be. What more could you do for a person like this than listen and hear, trying to understand what it is they saw, and doing this within the best of my abilities.

And at this thought, a friend of mine comes to mind from the community of trees, one who loved men and women like Berry when no one else would. Men and women returning from war, cruel war, a way for us to achieve more sawdust influence around the world. But what this dear woman saw was not cynicism or coldness in these people; what she saw were broken people desperately needing healing, and so she pointed them in the direction of the one great physician, the source of all healing. And how as I think about Berry now, I wish I could have pointed him that way, but I didn't have the answer, and needed healing myself; so I did what I could do, inviting him into my circle of friendship.

Berry's voice quivered a little as he continued to talk, and some very hard memories, I believe, started showing their contorted faces. "I'm sorry Benjamin, I didn't mean to get all emotional. I don't even know you or why I'm telling you these things. You just, seem like a nice guy. But maybe we can talk another time? I don't want you to be late for work, plus I have some more people hear to check in… by the way Dave will be your foreman today, he's a nice guy, I think you'll like him." Berry concluded, nodding his head towards the small line beginning to form behind me.

"Yeah, I'd definitely like to talk some more, it was nice meeting you Berry." I said, sticking out my hand to meet his. Quickly he smiled at me, shook my hand, and then pushed his sun glasses back tight to the bridge of his nose with his index finger, and the plastered face of seriousness, he bore once more. For some reason, maybe I just have one of those countenances, or demeanors, people felt that they could, and should, share with me, more than they would share with the average person. And though I didn't particularly mind these advances at the time, it was still a long time before I really realized this was a gift from above, and could, and should, be used for great good, when used appropriately.

53

Walking through the security gates, a brick wall sat blocking my view of the yard beyond. "Foreman Dave here, foreman Dave here, come to me, foreman Dave here..." A man shouted, waving a paper in the air. Moving his way, I walked high on my toes, and my eyes were just glimpsing the apexes of mounds, mounds of sawdust above the wall! What, did I say mounds? I sure did! When is Christmas, how does it feel? And not just any time, but the times when there is a great gift longed for. As I kneel with my brother, looking through the spindles of our balcony to the tree below; how the soft glow of the lights, leaves us guessing if the present we desire with our whole heart, has arrived! We talk in a whisper not to wake my mother, 'the big one is mine I bet'; I promise my brother. And now, my hands beginning to shake, how an adult feels like a child, longing for a little thoughtless indulgence in play, and his gift beneath the tree. With excitement, our toy begs to be torn from its package. And my mind, if it had lost all ability to restrain my body, would have had me doing cartwheels and summer salts, maybe a few languishing limbs, beating fists on the ground, and some unintelligible grunts and squeaks; and maybe, just maybe, all this flopping about and noise would have properly expressed the joyful elation filling my heart, at the sight of those mounds!

Now, writing this to you, I can't help but be filled with some embarrassment at my folly; the type of embarrassment one feels when he reflects on child-like immaturity. How I wanted so badly to be immature at that moment, and go running past foreman Dave, around the wall, and dive head first into a pile of sawdust. But, some nether region of my mind, with self-control, I didn't realize I possessed, withheld me from this longing desire.

And we should not forget, and most assuredly should remember, that on occasion, though rare and quickly dismissed by a sound mind, I do see a pile of sawdust here or there and long for some consequence free enjoyment. However, when a moment is taken to decipher what it is that the sawdust really offers, it is quickly observed by a thorough conscious, that it is a pot of boiling pride, bubbling within me, heated by a match of lust, which has caused this, and nothing more.

But before we go further, let me implore you to not heed the sirens call, though beautiful beyond description, promising us profound happiness and contentment, their song first plays to the spirit and then to the flesh. Here the problem arises, and here the problem lies, that leaves us believing we may have control over this urge, and that it is nothing more than an urge, and can be overcome. But what that siren song of sawdust fails to sing, is that it raptures not only our ears, but our soul to sting. A stinging, with a poisonous dart of death, pernicious, slowly and subtlety harmful, it will take you for all you have and more. Yet, I knew these things not, and I would have perished in their pursuit had it not been for some undeserved favor from above, something given and not earned.

So in a sound cool voice, the type of voice overcompensated with fallacious ease, I introduced myself, "Foreman Dave, hi, my name is Benjamin. I'm here to work in the inventory department today. Berry said you were going to show me the ropes." Foreman Dave looked at me, with the look of knowing many things I did not, and replied, "Nice to have you on board, you picked a great day to start. As you could probably smell, yesterday we got in our cedar logs from the north, they are just starting to be processed, so you will be working on woodchip bunk consignment…"

Woodchip bunk consignment, well, that sounded like a very noble calling, and I was even more pleased with the idea of fresh cedar. The day, I'm not sure could get any better, than it was. "Ok, just show me what you need me to do and I'll do it". I answered with the cocksure confidence of a man who saw wallowing in sawdust, as life's ultimate aspiration. And even better than that, was wallowing in free sawdust, something you didn't have to work to produce! And foreman Dave only to eager to have someone with my eagerness, responded quickly, "Alright lets go, I'll show you what you are doing."

Following foreman Dave, we walked around the brick wall, and I was given my first close up view, of what I thought was heaven. Each compartment, approximately ten-foot wide, ten-feet tall, and thirty-feet deep, large enough for a large truck to park itself comfortably, held massive mounds of sawdust. And so we strolled past bunk after bunk of woodchips, heading toward, what might resemble a grain elevator, or quarrying belt, and I could see the fresh sawdust falling off a conveyer to a mountain bellow.

Getting close, the wind lofted the lighter sawdust upwards, vortex's formed between the lines of bunks, and I felt like I was in a shower of pure, unadulterated ecstasy. It was not just the ground wood, but what the ground wood promised, which really brought me to my knees to worship what it held. Because what it held for me, and so many others was the key to self-gratification, a place of conjuring ideals of fulfillment and purpose. How I thought, the sawdust was where I would find deep meaning and satisfaction in life. And as I drew close, I could feel pieces getting stuck in my hair, and in-between the collar of my shirt and skin, along with a bit of dust in my eyes. But what is morbidly strange, is that even the itching and watering eyes felt pleasant!

Yet, this pleasantness, was only for a time, and soon to be my foe. But what it brought then, unbeknownst not only for me, but for all of those who celebrate the sawdust festival, what it really brought, was punishment: blindness of mind, strong delusions, vile affection, a reprobate sentiment, and horror of conscience, to name a few. So getting near the base of this mountain of sawdust, my delusions had left me with a romantic notion of love, my senses had been rendered just crooked enough, to think I was the most fortunate man in the world, at that time, and for eternity. Part of this mirage of the mind, a marriage to death, was that I had never considered what it was to work as a slave to sawdust. And so when foreman Dave handed me a shovel, and pointed me to a wheelbarrow, I must admit, I was a bit perplexed, and unsure of what to do?

"Ok, Benjamin, now what I need you to do, is start filling this wheelbarrow, and then go dump it in bunk six, when that one gets full, go to bunk seven, and fill that one, then when that one gets full, go to eight, and so on. Get the picture? Pretty simple, any questions?" Foreman Dave asked, yelling over the obnoxiously loud wood chipping going on nearby. Looking around, I held the shovel with a bit of dumbness, dumbstruck that he expected me to do these things with my hands. I mean, I play the violin, I can't have overworked muscles, doesn't he know it will lead to tenseness and poor quality sound when I play? "What's the shovel for? Isn't there some heavy machinery to do this stuff?" I asked, a little annoyed at the joke foreman Dave was playing on me on my first day. "Yep, you're it!" Foreman Dave replied, patting me on the shoulder, and heading back towards the front of the inventory yard.

"By the way, you're expected to fill two bunks a day, any less and I may have to report you to Mr. McNabb." Forman Dave yelled back from the top of his lungs to overcome the wood chipper noise. Glancing at him, and then the infinite mound of growing sawdust, a hint of dismay fell over me. First I thought of foreman Dave's words, and the threat to inform Mr. McNabb of any slothfulness endured on my part, and this was enough motivation to get me going.

The initial strike with the spade to the mound of fresh ground cedar, sent me into thought. Then after an hour or so, sweat dripping from my face, I took a couple swigs from my flask, and I became pensive. Half-way through the day, blisters began to form on my hands, my knees were weak, and I had appropriated sawdust to every nether region of my body, and a brooding philosophy was now my companion. I was breaking my back, obsessing over ground wood, only to find when I had access to it in a way; in a way I had always imagined I would want, it didn't fulfill in the way I had hoped. And suddenly, woodchip bunk consignment, had lost its noble appeal. Wait, not just lost its noble appeal, but rather was a new form of torture, especially for an intellectually minded fellow as I had seen myself then.

By the time foremen Dave informed me of lunch, I was ready to fall over. Dead tired, I had probably moved several tons of woodchips.

The novelty had worn off after the first few wheelbarrows, and alone, moving an endlessly growing mountain of cedar, dirty and tired, I was compelled to examine myself for the first time, in a long time. And so I began asking myself, why was I spending my life this way?

Falling into exhausted repose, or better said, a heaping pile of compost, after four-hours of hard labor, I rested my shovel against the side of the wheelbarrow, and stumbled towards the fence to rest my aching back. Leaning into the fence with my arms, and resting my head against a board, I could just make out the shape of Mr. McNabb's house in-between the crack in the planks, and the trees beyond. And I thought of some words I had for him, better left unmentioned for now. And at these thoughts, I couldn't help but grow in boldness at Stephan's idea to try and bring some humility to this pompous man. And wouldn't you know it, as I leaned against that fence, and considered many dreadful idioms of Mr. McNabb, I noticed the fence moving a little at its base where it came into contact with the ground. This would be the perfect place to sneak into Mr. McNabb's compound for Stephan's plan of sabotage. Ah, yes, providence had shown her favor upon me. Sitting up against the rickety board, I looked, and saw the nails were rusted, and had begun to work their way out from the fence post.

I could almost get my fingers behind them to give them a little pull. Glancing about the yard, I watched for anyone watching me, and seeing the coast was clear, I pulled a small pocket knife from my pocket that doubled as a bottle opener. And as you would probably guess, I used this tool much more frequently for its cap removal capabilities, than for the knife. But here and now, it came in handy, and I began to gouge the

59

wood around the nails, and preyed at them until they came loose. I gave the plank a little jiggling at the bottom to ensure I had removed all the nails, and then gently slid some dirt back against the board to hide any signs of tampering.

I couldn't wait to tell Stephan about my contribution to our plan, and how fate had so obviously shown her light upon me, and how we now had a starting point for the break in. Though I know today it was not just coincidental serendipity serenely shining towards me that was allowing me an opportunity to bring some justice at the mill. But instead, immutable decrees from heaven, that had chosen me to bring some fairness to this tree grinding factory.

Now that my mind had been properly sent thinking about other things, mischievous things, I wasn't so disgruntled about going back to work. And when things got tough, I would just think of conversing with Stephan or playing my violin, and the sweaty stinging eyes, and aching muscles, and burning blisters allowed these aggravations to fall from the range of my senses.

And before I knew it, the day was over, and I was ready to meet Stephan to begin planning what would become known around the mill, as 'the great cupcake controversy'.

4

Before we begin, may I call to all of you? Those who have ears let them hear? The more I press, the moral pressing of the unseen schisms between truth and knowledge, is where most difficulty arises. And not only for myself, but also for you, as the dead cannot hear, even when words of life are spoken. What I shall distinguish, is that, information may be truth, and may not, but if it is true; true information, will accumulate within us. But if we do not see the source, we have missed the mark, and then this accumulation is all for not. And so, we become as useful as heat in the desert. And as I write, and close my eyes to see, and envision this heat, where I find myself is a valley of death.

When I close my eyes and stare into the fiery valley, I see it is very dry and full of bones. There is nothing green, nothing alive, but the life within me. I count myself very fortunate, much loved, that I have not been left in the valley of dry bones. But how I still call to all that lie in the valley that they may waken from this dry dreamless sleep. Those who have ears let them hear?

As I stand on the precipice and call into the valley, these are the words that are echoing off the canyon walls: 'dry bones come alive, dry bones come alive, let the breath of life fill your empty ribcage. Dry bones, I will give you tendons, and flesh, and when I call, I will give you breath and life. Dry bones come alive?'

And as I spoke, there was a noise, a rattling noise, and I saw that the bones moved. And bone came to bone, and the rattling became loud, and I was very pleased that they had heard my call. Flesh and tendons came on the bones, and appeared, but there was still not breath. But I was asked, 'give us breath', so I said let the four winds come, from the north, and the south, and the east, and the west. And the wind blew in a great tempest, and the breath came to the slain, that they may be made alive. The alive moved from the valley of death, and I was very pleased.

But as I looked into the valley, I saw that there were many dry bones still there. And I was saddened, asking, 'why have you not been made alive dry bones, with your brothers and sisters, who have walked from the valley of death?' And the dry bones groaned back to me, 'we have not knowledge, because we have not love, and without love, our truth is dead'.

As we return to my story, I open my eyes, and leave that for you. Flee from the dead truth, and empty hopes of the hopeless, the blind who lead the blind, learn from the learned, I will beg. And as the memory of my walk to the river returns, how I wished I would have learned sooner. But my time, was my time, and so I must wait.

I was first to the river, and lying on the grass, my muscles felt like jelly, my feet hurt, and all the skin on my hands was fresh and raw. All these things only promoted ideas of mutiny, and I can't say, even if Stephan had backed out of our plan and told me he had changed his mind about becoming a saboteur, that I would have followed.

But a gentle rustling of grass, and clinking of glass awakened me from my morbid pot of self-pity. And as I saw Stephan and his smile, the thoughts of my troubled body moved far beyond me. "Hey, what do you have in the bag?" I asked Stephan, as he began working himself into a comfy spot in the grass next to me.

"I brought us some tree-root beer. I figured you would be pretty tired after working all day in the inventory department, and would like something cold to drink." Stephan replied, with the thoughtfulness of a true friend. "Dude, what are you doing? I thought you had sworn off all wood infused drinks? You better not let Dr. StrusselCööK know about this." I implored, feeling a bit shocked he had given in so easily.

"Oh don't worry, this is a fiber free beverage, so it only has some vague notions of the real thing. Plus Dr. StrusselCööK gave me the idea. She said as long as I hung around people with the same problem, this would be a way for me to fit in without feeling uncomfortable. No offence." Stephan said, twisting off the cap to my drink and handing it to me. "None taken, but I can't imagine why someone would want to just flirt with sawdust drinks. I mean, what's the point?" I replied, taking a drink, and noticing I was experiencing some dissatisfaction with my beverage, and its lack of bite. Stephan refrained from answering for a moment, taking a drink himself to consider my words, then he spoke. "I'm not sure, I guess I haven't really thought about it before. But she's a doctor, she should know what she is talking about, right? Plus it's not like I've completely sworn off sawdust, I mean that's kind of a crazy thing to think about. Because I still have it in my food, and I watch tree-vision."

"Sure man, whatever you say, you know much more about that stuff than me... But I've got some really great news for us, though. I think you'll be proud of me, I have been considering your plan to break into Mr. McNabb's house." "Yeah, so, what did you come up with?" Stephan asked, and letting the question hang in the air, I tried building the anticipation, and then I spoke. "Well, while I was on my lunch break today. I was so tired I went to lean up against the fence. And I noticed something, the first thing I noticed was you could see Mr. McNabb's mansion from where I was at, but then, as my weight pressed into the board, it moved. When I looked more closely at how the wooden fence was constructed, I saw some nails had been working their way out of the wood. So I just gave them a little extra help with my pocket knife, and pushed some dirt up against it to keep it in place. I think both of us will be able to fit through the hole there, once we pull the board out of the way; that will be a great entrance and exit spot for us."

"Ok, that's a good start, but how will we get past the extra security, to get into the inventory department?" Stephan inquired, obviously thinking he had found a hole in my plan. "I've also thought about that! When I was getting checked in today, I made a friend, Berry. He's one of the security officers there. Since we have to get in early to turn on the PA system before morning colors, inside Mr. McNabb's house, I was thinking, I would tell him I had some extra sawdust to be moved from the day before and that I don't want to get reported to Mr. McNabb for not moving it..." Interrupting, Stephan forced his question in-between my excited retelling of the plan, which had worked its way out so well in my mind. "What about me?"

"Well, I'm glad you asked that. You see, Berry and I have formed a special bond. I put some of this in his coffee this morning, and he started telling me all about his frustrations with enforcing law in our sawdust nation; I figure, I'll do the same thing again tomorrow morning, and you'll be able to slip right by him; no problem." I recited confidently, holding up my silver flask. What more could you say, I had thought of everything. A smug look now wrapped my face as I internally reflected on my brilliance.

"What about the dogs?" Stephan questioningly suggested, scratching his chin, clearly analyzing my well thought out plan, and deciding if he was onboard. "I guess, we could just give them steak; isn't that what they do on tree-vision all the time?" I proposed, believing tree-vision to be the holder of all things true. "Yes, I suppose it is, and for our purposes, tree-vision may have something to contribute to our thinking here... I definitely like the idea." "Alright it's settled then; when will we commence operation... operation beyond good and evil, let's call it." I thought out loud, not realizing which part of my brain had conjured such deep things without me knowing.

"Operation beyond good and evil, I like it, I like it a lot. Let's only hope we can live up to the name..." Stephan replied, searching me for clarification on my clever title for our act of rebellion. But not knowing where the idea had come from myself, I began asking him about something that had been on my mind for a while. "Hey Stephan, I was wondering, I want to go get cleaned up first, but if you would join me at my house this evening for a drink of your choice, I would like to hear more of your story; and maybe you'll allow me to play my violin for you?" I asked, holding the question with gentleness, hoping Stephan would allow me the privilege of his company. "Sure that sounds great, I'll bring my own beverage though, and maybe something for us to snack on."

At that, the rest of our conversation was of unimportant minutia, and so we parted with plans to return together soon. Sometimes, as I write, I can't help but think of other things, more important things than what I'm telling you now, so I will ask for you to hold fast to your minds, as I struggle to cover all the bases of my life.

Making my way home, I thought about the day past, and considered many things, as I have been known to do, I found many frustrations between these things. What is frustrating to me, is when thoughts come, and there is no way to quantify them, or way to analyze the feeling they give me. Forgiveness of self, a most difficult task, inherently absent from my nature. And for the first time in my life, I was being confronted with new thoughts, new feelings, which left me itching in my skin and asking questions, questions I'm not sure had answers. Questions concerning forgiveness. Why forgiveness you might ask, what did I do wrong? I'm not sure I can answer that in a satisfactory way, all I can say is there was some deep prodding, the poke before the poke, if you will, nudging me towards a different way of looking at the world. And this promontory, a strutting, vaporous idea, demanding forgiveness, for those, for what rather, is more abhorrent than to not see things as they really are, and maybe just that, required forgiveness in and of itself? Because I had been following a particular way of thinking up to that point in my life, but sawdust now covering me head to toe, reaching places I didn't know sawdust could reach, giving me perplexing considerations, where none had been before. And so this lent itself to more questions, and I started asking myself, why do you love sawdust so much? What has it done for you?

Once I had returned home, after the long walk, and the long broodings previously mentioned; I began cleaning my mess of a place, sweeping sawdust crumbs from my end table, and vacuuming up all the wood flakes that had worked their way into my carpet. Showering and cleaning myself up, I fell to my couch exhausted, and looking at my violin from across the room, I decided I was too tired to play. Being overworked from moving hundreds of barrels of sawdust, the one thing in life that gave me pleasure above all else, sat unmoving, in a pile of sawdust slothfulness.

My mind being peculiar, and most certainly left to its own direction, began to wander to the nether regions of troubled sleep. As I fell unto this slumber, on my couch, it took me on a strange journey. Though I don't pretend to have the greatest self-awareness, I do pay attention to my thoughts, and must admit, I'm not sure where these originated. And so, this was the dream I began to dream, as I fell into that uneasy slumber on my sofa.

Standing before Mr. McNabb's house, an empty echoing, left this black and white world without the beauty of diversity attributed to life, a colorless world, but for the orange shell of Mr. Zooty impersonating a cloud above. I stared into this cloud, and wondered why it was orange, when the rest of life seemed to be only shades of gray. It was not a beautiful orange, but a neon orange, artificial and self-imposing on the world around. And as I recall what brings beauty, now in my current capacities, here I shall think of my dearest Margaret from the community of trees, and how she has shown me what beauty really is. I know you are not familiar with Margaret or the community she belongs to, but this place, in my story, will be a place she will soon be, and you will soon see. And nothing of what I saw here, now, reflects beauty as it is in my mind today.

Returning to the dream, digressing for but a moment, a mob began to gather, a rabble rousing mob. Throwing sawdust everywhere, this rabble stole my vision from the firmaments, and my eyes were drawn from Mr. Zooty above, to the sawdust below. And as they threw sawdust into the air, I began to throw sawdust with them, forgetting all about the giant Mr. Zooty hanging overhead. Joy, Joy, ode to joy, a sawdust joy like no other, ecstatic uncontrolled muscle twitching's yielding ecstasy! I could have lived in this moment, tossing and rolling in sawdust for the rest of my existence. But as I fell to the sawdust covered earth, looking back into the sky, Mr. Zooty clung to the gray backdrop unwavering in his vile stance. And then Mr. Zooty began to speak, not just addressing anyone, but addressing me, calling me out from the rabble, and this caused me to pause. But it was not the high, squeaky, unintelligible voice of snail talk, we are used to hearing Mr. McNabb translate; it was Mr. Zooty in the sky with the voice of Ohm Matzo:
"I see you Benjamin Silversin, I have been watching you for many years, growing in delight as you wallow in sawdust with hoppy tears;
since you were but a sprinkling of life in your mother's womb,
I have begun a sprinkling, with a plan to groom;
a grooming for the bad and not the good,

68

for your devotion to me and not to him, has time withstood;

for what has been put in you Benjamin, is different from the others,

though it has not been awakened;

my hope is still, you may be forsaken;

though is written you were fearfully and wonderfully made,

it is the truth into a knot, I shall have you braid;

braiding all that is right and true,

twisting it into a plank of wood with a vile, detestable screw;

it is written you have been known and loved from before time began,

but you Benjamin have done nothing but always ran;

and for that I am quite hoppy!

Thus speaks Mr. Zooty"

Sitting up from my sleep in a panic, sweat poured from my face, pulling my shirt away from my body, I tried letting the air cool my skin. I wiped my forehead, and paused until the knock that had awakened me, returned, with a short rapping. My heart began to slow, as the surroundings became familiar, and I confirmed there indeed was no giant Mr. Zooty overhead slimily propelling himself across the sky speaking in senseless rhymes. This revelation, as I'm sure you can imagine, was of great relief to me, but it was only replaced with anxious considerations of my failure to prepare my abode for visitors. And so, leaping from the couch, hurriedly I swept up the remnants of my bachelor lifestyle.

Answering the door, looking a little disheveled, thoughts of a giant Mr. Zooty not far from me, I saw Stephan holding a grocery bag. With his brows furrowed at my sight, he began to speak, "Are you ok? We can always do this another time if you're not feeling well." "I'm sorry dude, I just woke up. And I had the strangest dream, I'll have to tell you about it sometime... But please come in, I'm sorry if the place looks a little unkempt, but I was just so tired from work, and I fell asleep right after my shower..."

"Don't worry about it, it will take a few weeks for you to get used to the inventory department, foreman Dave is a slave driver, for sure!" Stephan returned, walking in to my house, appearing to take in the simple accommodations. His eyes falling on my violin from across the room, he walked over and picked it up. "So you play the violin... that's cool, it's a very emotional instrument... I've always wanted to learn music, but it's a lot of work" "Yeah, unfortunately I haven't had any time to practice today... So what's in the bag?" I inquired, opening the windows to allow the cooling evening air to fill the house. "Well, I brought some mineral water for myself, and for you, I got this hand crafted wood ale from our sawdust loving friends in Europe... they say it is one of the best ones on the market, but then again the Europeans always say that about their wood drinks. I also brought some fresh fruit, and a maple aged cheddar. I hope that's ok?"

"Oh man that sounds great I don't usually eat this well, or drink this well, I'm usually an instant gratification kind of guy, doing the fast food thing." I said with excitement, becoming giddy at the idea of this high priced treat, I mean the Europeans have been doing this sawdust thing a lot longer than us, they should be better at it than we are.

"I thought, since you opened up your home, and will be providing me with a violin concert, that this was, well, the least I could do." Stephan replied, giving a gentle nod of the head in thankfulness.

70

"Cool, thanks for thinking of me. How about I take that from you and put the cheese and fruit on a plate, and the drinks in the fridge… And, we'll go on the porch to talk, we'll get a nice breeze there." I suggested, being more anxious to slam a wood beer, than to taste the cheese and fruit. "Ok, sounds good to me."

I took the bags from Stephan, and going to the kitchen, the first thing I did was crack one of the pretentious European ales, and boy was it good! Even in hindsight, knowing wood drinks are not good for me, I still find it difficult to forget the hiss they make when you open them, or their sweet bitterness on my tongue at the first swig. Anyways, as I cubed the cheese, and arranged the fruit, I maintained many breaks for my friend Mr. Wood-Ale. And I must admit, I had finished more than one by the time I made it to the porch to sit with my new friend. As I reached the porch, my mind becoming subtly foggy, like the Themes in the spring, and so, a tired man melted into his chair, feeling like the mist above the river.

The waning sun on a hot humid day was finally beginning to set, sucking itself beyond the horizon. And the cooling air left us both enveloped in our own thinking for a time. Slowly picking at the snack tray, eventually I asked, "Should I play my violin first, or do you want to talk?" "No we can just talk for now, I know your tired from work, and plus, you should enjoy your drink since it's already open." "Alright." I agreed, I mean, who am I, to argue with such a pleasant suggestion, as to finishing, or rather consuming my sugary salve for the soul?

"So I'm curious to know why you don't drink wood drinks any more, I mean, you said you still have sawdust in your life in other ways?" I inquired, unable to understand what purpose life presented to the participant, if there was not pleasure to be endured at every moment along the journey. Thinking now, maybe small enjoyments were only leading up to the big ones, and if we couldn't enjoy the small things, we could never enjoy the large things, for what 'these things' were, as 'these things' were meant to be: as I can see this now, I didn't see this then, as sawdust stayed true to me as my measurement of fulfillment during that time, and throughout all time. But Stephan, clearly with more discernment than myself, replied, "That's kind of a difficult question to answer, maybe it would just be easier for me to start from the beginning; that is, the beginning of my story." Stephan said speaking quietly, looking out over our town as the dark purple sky from a closing day provided us with a backdrop of thanksgiving from above. And so, only to eager to learn more of him, I consented. "Ok."

Stephan thought aloud to himself, then he began to tell his tale, "Where to start? Where to start? I guess I can start with my parents... I'm from the south in our sawdust nation, originally, and my Mom was the one who raised us. My dad, well I don't really see him much anymore, and I didn't really see him much growing up either, now that I put it that way. The only time I really saw my Dad was Sunday afternoons. He worked all week, very hard, at a factory that made wood cutting tools. Then Friday and Saturday he would come home, but he would leave as soon as he did, and be out all night, and sometimes during the day too, carousing around. On Sundays he would come home with whatever money he had left from his check, after partying sawdust festival style all-weekend, and give it to my Mom for food and rent... and then, I remember him starting to drink, at home, as I got older, or maybe I was just more aware of what was going on. But anyways, when my mom would ask him where all his money went, or what he had been doing all night, well, he would get so angry, I still can't understand how someone could get so angry like that, especially with someone they are supposed to love… Usually he would just drink more when she would ask him those questions; but sometimes he would call her names, and on rare occasions he would hit her…" Stephan's voice began to quiver, and I sent my eyes blinking more quickly to remove the forth coming tears. I have always found it difficult to separate my emotions from people, and learning about Stephan's life, I couldn't help but empathize. "It's ok, you don't have to tell me this if you don't want to." I offered, squinting and looking away to avoid showing the sadness that had begun to fill me, with the telling of Stephan's story. Stephan, clearly determined to push onward, took a sip of water, cleared his throat and continued. "No, it's ok, I think it's important to tell my friends these things, plus it will help me to illustrate something I want to share with you more effectively… Anyways sorry about that, as I was saying, I remember one time, he, he being my dad, had accused my mom of being with another man, of course it wasn't true, but he thought it was. But this time, being different from the others, he wanted to prove his point, so he pulled off his belt. I remember this vividly because that day my mother was wearing a white dress, she had worn it for church that day. My father called us, which is me and my brother, into the living room and had us sit down on the couch. My dad looked at us and said 'remember this boys, this is what happens when you break someone's trust' and then he hit my mother with his belt, he hit her some many times, and he hit her so hard. I still can't think of it without

73

shuttering inside. And the belt he had, the belt he used, had a big metal buckle on it, and I remember the noise it made when it struck her. And my mom, she just looked at us with the saddest eyes I can ever remember seeing, tears falling silently from her eyes, to her cheeks, to the floor. And her white dress, the one she had worn to church, began to turn red…"

Holding my wood drink tightly, my emotional inhibitions partially removed from my liquid spirit softener; thus my eyes became cloudy once again, as I envisioned a small Stephan, watching his mother beginning to bleed as his father stood whipping her like a dog; and as you might picture, I couldn't help but bring my knuckle to the corner of my eye, with this in my mind. And Stephan, watching him patiently as I made this motion, seemed to have moved beyond where him and I now sat, watching the sky as the stars eclipsed the sun, a temporal world of pain and strife, no longer affected him the way I would imagine it should. But, after a time of consideration, he appeared to come to some satisfactory conclusion as to the purpose behind this revelation, and he looked at me and smiled. And he began telling me of his sawdust addictions, and confinement, and so many other things.

And here, in our conversation, we shall halt, for the things he told me next made little sense. And as I know now, that couldn't help but be true, and to try and explain them in a way that yields them the proper honor with which is befitting, would be to diminish their power. What I will say, is these things, 'spiritual things' which Stephan spoke of, had a shining in his mind which I could see on his face. And to some of our friends, these metaphysical qualities attributed to us people, are only signs of an archaic desire to understand the world in which we live: what profound sorrow, what pity, I observe in their simple-eruditeness, their presumptuousness, their self-will, these lovers of self-style living; don't you know, then, I was one of them though! Yet I dared to inquire further.

"So why do you believe what you believe, I mean, if you can't see it?" I asked, and Stephan closing his eyes in thought, finally rendering within his mind a picture with which he was satisfied to share. "That's a good question, I'm glad you asked it. I was actually thinking about it earlier today after you asked me to come over, and to hear more of my story. Because I've been asked that before, and maybe I haven't always had the best answer. But the way I think of it, or the way it makes sense to me, is maybe more appropriately seen as a picture. And I was thinking, if you have ever gone sailing that is kind of what it's like. I was in one place, a very dark lonely place, ready to give up, and then one day someone offered me a ride on a sailboat. They said they couldn't go with me, but the trip was free. They said, they couldn't really tell me where I was going, but once I got there, I would know I had arrived. They said, I would know because, I had arrived somewhere much better than I could have ever have imagined. And I can't tell you the speed of the wind, or its direction, the temperature of the air or the water, on my trip, but I do know I was in one place, a very dark place, but now I'm in another place, a very beautiful place, and the place I'm in now, is so far away from the place I was in then. And the two are so far apart, I know I couldn't have gotten where I'm at now, on my own. That's how I know what I believe is true, well, it's true because the journey is true. If that makes any sense?"

5

Let us not be futile in our thinking, seeking only entertainment and distraction, falling into a pit of thoughtlessness and close-mindedness, as the venders and poets do our thinking for us. Or as ideas come forth to pay their respects, let us not lie dead in our caskets, but sit up to great them. Hello. Before, as clams, sitting in the silt of thought, we should filter our water with discernment, until we have caught a gritty idea, and shall ruminate on this idea, until it turns into a pearl. Or as a caring passerby, has spotted us turtles crossing a busy street, and not knowing that we are in danger; that when we see them, we would retract into our shell of familiar-ness. Because at the sight of their challenging principles to our safety, or to our pride and self-reliance; we would rather pretend no one is there, than to take a few moments to dive into the pond of self, examining what has caused us to leave our home of soft-niceties, to fall onto the pavement of hard-heartedness.

Rather, as we push the envelope of our understanding, we should first attend the economy of intellectual systems. Observing the grand spectrum of principles, and philosophies, we should bake, and taste test each cake properly. And in doing this, we will ultimately decide which one should be our fare for life. As we begin to tread the bizarre, the market place of ideas, we will pass each vendors stand, looking carefully at what they have to offer. And as we begin to purchase the ingredients for our cake, for our purposes here, we will make but two.

The first cake we will bake, will include a cup of self-indulgence, a teaspoon of vanity, one large ego, and some glutton-full flower. Mixing well, and putting our cake in the oven, we will watch as heated perseverance, gives our cake a haughty spirit, and then, when the cake is full of itself, we will know it is done cooking, and ready to eat.

We will forgo icing our cake with lasciviousness, or any other vulgar temptation that should neglect our duty, to bring forth from our minds, an accurate account of our cake. So when we take a bite, any honest individual, with a well-constituted mind, should only taste a cake that is bitter-sweet at best, one that looks more moist than it really is, and does not live up to its name.

Our next cake, is much different, because we start with different ingredients: it will be a glutton-free cake, with a dash of sensible salt, a cup of virtue, and mindful milk to replace the egos. And when we place it in the oven, double checking to make sure our cake is at just the right temperature. Not letting it cook to long, and ending up with a self-righteous-cake, or cooking it to shortly and ending up with one that is without character and hypocritical. We don't want either one of these cakes, so as you can imagine the time spent in the oven is very important. But when this cake is done, there is something different in the air, an aroma of sweetness fills the whole kitchen, and it almost seems a shame we should have to cut into it for our experiment.

But we will cut into it none-the-less, and what we observe first is its texture, how when the knife of life presses in, our cake bounces back.

77

We see, and soon taste, our cake is not dry, lacking cohesion with the world around, but rather seems to know that it is a special cake, and is in the world, but not of the world. This perspective allows our cake to appreciate, it is what brings flavor to life, that it has become the salt of the earth, or here, our sweet dessert. Allowing our sweet dessert to melt in our mouth, there is no unpleasant after taste, only a bit of sadness that life seems to have lost some of its goodness as it is swallowed. But what we quickly recall, is there is one great baker, the chief cornerstone of culinary, and he is always backing new cakes, and our hope is in him, not in our own taste testing abilities.

Keeping our experiment in the back of our thinker, I will not ask you to lend your mind to my ideas without proper investigation, but please don't think too long, and lose yourselves in the process. What we will begin to soon see, is I was beginning to work with different ingredients in my life, though not far off, as I woke early to my alarm, preparing myself for 'operation beyond good and evil', I was still my own leader, my own boss, and what a terrible leader of myself, I had become. Yet, the sparkle in my friends eye, had me considering something new, and the trials to come, the cupcake exploits, were mischievous things in my mind, but had worked themselves out so well, for me, who was called according to his purposes. And that was a good beginning, for now.

Rolling out of bed, sleepy eyed and sore, the crickets and the bull frogs were the only critters to keep me company at this early hour. Revolving my check list for the day around in my mind; Stephan was bringing the steaks, and I was bringing the panty hose, another idea courtesy of tree-vision, I might add. Check and check, I thought, so let me get going. Yawning and walking onto the porch, I had made myself my usual cedar coffee. Allowing the cup to warm my hands in the cool dark hours before sunrise, I looked at the stars, with apprehensions. All this I thought, only burning balls of gas haphazardly strewn around periods of emptiness, was it true?

For another time, I shall lend my pensive inner workings, a place to organize these considerations, and then when the truth is known, how it has set me free, freedom of my affections from the vile and self-destructive to the good and the pure, I shall then see, and will better able to answer these dwellings of my mind for you.

But now, observing strange mental agony, before one endeavors in something new, something terribly wrong, but feeling oh so right; how butterflies began flying, and geese began bumping, along with a few frogs searching for a home in my throat, with the anxious forebodings of operation 'beyond good and evil'. These animals appeared to be having their time of fun with me, and I wasn't sure how to escape them. Seeking my sensitive spot, which is, after picking up my violin, I noticed the bow trembled on the string as I drew it, and figured just getting on with it as Mr. Zooty says, was the best thing I could do before any more animals joined my neurotic party, and my nerves truly came undone.

Placing my violin aside, and fast-forwarding, I began my long walk to the bushes near the mill, where Stephan was to meet me with the steaks, and I myself, would come bearing the gift of panty hose to cover our faces. How foolish we would have looked, if anyone was able to see these amateur criminals, us, preparing in our naïve way, for the truly spectacular performance, which was to come next. But there was no one to see, and the best I can do for us now, in my current place of safety, as there is still a resentful warrant for my head form Mr. McNabb; is, I will use my words the best way I am able.

The streets around the mill were empty and dark, the only lights to be seen were from the guard shacks, and some feint glowing emanating from the landscaping of the white house. The rest, everything else was dark, a darkness so dark, it seemed to bring to light the deep hidden objects of my unseen spirit. And that, for now, is all I will mention about darkness.

Mr. McNabb's mansion was far out of view, as it sat bordered by the mill on one side and the river on the other, not to mention the large trees that eclipsed its imposing structure. But as I walked, taking in the blackened day, the first light to not just catch my eye, but my attention, was a flashing light, coming from the brush on the side of the road. "Hey Benjamin, is that you?" Someone whispered to me, from the direction of the flashing light. "Is that you Stephan?" I asked queerly, I mean, who else would be calling my name from the bushes at this ungodly hour? "Yeah, it's me, just follow the flashlight; I'll shine it on the ground so you can jump over the ditch." "Ok." I quietly replied, feeling like a commando on nighttime ambush. The long grasses that bordered the road, lent my skin their morning dew, and seeds and fibers of all sorts, worked their way into my clothing as I did this, and a physical itching, not as pleasant as sawdust, overtook my scratching mind.

"Hey man, glad you made it…" Stephan acknowledged, after I drew close and made my seat next to him. "So are you excited for this, ah, little endeavored of ours?" I offered up anxiously, placing my small sack on the ground. Clicking the flashlight back on, Stephan pointed to a piece of paper, and began to speak, "I sure am, check this out, I was able to get a map of the interior of Mr. McNabb's mansion. It looks kind of sloppy with my hand drawing, but that was the only way I could copy it." My mouth fell partially ajar at this sight, a very brilliant idea, some detail we no doubt needed, and I surely missed in my planning. Stephan has really been thinking about this break-in thing, I observed to myself. "That's a great idea, but where did you get a map?" I asked, squinting my eyes, trying to orient myself on the topographical lines to find the mansions proximity to the inventory department. "I went to the local historical society, and found the old mansion's building records, some permits that had been pulled, those kind of things, I thought it might come in handy…" Stephan answered, tracing his fingers over the lines on the paper. "Cool, yeah, I think it'll come in real handy." I replied, admiring Stephan greatly for his foresight. "Ok this is my idea…" And Stephan began to tell me the intricate details of our coming escapade, until, finishing his pep-talk, he folded up the paper map, and grabbed his bag. I watched, as he did this, putting the map up for safe keeping, and saw the steaks, just barely, beneath a bunch of weeds. But why would he have a bunch of weeds covering the steaks, filling the top of his sack? "Hey, what are the weeds in your bag for?" I inquired, perplexed, wondering if dogs liked steak with herbs. "Oh, well, those aren't weeds, its hemlock, and you'll see what it's for later, so don't worry about it for now."

"Ok, whatever you say…" I answered, a little resentfully at first, wondering why Stephan would be hiding something from me. I impart unto you, why would he not trust me with hemlock knowledge, we had come this far together? But analyzing and concluding this was but a small detail better left for another, more timely discussion, I continued. "I guess I'll lead us, and start us out of the bushes here, into the mill, just split off to my right after we go through initial security, so they don't see us walking towards the inventory department together. Ok... And once we get to the inventory department, I'll pull out my flask, and Berry will take care of the rest..."

"Sounds good... I'll meet you at the rendezvous point by the loosened fence boards behind the sawdust bunks. Alright...? Good luck!" Stephan acknowledged, picking up his bag, and walking into the darkness beyond. Our plan commencing; for the first time my mind moved from a theoretic place of abstraction, to a place of action. Though this change was subtle, it offered a new heightened sense of the world around, and everything became clear. Our conspirators chariot had been pulled from the armory, now moving forward, it was being pulled by a war horse unseen; and soon, we were entering enemy held territory. My only hope now, was that I would not neglect the reigns, and a novice charioteer might not crumble under the pressure of vital circumstance.

So walking and thinking, my mind like a braying metronome, baying to stop endlessly swinging to and fro, from one idea to the next, primarily engulfed in scenario construction, and how our day would unfold; it must stop, so I may rest. Yet, if you have ever dropped a marble and tried to recover it quickly, your frustrated effort probably only yielded a marble scattered across the room, defiant, flaunting its ability to slip through your fingers, and thus was my mind, the more I tried to subdue it, the more rebellious it became. The best I can do for us now, is observe an anxiety so great, which was, if we were caught doing what we were about to do, it may very well be the end of us, and my story.

Still, I arrived safely inside the mill, making it through initial security unmolested. I began my long walk up the hill towards the inventory department and Mr. McNabb's mansion. The weight on my shoulders at the moments to come, becoming heavier at each step up this knoll, each step made in the direction of Berry's guard post. From a distance, crowning the hill, I observed Berry sitting with his feet propped on the desk and hands behind his head. Sheepishly I moved in his direction, and out of the corner of my eye I could see Stephan stooped behind a garbage container ready to dash through the gate at his first opportunity.

"Good morning Berry, how's it going?" I asked, leaning in the window, allowing my forearms to hold up my weight. "Not bad Benjamin, it's nice to see you made it through the day yesterday, and were able to make it back. Foreman Dave is a nice guy, but he pushes you hard for sure." Berry said with a smile, bringing himself from a reclined position, to one of uprightness. "Yeah, you bet, I'm sore as heck though from working… but I didn't get all the sawdust moved that I was supposed to, that's why I'm here so early, Foreman Dave said he would report me to Mr. McNabb if I didn't get it all moved before my next shift." Pleases believe my lie Berry, please believe my lie, I thought. And I began to consider, that maybe Berry knew there was no extra sawdust to be moved, or he had seen my bunks were already full, or any other way he might have been able to conclude that what I promised was not true, and so, sweat began to form on my brow, and my fingers began to tremble. At this, I kept one hand over the other, held them together tightly, and tried to look as cool as a cucumber while he considered my words. He took longer to answer than he should have, and I surmised it may be all over before it began. "Oh, I wouldn't take him too seriously with that threat, it was your first day, plus, that is more likely just something he tells all the new guys to help keep them in line. But since you showed the initiative and came in early, you should at least try to get done whatever it is you need to do." Berry answered easily, not suspecting a thing, and a relief fell over me, like a cool rain shower on a sweltering day. "Well, good... But cool that means I have a few minutes then, I thought I was going to have to hurry to get that sawdust where it was supposed to be... So, anyways, how's the coffee Berry?" I replied and inquired with a smile, giving a little wink and furrowed brow, to let him know, or make him feel, I understood his troubles. "It's a little weak, if you know what I mean...?"

Pulling forth my sterling silver angel's share, I offered tacitly, a bit of molten grace, or more reasonably, unspoken forgiveness, with a small nod of the head towards my hand. And without hesitation, or rather with a quick glance around, he pushed his cup near the window, and I leaned in to let a handsome splash fall into his coffee. And just as I suspected, some of my liquid inhibition remover in gullet, a new Berry began to emerge, one who could transcend the dismal realities of law-dust enforcement. One who floated strait towards speaking, with a frictionless efficiency, telling of his aggravated career resentments, and the anti-hopes he possessed for humanity.

"Truth be told Benjamin, I get so upset sometimes..." Berry began, as he took long sips of his coffee. "I've been working an awful

84

lot, there is never an off hour for the criminal in our sawdust nation, or so it seems… Did you know, just the other day I caught someone stealing wood shavings from the inventory department. It's one thing if when you use the blower at the end of the day to clean up, you miss a couple flakes that are stuck in your hair, or under your collar, I mean that's fine, no big deal… but this guy had a baggie packed full of shavings and it was stuffed in his pants. Caught red handed right…? No, guess what he had the nerve to tell me? He said, he didn't know how it got there... That's crazy, does the guy think I'm an idiot. I'd be a million pound sawdust-air if I had a woodchip for every time I heard an excuse for how someone else had some stolen sawdust, or how they didn't know how it got there. It just doesn't make any sense sometimes, I wish, I wish people wouldn't love sawdust so much, I really do hate having to arrest people… I remember one time I arrested this one guy and he asked me to call home and tell his mom where he was at, so she wouldn't worry, I didn't give it much thought beforehand and I called, do you know that was one of the most painful calls I have ever had to make. The mother started crying and telling me how her son was a good boy, and had been on the honor roll and played sports in school, that he helped raise his little brother after his dad left, but because he was lost and had no one to raise him, he got caught up in the sawdust gangs… she paused, and didn't say anything for it seemed like forever, but then she started telling me how his little brother, the one he helped raise, who admired him so much, got caught up in the gangs too… and one day she came home from work to find a police officer at her house. The officer was there to tell her, her son had been murdered… and then she started crying, and couldn't stop, through her sobs she said all she wanted, the only thing she wanted in life, was for him to get out of that sawdust life, so she wouldn't lose another boy… I have to say, I had a tear coming down my face by the time I finished my conversation with that woman, I will never forget her… these things, all these things are so heart breaking, I do my best to try and help keep others safe, you know? And guess what? I end up being the bad guy, who would have thought?"

Berry stopped speaking again at the time he became emotional, and I don't blame him. I, being the particularly sensitive guy I am, felt a little bad, that I had called a man to start sharing his deepest thoughts, only for my own selfish ambitions, to get Stephan inside the inventory department. But yet, maybe there was some good here. Everything penetrates me if you haven't noticed, but that is how I make sense of the world, and though it certainly has its drawbacks, it has its advantages also, and perhaps one advantage here, was I was able to carry away with me some of Berry's burden, and he left, or rather we parted that day, with Berry being a lighter man, for the time we had together.

"Yeah, I think I understand what it is your saying, I'm really sorry to hear that, you have a tough job…" I offered Berry, in hopes that my words might be an aloe, my own cool words to him. "Well, thanks for listening, maybe you can stop by again tomorrow? I should let you get to work, I don't want you to get on foreman Dave's bad side…" "Yeah, I'll see you tomorrow." I replied as casually as possible, not wanting to come across as being too anxious to leave.

Waving as I left berry, I began walking through the gate and around the wall into the inventory department. Arriving in the yard, a few

86

fire flies danced about, and a thought of a lightning bug sender came to mind, perhaps there was someone, somewhere, thinking about me, as I was thinking about them, and they sent these lightning bugs here to remind me there was light even in darkness? As this place, the mill, was desolate of life, except for some dimly lit areas near a few of the buildings, everything else was dark, and these few fireflies, were all I had to bring me hope, hope that there was someone out there who cared about my darkness.

Slippery ideas, slipping slowly forward, past my bunks full of sawdust from the day prior, and towards the fence. Several flashes of light, clearly artificial in origin, of a flashlight, alerted me of Stephan's safe arrival inside. Moving in his direction, my head felt light and my stomach began to twist, along with the anxious meanderings of a mind before risk is taken, and I couldn't help but become a little nauseous at the idea of entering the abode, or rather the castle of McNabb the great.

"Hey Stephan, I got-to sit down for a minute, I'm not feeling so well…" I admitted, as I entered the thick grasses near the fence line, his face coming into focus. "Oh man, you're not giving in already are you? We have come this far, we can't turn back." Stephan pleaded, with the pleading voice of peer pressure. Not that I had actually considered returning from whence I came, but the thought of being at home with my violin was a tempting and pleasant thought indeed. "No, I'm not giving up, I've just never done anything like this before, and my nerves are not necessarily agreeable to this type of anxiety… Alright?" I barked back, a little upset he couldn't understand my uneasiness. "Alright, I got it man, no pressure, just let me know when you are ready to go, I have the dirt pulled back from the fence board, so all we have to do is move the plank…" Stephan said, patting me on the shoulder for encouragement. I took some deep breaths, thought about the potential consequences, both good and bad, my promise to Stephan, all of our planning; and weighing these things; as I weighed them, the crooked grin of Mr. McNabb carrying Mr. Zooty came to mind, and the evil grin he held as Stacey went running from the grand ball room crying after he had called her ugly on orientation day; and this picture of a tearful Stacey, sealed for me, my decision to push forward.

"All right, let's go, and get this over with." Watching Stephan, he smiled his big white smile at my proclamation, and immediately waved his arm and began crawling towards the fence. "Hey set the board next to the opening so we can put it back in place when we get on the other side, I'll pull out the map and steaks as soon as I get through; ok?" "Got it." I whispered, and so we moved the plank, squeezing through the tight space, I found myself shortly, on the other side. And where I found myself was a forest, the first forest I had ever been in, with real trees, and I couldn't help but think I had passed through the wardrobe to Narnia.

"I think we can duck low along this tree line here, and that will take us to the servant's entrance on the west side of the house." Stephan suggested handing me a white paper bundle, butchers paper, filled with meat. "Sounds good to me, I should probably unwrap this some, so the dogs can smell it…" I replied, pulling back the paper corners to expose the steaks. "Alright, let's go…" Stephan commanded, waving his arm for me to follow. We made it up near the edge of the house rather easily, only the sounds of a few broken twigs, and some leaves rustling announced our arrival, and no dogs.

Tapping Stephan on the shoulder, I whispered, "no dogs, cool right?" Turning towards me, his mouth opened as if he was to speak, but he spoke not, what he did do, was point, point very emphatically over my shoulder. And soon, the warm breath, and the quite growl of eminence provided me with an accurate understanding of the dismay on his face. No fast movements, don't act like your scared, I told myself. Moving with the sureness of a man walking the plank holding a millstone, so I held the steak, and turning with providence, I uttered a short plea. Oh fortunate providence, my I ask, have I asked that the pup before me should enjoy filet mignon?

The answer was provided quickly as his friend joined him, and both dogs' tails began to wag as I set the humble offering before them, a humbled man I was with their ferocious Benjamin tearing devices smiling in my direction. Finally as one duo indulged in gluttony, another duo began slowly backing up, moving near the entrance we were to use. "Good job Benjamin, you handled that like a pro." Stephan encouraged, pulling me by the arm across the open ground separating the edge of the woods from castle McNabb. We reached the door, and suddenly it occurred to me we didn't have a key, what if it was locked? Yet, didn't I feel a little stupid when the man who had retrieved a copy of the floor plans from the historical society, pulled a shiny golden lock opener from his pocket? "Where the heck did you get a key?" I asked emphatically, watching Stephan fumble to get the key in the slot. "I used to date one of Mr. McNabb's servants, that's probably all I should say about that."

Wow, this guy, he's something else I tell you, he could find fresh ice cream in Mozambique!

"Before we go any further, let's put theses on, we don't want anyone to be able to identify us." I said, handing Stephan one of the panty hose. I pulled mine over my face first. The new view of the world I had from inside woman's underwear was certainly an interesting one, and though I would not suggest this to our more refined readers, perhaps, there was something to gleam from a woman's perspective on breaking and entering. Stephan obviously recognizing my new profound insight into life, seeing things differently himself, started to laugh so loudly I was forced to cover his mouth with my hand. "You're going to get us caught dude, stop laughing so loud." "Sorry man, but if you could see your face, it's priceless." Stephan replied as he composed himself. "I don't want to be here any longer than we have to so let's go, you lead the way." I made known, and an understanding, or maybe a new gravity given by our situation occurred as the first bugle call of the day began echoing throughout the grounds of the mill.

"We have to hurry, we have five minutes at most…" I implored, pushing Stephan towards the door. We entered the home slowly. The hinges were properly lubricated, so there was no squeaking, ok, good start. But as we shut the door, the light glow of early morning no longer our companion, an absence of light, or maybe of glowing goodness, placed us in a position where we were forced to consider what would be our guiding force? Clicking on the flashlight, it seems we could see what is, by knowing what is not, and here, what is, is that those small cylinders of chemically reacting goodness within a world devoid of its own good power, could help us along.

Paintings, artwork of all types, suits of armor, swords, gold inlay; shall I continue, were what willed, and or filled, the McNabb corridor consortium. Stephan led the way to the slaves, excuse me, servant's staircase, and we soon found ourselves on the third floor of the residence in the office of great evil, the officially vile mill owner's place of work.

"Ok Benjamin, find the switch for the PA system, I have to find Mr. Zooty." "What? Are you crazy? Leave Mr. Zooty alone, Mr. McNabb will have our souls if we mess with him." I begged as I searched and found my destination, the on switch large and red for the mill's microphone. "I'm Sorry Benjamin, but I can't do that, I've been working here at the mill too long to just let an opportunity like this pass me up…" Grabbing Stephan by the arm, I pleaded first with my eyes, and then with my words, "Please, I beg you, I'd like to live to enjoy another festival?" "Forgive me…" Were the words that trailed off into the darkness, as Stephan moved, pulling away from my grasp towards the grand wooden desk of the greatest authority in the land, the power and principality of the air around the mill.

What could I do? Certainly nothing which could change my friend's mind, so I did my part. Turning the switch from off to on, I hurried to Stephan's side, next to Mr. Zooty's cage, as he pulled the weeds from his sack and placed them within the beautifully orange snail's reach. "Alright, good, now let's go." I beseeched pulling Stephan by the collar.

And so we retraced our footsteps, made it downstairs, and locked the door behind us.

But as we made it back to the woods, observing torn butchers paper on the ground, our terrible duo nowhere to be seen, a thought occurred. You whimsical thought, most certainly you have come too late to be of any good, which is, in my terror, I provided those hell hounds with all the meat I had, and we still had several hundred yards of forest to cover before we could escape over our fence of safety. And wouldn't you know it, these creatures who seem unable to anticipate anything besides their next meal, were anticipating us slithering forth from the servant's entrance. Maybe we are their next meal?

Frozen in time, time stood still. Slow the song in your mind, think about the next note to be played; don't think ahead of yourself, you will mess things up. Some sage advice courtesy of my violin teacher that maybe, if I could focus on one thought other than falling into the hands of these guard dogs, or Mr. McNabb, I could decide what it is I should do to avoid tearing and gnashing of teeth. I could climb a tree, that might work; wait, I don't know how to climb trees, I've never seen anything larger than a shrub prior to working at the mill! Stupid thoughts, think your way out of this one dummy, ok, what's next? Here, perhaps, profundity found an ally in the simple, and for a moment we could acknowledge that true insight into my existence, my current state of being, or any future lack thereof if I fell under the paws of these beasts, would be found in this most brilliant tree letter word, "RUN!"

As I am a bit slower than most, Stephan seemed to have taken the same line of thought prior to my wise exclamation, in that, he was nowhere to be seen, only the swaying branches in the forest in front of me proclaimed his parting of the woods and a b-line already made towards safety. Dashing in his wake, it seemed every branch that could swing, and every twig that could whack, and every thorn that could poke, found a place on my arms and face and legs. Tearing with a speed I didn't know I possessed, towards safety, the most detestable creatures one could imagine, were now hot on my trail, and I was deathly afraid beyond words.

Running, running, running fast, finally, I saw the fence, and a finale to a splendid excursion out of Plato's cave was nearly at its end. I saw Stephan peering over the top of the fence as I exited the woods. Making my way near the wooden separating staves, I leaped with abandon, and as I leaped so did the pernicious pups following me. On top of the fence, Stephan caught my arm and the pursuing blood beasts my pant leg. I tried my best to pull myself over, with all my might, but I went nowhere. And so Stephan found himself in a tug of war with the hell hounds, me as the prize.

"Whatever you do Benjamin don't let go, on three we are going to pull as hard as we can, one, two, three…" And so I pulled, heaving myself with every morsel of strength I could muster, straining with my very being. My pants tore near the ankle, and I went toppling over the top of the fence, falling right on top of Stephan. He looked at me, and I looked at him, breathing hard, sweating profusely, I tried to gather myself. And in those short moments, his first reaction, what he choose to do first, was chuckle, and then he began to laugh, laughing the most enormous laugh.

"Dude, what are you laughing at, that's not funny, I almost just died." I exclaimed, as I stood, brushing myself off and looking around to see if anyone had seen us. "That was epic man, we are going to have to record that somewhere for posterity... Hey I think I can hear something coming over the speakers, we will talk about this later." And sure enough, faint and distant, you could hear Mr. McNabb talking over the loud speakers of the mill, and these were his words.

"Good morning self, oh you beautiful self, with what a pleasure it is to wake to the sight of you, may we thank the heavens for our beauty, and always know the mold was broken with us, and that the world will be blessed because it has our presence for yet another day... I have been thinking self, and Mr. Zooty, and what has come to center my thoughts, is, genius, that there are two types of genius, a genius which births new ideas, and a genius which twists the existing ones to his purposes, for his gain. I would say, I am of the later genius, for how I have twisted the minds of the herds of sheep that go running about, thinking they live in a nation that is free, ha, ha, ha... these sawdust slaves, they are no freer than mold is to cheese, or bark to a log... they are so pathetic... wait what is that in the mirror, is that a blemish we see in the mirror, we have become ugly have we, well not as ugly as them, and that is what life is all about, let us think ourselves just a little bit better than those around us... I get so angry, Mr. Zooty, because they say we have chocolate chips in us, they say we are part chocolate chip cupcake, but we have no chocolate chips in us, I don't care what they say, chocolate chips are far from us... I hate chocolate, I have done my best to grind up all the coco trees, but they just won't die, and they say we are part chocolate too, they are liars Mr. Zooty, big fat

94

liars; we are too beautiful to be part chocolate; I am my own flavor! I say again, I am my own flavor cupcake! My own flavor I say, why can't people understand that, a very terminally unique flavor am I… Why Mr. Zooty, am I wracked with such fear? How can you love yourself so much, but still be frightened like a little child inside, this is such a terrible paradox Mr. Zooty, love and insecurity? Will you, give me a big wet snail kiss this morning, to raise my spirits? It will be much appreciated; pretty please…?"

"Mr. Zooty what is wrong with you this morning? You are speaking in such a hushed voice, you must raise it; I can barely hear you. No kisses, you are sick, you said. No, not sick, but dying! WHAT, WHAT MR. ZOOTY YOU CAN'T DIE! You said, some slugs have crept inhere while it was dark, and snuck some hemlock into your cage, you said, it looked so pretty you couldn't help but take a bite. Could you see who it was? No, it was too dark, you said. What, what was that Mr. Zooty? You said, 'in your short life, you have realized, you know that you know nothing, so just remember, we owe a cock to Asclepius. Pay it and do not neglect it...' Oh no, Mr. Zooty, stop being so morbid, and dramatic, hemlock is not poisonous to snails, it only tastes bad. What, what was that? Am I sure, of course I'm sure. I remember that specifically from my botany class in college… But I promise you heads will roll for this dirty trick, and if we find out who did this, we shall have an auto-da-fé here at the mill! I promise that! We, will talk more about this later, we have to address our stupid workers, or slugs as you like to call them, they are so stupid and we are so smart, but we must address them anyways, because it is protocol… Wait, why is the speaker system already on? You didn't turn it on, did you? You couldn't have, I don't see any slime on the control panel. Oh, those despicable rogues, they are saboteurs as well as assassins. If we get our hands on them Mr. Zooty, I dare not think what I shall do to them… but let us begin, as I said we will talk about this later…"

The voice of Mr. McNabb became louder as he moved closer to the microphone, and there was no denying there was an anger in his voice, which few have ever herd, or lived to hear. The anger, the rage; well, it sounded like, Mickey Mouse just after he got done huffing on helium. He was so mad, and spoke so excitedly, a high pitched screeching billow emanated from the speakers, in place of the usual condescending tone.

"Good morning mill workers, first I shall inform you we have traitors in our midst, here at the mill. And we all know there is nothing worse than for someone in our sawdust nation to claim allegiance to something else, to anything else, besides our sawdust nation… As we will remember a great man once said, 'my only regret is that I have but one life to give for my country.' And as we think of this quote, though I would never give my own life for our sawdust nation, because it is a very precious life; yours are not so precious, so a quote like this should cause your patriotic temperaments to flare, and when I tell you, what I shall tell you next, that is, that someone tried to kill Mr. Zooty, in the wee hours of the morning; an anger should befall you, a patriotic anger, and a determination to catch these terrible people. So I, Mr. McNabb, in an effort to catch these threats to our society quickly, am immediately issuing a warrant for the attempted assassination of Mr. Zooty, we are very fortunate our assassins are simple, and do not know hemlock isn't poisonous to snails, but this will not negate their punishment or their pursuit. I will offer one million pounds of sawdust as a reward for the apprehension of these criminals dead or alive! Though I hate you, and detest your being, I do need your help, so may I use the word 'please', but please take this as no kindness, only a 'please' with the most contemptuous connotation. NOW GET TO WORK, YOU STUPID SERVANTS, and HAVE GRATITUDE FOR MY EXISTANCE; that is all."

And so the speaker system clicked off, and a day of stupendous serendipity for the mill, moved from the present, to the past, to live long in the fair grounds of infamy. In the meantime, as Mr. McNabb and Mr. Zooty had conversed, Stephan and I had made it to the formation which looked upon the McNabb residence, the place where most stood for his anointment, excuse me, his announcement. No one listened to Mr. McNabb, and no one went to work as they had been commanded. What the crowd did do, was begin to whisper, whisper things like 'Who do you think did it?' and 'What would you do with a million pounds of sawdust?' And this reward, started the obsession to catch the traitors at the mill. And though, most people when pressed about their feelings towards Mr. McNabb and Mr. Zooty, would probably admit they found the attempted abatement of a snail's life, rather funny, their love for sawdust was so much more, and so, their eyes were peeled for the least parcel of incongruity around them. With the heightened sense of patriotic duty, or rather sawdust lust in the air, paranoia set in where none had existed before. And strange things began to take place around the mill.

6

Since I am in one of my pensive moods, try not to take me too seriously, yet take me as seriously as possible; for as we may acknowledge the tickling of our souls when it feels agreeable, we neglect it when it aches. What hurts is the sandpaper of vice, the gravel of pride, the poking of vanity, do not be drug a-crossed them now.

For if you are to analyze what comes soon, with any insight whatsoever, a soon-ness of spirit is required, an urgency above all urgencies, so that you are not continually pulled down the torrent of strife, into the deluge of death. I will be first to acknowledge my word plays can become a bit tiresome, but there is an aim I wish to mark. I see you all running to and fro, obsessed with beginnings and ends, starts and finishes, birth and death, but nothing of the in-betweens. Do not let me lose you now, loose you minds, untie the string. As we elevate our minds, engaging in fine thinking, the fine art of the mind, let us drop all subtitles and pretense.

A silly sadness fills me when I observe, 'these chasings', all of you simple silly minds, you are such a sad sight 'chasing about'. Please let me not follow with an apology, or appeal to friendship, for I cannot befriend, simple silly travelers, those making their way through life, unable to pull their hearts from the 'perishables' to consider the 'perpetuous'. I cannot reason with the ants on the honey, as they seek their temporal sweetness, and watch as they are squished by the firmness of eternal time, times firm movement above them. Stop, stop gorging yourselves, you honey slaves, and add some meat to your diet! But first, if you are to do this, let you, make your burnt offering, burning the fat first?

I will not try to win your affection by appealing to your self-love, you lovers of self, always in awe of your reflection, and inspired by your own thoughts, I pity you. Are you offended yet? Probably not, as the evil doers and self-lovers, never consider themselves to be among that class, yet you are there, you are here. May you sacrifice your worthless lives, the lives spent in 'vain chasings' for one final act of goodness before your final act is over? Nothing you have built up and stored up will last, the bugs and the worms will eat their holes through them. You commoners, worth nothing to the high places, for what is common is of little value. Common is hate, common is envy, common is pride; you surfs of indulgence, I lament your vain toiling's, your vain common existence, so I appeal only to the uncommon?

If distinguished thinking could be observed with light, I am afraid most of you would be utter darkness. And if we could examine further your darkness; I would say pathetic, uninhibited thoughts of perpetual debauchery would yield, with words, a most accurate account of their consistency. Forgive me for prodding a sore spot for nearly all, but our thought life, is the only life that distinguishes us from the heathens, and the heathens from the animals. Many monkeys, have had more profound insight into their existence than you! Did he just call me a monkey? I sure did, and with some pleasure I might add, I would call you many more names, but we do not have the time, and I believe in doing so, it would detract from my purpose, in doing so. In doing so, I hope to wrench the bananas from your hands, let go of your bananas and allow your taste to be elevated; will you?

Yet I will offer my hand to you as well, in truce, one final showing of mercy, a mercy agent, as my mercy is great, but not never ending. Remove yourselves from the sawdust before it is too late. Consider not, the dark ashes of the past, and put on your sackcloth. Turn from hopeless festivals, and futile thinking, the wisdom that is foolishness, and seek what is true, to true sagacity. May I plead, many pleadings?

Please pardon my short diatribe, I know it was certainly out of character, but I couldn't help but feel some things needed to be addressed before we went further. Further clarification demands I say: I was really speaking to myself more than anyone else, my past self. And if I could move through time, back at the mill, how I would have shown myself to myself, and pleaded many pleadings to draw away, as far away as possible from the sawdust. 'You don't understand Benjamin, you will have nothing when the festival is through with you, no friends, no family, no occupation, no love, no dignity, wait let me rephrase, you will have something's, you will have hate, and envy, you will have regrets, and resentments, misgivings about everyone, and you will have the ability to trust no one…' These are some of the things I would have told myself, but even if the possibility were there that I could have spoken these words to myself, I either could not, or would not have listened; if it were possible?

Setting aside my pleas to myself, time went on and time went well at the mill. Many things changed and many things stayed the same, there were good days and bad, friends who came and went, fun had, and sadness endured. My violin spent much of its time enjoying life without much thought of consequence, or future. The hedonistic tunes of my brave instrument went on and went well, many enjoyed my playing, for their minds played an equal melody. Though wouldn't you have noticed, if you had been listening closely that, with increasing regularity my special instrument was sounding sadder and sadder, lamenting long notes as the ever decreasing return of pleasure which the sawdust offered, grew?

To be more exact in our timing here, several moths had passed, perhaps a season turned, and all the investigations into the attempted assassination of Mr. Zooty led to dead ends; for that I was quite grateful. Yet, this point in time brings me to a week in my existence, which hurt more than I can possibly tell you. My eyes become heavy with tears at the thought of this week, and perhaps the hurt has penetrated so deep, it may be a gulf which is never filled, not filled until I am called home?

The day was a Thursday, a Thursday like any other, I had an expectant hope that day which would not have permitted me to consider the pain that was to come, even if I tried. For who can anticipate the un-anticipatable, who can know when a heart will be broken? And this is where the story picks up; who can foresee the broken heart indeed?

Backbreaking labor, moving wheel barrow after wheel barrow of sawdust for Foreman Dave, at this point in time, so much sawdust in my life, moving day and night, both in my dreams and in my reality. My hands had become calloused from the work, the slavery; my muscles tight, my heart hardened, and some days when I sought escape in my violin, how it scarcely made a sound recognizable to the beauty of which that virtuous instrument is called?

Standing by my sawdust bunk, I leaned with my arm pressing high against the cement wall which kept the wood shavings piled tall. As I tried to catch my breath and took a swig from my flask, I saw Berry, Officer Berry, walking my way with paper in hand. I must tell you, I was certainly nervous at his sight, every moment I considered this dark secret of mine might somehow find its way to the light, the secret of the clandestine assassin's part in the famous, the infamous conglomerate which sought to bring about the end of a tyrant, a regime.

"Hey Benjamin, how's it going?" Officer Berry asked, placing his sunglasses atop his head to allow for personal contact, with a man he had become quite personal with. "Oh not bad, a little tired… you know how it goes?" "I certainly do, I have something here for you. It is a summons from Mr. McNabb, I was asked to deliver it personally to you, and I am to return to him with your response fore width." Berry said, handing me the parchment. I received the letter from his hand and looked at it. A giant red wax seal with the McNabb coat of arms authenticated its origins, holding it closed, and acknowledged to me the special care with which it was made. I broke the seal and began to read it aloud, "It says… Benjamin Silversin, It has been brought to my attention, by Foreman Dave, that you have been a most productive worker for the mill. As I inquired more of you, from Foreman Dave, trying to determine the consistency of a worker of your caliber, so your attitude may be replicated in others, for future sawdust production, I came a crossed a photo of you in your personnel file. While I examined your special countenance, I suddenly remembered meeting you on new employee indoctrination day several long months ago, and how when I inquired of your personal leanings, you informed me of your love for the violin. I must admit, it is rare, or you are of a special breed of man who seeks such elevated things in life, and that there might be hope for you, and others among the proletariat, yet? If you have not forgotten our brief encounter, then you should also remember Mr. Zooty is particularly fond of this emotional instrument. So as Mr. Zooty's birthday is this 'eve, I wish to surprise him, and offer you a special dinner, as a showing of gratitude for your hard work. We are having a chef flown in from the Burgundy region of France, to prepare a special French radish dish for Mr. Zooty. My hope is that you will be able to join us and that you would bring your violin? Yours ungratefully, Mr. McNabb…" As I stopped reading, I felt a little sick to my stomach, and vomit was not far off. There was nothing good about this invitation, nothing good about it at all! Sure I could hold a conversation with the most educated our sawdust nation could produce, sure I could offer a bit of heavenly pleasure with my violin, but that hardly permitted me to be among the snobbery of the McNabb court. Or what if this was a trick, what if somehow I was being invited, but this was not really a surprise birthday party for Mr. Zooty, but a surprise torture party for Benjamin? No one as of yet had been implicated in the attempted assassination of Mr. Zooty, what if, what if, this was a ploy, or Mr. Zooty recognized my voice and could tell Mr. McNabb who I really was? If such thoughts were arranged close, as philosophy is to mental torture, as it is often difficult to discern which is which, I either became a philosopher at that moment in time, or perhaps one acquainted with the fine art of the mind, the minds torment? And the torment came in this form, if you have ever been in a relationship, as you begin to hold that person dear, through no effort of your own, some deep inner working of your spirit begins to construct a future with this person apart from reality. Perhaps this is an exercise of the soul which longs for that companion from above, yet, when this individual is taken, as the relationship breaks down, so must we begin the painful deconstruction of our minds eye on the future with which our mind produced so easily, as it is no longer there. How painful and grueling this hurtful activity is, but a necessity. And the mental bridges which I considered upon this invitation to a diner party, far apart from my desire to be there, forced me to cross; were high and rickety. These bridges swayed high in the air and a mental deconstruction was forced, dismantling any notion I had of flying under the radar and living in safety at the mill; a mental torture that would hold its own with the greatest relationship ending escapades!

"Ah, I don't think I really want to have dinner with Mr. McNabb and Mr. Zooty, Berry." I admitted, completely dismayed that this was the direction my day seemed to be going, apart from any direction of my own. "I see, I guess I can understand your reluctance, all the silverware and plates, who even knows which one is used for what…? But ah, I don't know how to tell you this… but you cannot refuse an invitation from Mr. McNabb, he really just sent the invitation as a courtesy." Berry informed me, apparently recognizing the discouragement this letter brought me. "Look on the bright side, you are always telling me how much you enjoy playing your violin for people, at least you can have that to look forward to." I considered Berry's words, and then considered our friendship, was it as deep as I thought; could I trust saying any more to this representative of the republic then what I already had? "What happens if I don't go?" I asked, wishing, hoping, praying, someone might have mercy on the humbled man I was becoming, had become, when faced with the proposition of a radish dinner. "Hum, well, I don't recall ever hearing that question before… I guess now that I think about it, I don't know anyone who has refused before, but I can assure you, getting on the bad side of Mr. McNabb is something you don't want to do."

My chin dropped to my chest, my cheeks puffed out; a sigh was let loose, defeated; a defeated man I was, like a child who just lost his lollypop, no more able to reclaim his piece of candy, than his dignity. What can I say, exasperated, distraught, forlorn… shall I continue? For how many a day have I already listened to the morning announcements of 'McNabb the Great'; how many stories have I been told by Stephan and others of his merciless pursuit of a sawdust empire? Such a terrible image I had in my mind of this man, and now I must eat dinner with him and his talking snail? Oh, no! Yet, maybe, Mr. McNabb was not as horrific a gentleman as I had conjured in my mind, maybe all this terror on my part was simply an overreaction to an overly powerful imagination, as I surely possessed? I don't know?

"Alright Berry, thanks for bringing me the letter, and for the encouragement, I guess, you can just inform Mr. McNabb I will be at his house around six-ish…" "Alright, good luck Benjamin, I hope the dinner goes well, if you need to get cleaned up before, I'm sure Foreman Dave wouldn't mind if you left early." Berry offered, presenting me a small consolation prize, some time off, for submitting to his suggestion before the great event.

I took off from work, and headed home early as had been suggested, and made myself ready for the hour quickly approaching. And though I don't tell many people this, lower your ear and I will whisper it to you, please don't repeat this to anyone else but, I wanted to go home and cry, beat my fists against my bed, and hold on to the staircase railing, refusing to budge, to move anywhere. A temper tantrum above all temper tantrums I wanted to throw, but there was no one to listen, no one who cared, no one who would wipe away my tears. So resolutely I faced the prospect of the diner to come. Possibly, if I would have known what was to come, I would have risked confinement to avoid the noble evening which providence had placed before me. But I did not know, and so I didn't risk, and begrudgingly after a few sawdust drinks, my nerves becoming gradually more agreeable to a fine meal, I packed up my bow, my violin, and pushed on into the day, the day quickly coming to a close.

It appeared many were attuned to my arrival, for scarcely had I made it through the gates of the mill, before I was being escorted to the grand porch of Castle McNabb. A young servant opened the door for me as I approached, unable to knock for myself. "I'll take that from you." The servant said as I stepped inside the mansion, that is, she was grabbing at my violin case. Clutching tightly, feeling vulnerable, violated, I answered, "No, thank you, I will keep that with me." "Suit yourself." She replied curtly, turned, and then waving her hand said, "Follow me please." I looked around, admiring the artwork, the weapons of death on the wall, and considering what was different about theses hallways now that I was able to observe them in the light, certainly nothing worth our time here, nothing beyond the darkness which came so natural to Mr. McNabb, and has already been mentioned many times.

The servant woman guided me to a grand room, walking in my mouth agape, I looked upwards into the open expanse. A ceiling so high it seemed to reach to the very heavens, open glass to the firmaments, allowing the setting sun to pierce the room, a room, now aglow, in fiery red. Wood of every noble species, color, and hue, girded the walls, the floor, it was like nothing I had ever seen. Indeed, at that moment, the words of Miss Rachel came flooding back to me, 'just wait if you ever get a chance to see Mr. McNabb's house you'll never look at the world the same again'. In fact, she was more right than I could have ever imagined.

A chair was pulled back for me at the grand table, and I sat placing my violin on its shiny surface. I sat there for a long time, so long in fact, I began to pull my violin from its case and fiddled around a bit. I rosined up the bow, did a quick tuning and warmed up the strings. The sound my precious spirit whisperer made in that grand room was magnificent, I wish, I wish I could reproduce that reverberation for you now, and save you from the melancholy evening to come, and provide you instead with, a morsel of angel's breath, that heavenly wind felt in a beautiful song. Lost in my own way, in my own notes, I was startled when I saw Mr. McNabb standing under the archway watching me play.

"Very nice, very nice indeed…" Mr. McNabb acknowledged, clapping his hands, with his giant wooden cane placed under his arm. He looked as I had remembered from orientation, his purple suit, the cane, everything but the hat with the woodchip sticking out, but no Mr. Zooty.

"Thank you." I replied, looking about for the clear plastic cage. "Where's Mr. Zooty? I could take a request." I offered, hoping I could keep our conversation to a minimum, lest Mr. Zooty recognize my voice from that early morning as I advocated for his life with Stephan. "Oh, he's taking a nap, he will be joining us later, so I was hoping you and I could just converse for a while, at least until we are ready to surprise Mr. Zooty…"

Placing himself at the head of the table, in a throne like chair, Mr. McNabb nodded and gestured towards my seat. I followed this implicit suggestion, and placing my violin on the table between us, I sat and listened as Mr. McNabb began to speak. "So Benjamin, you seem like a pretty smart guy, at least your taste in music, and your mill application test scores would suggest such, so let me ask you why did you get a low level job here at the mill, I mean, you could have been a sawdust equipment engineer, or worked on biological tree growth enhancement, maybe even researched synthetic sawdust formulas…?"

Wow an interesting question no doubt, one I had yet to really consider. I thought about it, the question that is, and perhaps if I would have continued to think, as time opposes truth, so my answer would have grew gradually less honest, so I said what came to mind first. "Well, I really love sawdust."

"Fair enough… as do most in our nation…" Mr. McNabb replied, looking intently at me, then nodding his head and scratching his chin he continued, "Anyways if I may inquire of a sharp mind, I have a bit of a problem on my hands… you see, we have the upcoming festival, and the festival just keeps getting bigger, grander, it seems people are never content celebrating the same way twice, I'm not sure exactly why that is, maybe, that way people can tell themselves there is something important happening in their lives… a way to fill a hole which can't be filled, not that I really care, it's just with the exponential growth in sawdust consumption, frankly, I'm finding it somewhat difficult to meet the demand… well, now, we have arrived at my problem, I'm sure you have heard of the conservators, or the tree community to the north, anyone who has spent any time in our sawdust nation has…" I wasn't sure exactly what to think about where Mr. McNabb was going with this line of thought, so I just sat there contently, listening and nodding my head as he went on. "Well, they have the trees, trees which would fill this void, close the gap if you will, between the ordered sawdust, and the scheduled production… I tried to force them from their forest, to sell their land some years ago, but it seems there is some ancient law, an archaic law, which separates something and something, I have been told by my legal advisors, that some silly amendment has placed a wall, between us and them, but here is where it gets sticky, as glad as I am that this exercise clause prevents them from forcing their rules on me, it also protects me from forcing my will on them, and I don't like that… I WANT THEIR TREES, I WANT THEIR TREES NOW!"

The screeching high pitched yell of Mr. McNabb saying "I WANT THEIR TREES" still rings in my ears till this day, and I began to see Mr. McNabb was pushing a deeper agenda with our evening here than what the invitation had let on, an evening under the guise of a surprise birthday party, was much more. I wasn't sure how to respond, I mean, what do I know about the conservators or their trees? In an effort to appease his covetous spirit, I offered the only thing I could think of, "I can play us another song before dinner if you'd like?" Somehow, my pleasant, unimposing suggestion had the affect I desired and Mr. McNabb said "very well, very well..."

Standing up and pushing in my chair, I played my violin until a man in a fancy tuxedo with white gloves came into the room, carrying a silver platter. "Sir's dinner is served." He said, then placing the grand plates before each of us, the servant removed the covers and went to stand unassumingly in the corner. I looked at the plate before me, I can't say I was very impressed, the small portion, and the pretentious presentation left a bad taste in my mouth before I ever started eating, although, I will say, the wood wine was very good. I watched as Mr. McNabb took a bite and I followed suit. Clearly, very pleased with the meal, he snapped his fingers at the butler and said, "Call in the chef... Mr. Zooty is really going to enjoy this dish, Benjamin what do you think of it?" "Well, it's a little rubbery..." I admitted in the most complimentary way possible.

The chef came in, his hair was a little crazy, and he had food splattered all over the front of his shirt. "Chef, thank you for the presentation, and the delicate hands you have, no doubt you have a special culinary gift, the French breakfast radishes are superb, and surely you found a special meat to pair, may I inquire as to what it is?" Mr. McNabb asked, and I sat feeling uncomfortable, watching the exchange. The chef paused, as if to consider the question, then began to speak in broken English, with an accent that was without question from the Burgundy region of France, "Well, you see, da meats escargot..."

I observed a look of panic came over Mr. McNabb's face, he looked to the chef and the butler and asked, "Where is Mr. Zooty?" The chef responded first, "me know no Mr. Zooty, me only know escargot…" The butler responded next, "I will have him here for you promptly, sir…" as he walked briskly from the room. Time stood still for us in the grand dining room, and I began to roll the word escargot around in my mind; what did it mean? For a moment I was a little bewildered with this word, but suddenly like a rogue wave, it hit me; Escargot is Snail!

The butler came rushing back into the room with the empty plastic box, "I found this in the kitchen sir, its empty, and Mr. Zooty is nowhere to be found…" The butler pleaded in an exasperated voice, slightly out of breath. The implication of this statement by the butler was clear. And the room was filled, erupted with a billowing cry from Mr. McNabb, a cry so deep and terrible, first rate demons would have given it heavy applause, "NOOOOOOOOOOOOOOOOOO…"

All fell silent, my hairs still on end, Mr. McNabb looked to me and said, "YOU… you, this is all your fault, you and your stupid violin, the only reason I had this party was so you could play for Mr. Zooty…" Mr. McNabb declared, glaring at me with contempt, contempt like I have never seen, and imagine I shall never see again. And before I could stop him, or even know what was going on, he reached across the table and secured my violin in his evil grips. As if time had been slowed, like molasses on a cold winter day, so was the raising of my violin above Mr. McNabb's head, watching in horror, slow horror as he swung it with all his might against the table. An angel crushed by wretchedness, its wood shattering, its strings bursting forth, bursting onward. And from my brave instrument there came a cry, a sound of anguish, which was so disturbing, and cold, it would have chilled the most stoic heart.

"GET OUT, YOU AND YOUR STUPID VIOLIN GET OUT, NOW!" Mr. McNabb yelled as he threw what was left of my soul on the table before me.

Grabbing what remained of my violin, I dashed from the house of Mr. McNabb. I ran, and ran, ran as far as I could, until my legs would no longer carry me another step, falling into a heap by the river, the spot where Stephan had fist taken me for lunch some months ago, I began to cry. The more I cried, the angrier I became, until the anguish within me passed beyond a word, or an emotional expression, the anguish one has when what is loved most, is lost, is taken. Here maybe, as my mind continued to run long past my body, a separation occurred, and I imagined a cool dark place, a dark place in the wilderness, and I desired to die, take thee my life from me, for it is better that I should die than I should live?

For here, now, my mind is tired, for the music has stopped, I long for a day of rest, a day where I need not concern myself with the troubles of this life. For who knows where a violin can be fixed, in a nation without trees? Certainly I am not among the noble class which can ascertain such lofty repairs, and yet have my violin make a beautiful sound; myself? This is beyond me, I have failed, utterly failed in my pursuit, my pursuit to carve out a piece of happiness for myself, where shall I go for rest? I am so weary, my eyes are weighty; my back is bending under a heavy yoke, where indeed shall I go? And if time were dropped from our minds, and I was asked, honestly asked, if I should go on fighting, I would declare, life had taken the fight out of me. And if I were a man of greater bravery, I would have sought the redbud tree, as did Judas, allowing its purple flowers to cover my shame for eternity.

7

My dearest Friedrich,

      With what prayers, I wish you could receive this letter, but I write it now only for my own comfort. For I strongly think if you were alive, we would be dear friends, and I could tell you these things, in the comfort of your study, or on a long walk by the lake in the mountains. And we might have talks that went into the early morning hours, and have many warm memories together, in those places. From what I've heard of the teachings of your youth, and with what diligence your mother prepared your mind with truth, I shall only hope you found within yourself, before your last moments, a bit of humility. And maybe if this is true, I can count, with a morsel of reservation, that you were reciting passages from the good book before your death, with true faith. And there may be a day, I can inquire of your genius, and admire with what handiwork our father created your mind, in person.

      I must admit, when I think of you, tears come to my eyes, the way they do for my late friend Stephan. So please count this as no small, or petty writing on my part, but more accurately, the etchings of a man who has felt your pain, and had your thoughts. Though I don't pretend to know, with what a struggle a man of your brilliance faced, I have been endowed with a fine mind myself, one who's imagination can conjure the torturous thinking that must be endured, when no matter how many times, or how many ways you trace your lines, you can never find your way out of the maze. My deepest lament, is that your labyrinth, may have had many more dangers, than my mind is willing to recognize.

If I may apologize, and offer my deepest amends, asking forgiveness, for those who in your illness, treated you as a strange oddity to be observed for entertainment; the fallen philosopher. And when I think of them, and their callused hardened hearts, I wish to leave there bones unburied, and bleaching in the sun. Dishonor should be theirs, and their children's, and their children's, children.

Also, your dear love, the love of your life, whom you met in Italy. The one who thought of you as eccentric, that she neglected your feelings for her, and thought of you as no more than a curious evening guest to her society parties, for that, my heart is also with you. For nothing hurts as much as love, which is not returned, nothing so much indeed.

As I close this letter, let me hope, that those who see it, if one of them should come to see you, if and before, I have parted times ticking, that they should tell you of it, and that you might receive it with joy, as if your dearest friend has penned it for you, this would be my hope. And if I am the only one, let me be the one to tell you first, that our father loved you also.

Yours truly,

Benjamin

Here, if I could write a letter to all of you, I would, but time will not permit such a thing, and so I include in my story, a letter to one, which is meant as a letter to all. A letter like a few others I have written, which expresses something within me that must be communicated. A communication of my heart for you, my savants heart, may my writings serve you, as they were not brought about without much pain and toiling, not only in there compilation, but in the experience required, experience needed to produce something of depth, which my hope is, they may hold.

Let us now leave my letter writing and return to my story. I took the day off from work Friday, and scarcely left my bed, but for the filling of my flask, I lay about the house, a defeated man. Stephan had come around knocking, but I had not the courage to face him, or tell him what had occurred at Mr. McNabb's house, and so, I left his knocks unanswered. The weekend came and went, as time provided a bit of relief for my still open wound; as Monday came, I felt I could and should move back to work, even if times cure is barely a cure at all?

This was the beginning of my Monday: passing through security, by now, at this time in my employment, the whole security force knew who I was, and it seemed everyone was watching to see which line I would choose to enter the mill in; as no doubt this selection elicited a bit of smooth pleasure from my flask. Walking into the open expanse beyond the security gates, I saw a small crowd gathered around the white house by the cork board where job assignments and announcements were usually hung.

Drawing close, I saw Stephan stick up his arm and wave, yelling, "Hey Benjamin come check this out, new job assignments were just posted by Miss Rachel." Making it to Stephan's side, I looked on as he pointed to the board. "We get to work together in the processing factory, cool, right?" "Oh man that's awesome, I don't know how much more I could take, if I were forced to continue with all that hard labor for Foreman Dave." I replied excitedly, shaking Stephan's shoulder to show him my enthusiasm. Fate had certainly provided me with a pick me up when I needed one most, maybe, possibly this could be an opportunity for me, to have a whole new start, a fresh start working with my friend?

The processing factory took in all the new trees from the barges. Then the trees were de-limbed, and debarked, removed of any undesirable qualities before the trees were processed, all before wood-chipping time. That would be our job, get the trees ready, and cut them into shape for their future wood grinding projections. Exciting, right?

It seemed upon further investigation, conveyor belt one was in need of the most help, so that is where we headed. Getting to our posted areas I followed Stephan's lead as he applied safety glasses, and then hearing protection. The machine latched onto the trees, moved them about our work area as if they were toothpicks, placed them on the belt, and then sent them through two giant rotating cylinders that removed any likeness the tree may still of had to, well, a tree.

"Man, Officer Berry is really going to miss me, I hope he knows about the assignment change, I don't want him to think I bailed on him, you know, we were starting to have some really good conversations… he's definitely a nice guy…" I announced between tree shavings, a grinding which as the trees were latched onto by these giant drums, sent a vibration through the earth that rattled every bone in your body. "I think he'll be alright. How have you been, I stopped by your house a couple times, I must have just been missing you…" Stephan yelled as the next tree went shuttling past us. I wasn't sure what to say, I didn't want to talk about Mr. McNabb, although I did think this aversion could be compensated for by the fact I would get to deliver the news of Mr. Zooty's death, a death so befitting to a snail of the bourgeoisie, every time I think of it a giant smile grows wide on my face. Should I do it; ah, I can't resist.

"Dude you're never going to believe the story I have for you, last Thursday while I was working in the inventory department, Berry brought this letter to me, written by Mr. McNabb…" Pausing, I let a smirk grow out of the corners of my lips, keeping it there for some seconds, for affect, that is, the effect of allowing Stephan to see I possessed some very valuable information. "Yeah, so don't just stand there smirking, tell me already." Stephan ordered, and I was very pleased, it was clear he was chasing my carrot. "Yeah, so Berry brought this letter, it was an invitation to Mr. Zooty's surprise birthday party, I was asked to go, I guess foreman Dave had been telling him a lot of good things about me, and Mr. McNabb remembered me from orientation day…" I thought for a second, and as much as I wanted to avoid speaking about my violin, it seemed there was no way for me to tell this story without including it in some way; in the tale, maybe, if I crafted my story just right, Stephan would be to ecstatic about hearing of a special form of cannibalism that he would fail to inquire further? "Well, if you remember from orientation day Mr. Zooty really likes the violin? Having me over for dinner was a way to allow Mr. McNabb and I to celebrate Mr. Zooty's birthday and for him to enjoy my playing, or that's at least why Mr. McNabb said he invited me. But it was kind of weird, when I got there Mr. Zooty was nowhere to be seen, and Mr. McNabb kept asking me these questions about the community with trees, and if I had any clever ideas about how to get any of their tress. I told him, basically, I didn't really know anything about the conservators other than I wasn't one of them, and so, I just asked if I could play my violin, to keep the time pleasant… and that worked mostly. Well, here is where it gets good, he had had a special chef flown in from France to make a French breakfast radish dish for Mr. Zooty, I guess it's his favorite or something, I didn't think it was all that impressive, personally… and I don't know how to tell you this, so I guess I'll just say it… along with the radish dinner came Mr. Zooty, I guess the chef needed a meat to pair with the greens, so he was the one who got served up for dinner…" I stopped speaking and looked towards my friend with happily pleading eyes waiting for a reaction. "What do you mean Mr. Zooty got served up for dinner?" Stephan inquired in a yelling voice, as all the tree destruction going on nearby was really making it difficult to have a good conversation. "In France, where the chef was from, I guess snail is a delicacy, and Mr. Zooty propelled himself into the kitchen to watch the chef prepare his special radish dinner and never came back… the chef cooked Mr. Zooty, and Mr. McNabb ate him!" I exclaimed finding this news was even better when you were able to share it. Watching Stephan, a look of shock and awe radiated over him. Bright and gleaming, as the suns light radiates off glass, so was Stephan. If there was any way to magnify joy, or show the joyous way in which this news was received by Stephan, I'm not sure there is a way to communicate it. Placing his hands to his face, he fell to his knees, and for a moment, I could have sworn, he was going to cry. To cry the way a young woman

118

might when her gallant man finally asks her to be his wife. So perhaps, that is the best way to imagine it; that is having it most accurate to my recollection; imagining the joy of a marriage proposal, and the tear which comes upon the word 'yes'.

All was silent between us, as Stephan absorbed the weight of this water-fully beautiful news like a sponge, or so I observed. And the question, the inquiry I was hoping to avoid most, came next, as I imagine now it should come next, that is, in the mind of any individual whose mind is properly constituted with sense. "So what did Mr. McNabb do when he found out?" Stephan asked, now leaning in close to avoid yelling. As the question presented itself to the forefront of my mind, now in this moment, as I had imagined I would be able to tell Stephan of the destruction of my violin without much trouble, in the present such was not the case. As we consider, as I ponder what forces the mind to become honest with itself, maybe, an idea in our mind, is no idea at all, until it feels real, until it is really communicated to another. So when I thought this would be easy, as it became real, that is, that I no longer had my violin, I found it was very hard, too hard; so hard I began to break down…"Mr. McNabb… Mr. McNabb broke my violin…" Was all I was able to say…!

As a good friend should, as a man who exudes those special fruits of the spirit we all long for does, so was his attentiveness to my violin, and though it was clear he wanted to revel in the downfall of a Sultan Snail, he pushed his own desires aside to ask me, to ask me, about me. And this may seem like a rather insignificant thing to you, perhaps it comes natural in your case to do such things, that you neglect its importance. But for a man who had spent his entire life outside of human

119

compassion, these questions, and a listening ear meant more, mean more to me, 'till this day, than any words I am capable of sharing. "So how are you doing? I know your violin meant, I know it meant the world to you…?"

Turning from Stephan, I tried to hide my face, my lips quivered and my hands began to shake. What was I to say, what was I to feel? Though I still don't have an answer, and I dare not degrade the emotions I felt upon the final recognition of a broken violin, with some analogy. Whatever it was, whatever trauma I was going through, as Stephan drew by my side and put his arm around me he said, "It will be ok, I'll help you get your violin fixed, we'll go on lunch break to the music store, and you'll be playing again, playing for people again, before you know it…" and there was some hope.

Lunch came quickly, and I was excited, though I was still quite exhausted from all the emotions I had been feeling as of late, I had this strange feeling now, that everything was going to be all right. As the giant steam whistle blew announcing it was time for our break, Stephan looked to me and said, "Come on we'll have time to make it to the music store over lunch, it's only a couple blocks from here, and if for some reason you are low on wood-pulp currency, I can help take care of the cost…" "Ok, cool, yeah, I know the guy who works there pretty well…"

Walking briskly, we didn't talk much, and frankly I am rather appreciative we did not, as my ears were still ringing from that obnoxiously loud tree destroying machine. The music store sat on the outside of downtown, and we entered together to the giant smiling face of my friend John. "Hey, Benjamin, how's it going it's been awhile since

I've seen you?" John inquired standing up, and moving from behind the counter to pull me into a warm embrace. "I've been better, I'd like you to meet my friend Stephan." "Nice to meet you Stephan, any friend of Benjamin, is a friend of mine…" John acknowledged, as the two shook hands. And as they were doing this, as I was glancing about the store, I saw the shelves were quite empty. The percussion instruments were in there spots, likewise the brass and the woodwinds, but where were the strings? Looking more closely at the instruments that were available, I noticed they all possessed one quality in common, they were not made of wood.

Skeptical, but still not convinced this was something I should be too worried about, I began to speak, "Hey John, I need to get my violin repaired, I might even need a whole new one actually, now that I think about it, it will be hard to fix, it's smashed up good, well, my friend Stephan is going to help me with the cost, pay the price for me…" John looked at me, the smile falling from his face, then dropping his eyes and looking away, here were the words, the words I thought I would never hear, "I don't know how to tell you this Benjamin, but all the wood has been requisitioned for the upcoming festival, I don't even have an old instrument to sell you, I've been wiped out…"

Of this which I think, and try to tell, but where there are no words to tell it, let the music sing to you that the notes may tell you for me; for that which I cannot communicate to you with my utterance, can be heard in a simple melody. For the love of music, that I hear those notes, which stir something deep within me, that voice, that cry of my innermost self, which calls for that sweet song to never end. And when the notes play on, how I ask that they should never cease. And on that day when I took my beloved violin to have it mended, to get one anew, and it could not be mended, or bought anew, how that day resonates in my heart with notes of sadness like few days do.

"I'm really sorry, a few months ago McNabb Enterprises bought up everything, all the fresh wood, and anything I had left in stock, well, the government came and took the rest…" John pleaded, hoping, asking that I might understand. Without much thought, this is what I replied, "Its ok John, I know it's not your fault, it's just, sometimes I can't help but think the festival is taking everything good we have in life, and grinding it up…" Though perhaps you have just seen the profundity with which I spoke, I must say, I did not truly understand the weight of those words. And as I consider what I consider now, as I am likely to repeat this, the difference between those who celebrate the sawdust festival, and the others to come, is where they see beauty, a special beauty; I hope you see the beauty; will you?

"Hey Benjamin, we should probably get going." Stephan encouraged, patting me on the back, consoling a man who was inconsolable. "Yeah, you are probably right… thanks for your time anyways, John." I said placing my hand before him. "Oh, no problem, you know it's always a pleasure to see you, don't be such a stranger." And that was the end of our trip to the music store, leaving with a bad taste in my mouth, my resentments towards Mr. McNabb and a society opposed to good music, only grew.

Walking back to work, the pep in my step shot like a stray dog, I fumbled to think strait as Stephan looked my way and began to speak, "I don't tell many people this, because I am risking a lot, maybe confinement, or something worse, so I hope I can tell you?" "Sure, of course you can tell me…" I said, unable to get the thought of a wood drink off my mind, to numb the pain. "I, well, I became part of the community of trees myself, not too long ago, after being fed up with the festival life, and I know they have the wood to fix your instrument, maybe I could take you there?"

Wow, that was not what I expected to hear from Stephan, I mean declaring your allegiance to the conservators was very serious business, very serious indeed. In the past many have died for such a claim, they still do in many parts of the world. And now, in our sawdust nation, you were sure to be rejected, ostracized by almost all, and if somehow you fell under the authority of Mr. McNabb, confinement or worse would be your fate.

I didn't know what to say, or how to answer, but I was out of options, all my attempts to run my life in a good direction had failed, maybe now it was time to have faith in something else besides myself? "That sounds, it sounds good, I mean, if they can help me out…" Those were my words, and Stephan just smiled, shook his head, and said, "Cool, very cool, we will talk more about this later…"

Going back to work, I took a nip from my flask at every opportunity, it was the only way I knew how to deal with problems, with life… as the pain within began to bubble up; my broken violin in the forefront of my mind, so had I to keep pushing down the bobbing vanguard of broken noise with wood solvents, to keep it from overflowing, somehow, someway…

Work went on and work went well, and we both began to tire from the monotony, to become careless. Hazy vision, slow movements, warm fuzzy skin, a numb touch, my broken violin floating away like a fog over a ship as it enters a friendly harbor. So I became more carless than anyone as I was operating under the influence of wood spirits. Yet, for some strange reason my foggy mind thought all was well with my soul. It happened out of nowhere, I wasn't sure what was happening until it was too late; had my inebriated mind slowed my reaction? Looking over, watching in slow motion, Stephan's shirt caught itself on a branch as a large tree shuttled by our work station. I ran to help as soon as I trapped my feet on the shifting floor, and fumbling for the emergency off switch by the conveyor, I pressed the stop button. But it was too late, Stephan had been pulled into the rotating cylinders, the painful cry he sent forth made the machinery speak in whispers. Stephan crumbled to the ground, holding his arm, and he let out a scream of such anguish my whole body was immediately covered in chills; and that scream has caused me to awake from many a dreams, on many a dreamless night.

Dashing to his side, I pressed on his wound then pulled off my belt and tried to tie it as tightly as I could around his shoulder, trying to stop the bleeding. "Stephan don't move, hold this here… I'll be right back, just hold this, I'm going to run and get help…" My mind went racing and I could do nothing but think of rescue. "Ok Benjamin, don't be gone long… please…" "I won't, I promise…" I said over my shoulder as I left conveyor belt one behind me.

As I went running from the building, screaming for help, who else should I see, but him who I wanted to see, least? What morbid melancholy fell over me at his sight, and I considered whether it was even worth stopping, but what choice did I have, I had no one else, Stephan was bleeding to death as I thought, and surely a learned man could be of some assistance?

"Professor DuckÄtape… I need help, I need help quick!" I pleaded, out of breath, latching on to his suit jacket. "Calm down young man, just tell me what the problem is and we will think this through together, as the ancients did in Greece." "No I don't think you understand, it's not that kind of problem… you see Stephan, my friend Stephan's clothing got hooked on a branch, and it pulled him into the machine, I think it cut his arm all the way through…" I beseeched, as I tried to remain calm despite my flowing adrenaline. The Professor glanced at his watch, and then put his hand up to his chin to scratch, before speaking, "I see, a very interesting problem you have proposed, no doubt not entirely different from the one I faced as a graduate student…" Professor DuckÄtape proclaimed, as he plucked up the empty sleeve of his suit jacket, lifting it high into the air and dropping it to emphasize the superior experience from which he spoke. "Let me ask you first, are you sure he is not just experiencing the saw blade for himself, in his own way, to gain a deeper understanding, and deeper appreciation for it?" "Dude, Professor, what is wrong with you, don't you see the blood all over my shirt?" I yelled back, wanting to strangle this arrogant, vain man. "I do see the blood, but I did not see how it got there, so what makes you think, I can connect such an observation, with its origins in the natural world?" The professor retorted, quite proud of himself no doubt, but I fired back. "Because, I'm telling you, you idiot! Stephan is bleeding to death, I need

125

someone to run and get help, while I try to stop the bleeding." The professor placed one finger over his lips as if he was telling me to hush, and looked off in the distance before speaking, "Very well, very well, though you still have not proven to me with your reason, why I should believe such things, surely your overzealous presentation of the facts deserves some consideration on my part." The professor finally relented his position, and for any concession at all I was quite grateful. "Ok, thanks, please hurry, we are by conveyor belt one." I said as I went to leave, to run back to Stephan. "Before I part to claim assistance for you, young man, I just want to let you know, though this may appear to be an act of faith on my part, it is not, as I do not believe in faith, and I just want you to know, you still haven't proven to me that what you are saying about this Stephan character is true, I go, I go to get help simply because I was already heading that way…"

If I would have had time to knock his teeth out, I'm sure it would have been difficult to convince me this was not an appropriate action to take. But I refrained from any further discourse with this scum and went back to my friend, whose time was fading. Pulling up close to Stephan, I tried to provide some encouragement, "Here I can hold the belt Stephan, I got someone to run and get help; it should be coming any moment…" We stayed there, on that dirty floor covered in tree waste, for some time without anyone speaking, until after a long time, Stephan spoke.

"I don't think anyone is going to make it in time…" Stephan's words were light, yet heavy with forced effort, an increasing exertion, for a weakening body. "Sure they will, they have to come… I can hear the sirens of the ambulance now…" I promised, but there were no sirens, we were alone, as alone as you can be, scattered together on the dark side of the moon, and I was becoming scared. Some time passed, I'm not really sure how long it was, maybe five minutes, maybe an hour; I kept talking to Stephan to keep him awake and looking at me, pressing with all my strength against his wound to hold, to keep the life within him. I told him about my violin, and the many life lessons the simplest most complex instrument held. And how I loved to play, and couldn't wait to get it fixed, to have my violin mended somehow, someway, so I could play again, so I could play for him. And I told him to close his eyes as I held his hand, and that I would hum a few beautiful melodies, and if he closed his eyes, and imagined hard enough, it would be like I was right there playing for him. I said, envision the spot on the river you love so much, how the water brings you peace, and then think of me there with my violin.

And so I hummed, and as I hummed, I fell into those sweet places far from where we were, a sweet place where Stephan was not dying, and I was not covered in my friend's blood, dying inside. A place where my violin could play for eternity and never play the same sonnet twice. For a moment I drifted, drifted like wood in the tide to comfort, until, letting those sweet songs carry me far, far away, a heavy raspy voice interrupted my day wanderings, a voice thick with fluid which was beginning to back up into his lungs, as his heart struggled with the ever decreasing volume to maintain pressure, and this is what that voice said, "Hey Benjamin, do you remember that conversation we had at your house, the one where we talked about hope, and watched the stars come out…"

"I do…" I acknowledged, as the memory of a fine evening propelled its way quickly to the forefront of my mind. With it, a smile came to my face, and looking into Stephan's cloudy eyes as his light began to fade, these were his last words, "Benjamin, have you ever thought, that maybe the questions you are asking, that is, in the questions, is where substance lies, and not in any answers you may or may not have…? I guess what I'm saying, is, maybe the internal conflict that you are having, that I had, is more evidence of what is there, rather than what is not… I suppose all I can say, is if you want your violin fixed, if you really want it made new, take it to the community of trees, and they will be able to fix your violin…"

And here I must pause, as there have been few times in my life where there was such a torrent of passion, wading tears; an inner lament that went so deep, that it went to sweep me away. I'm not sure that in this life, we can experience anything so harsh. A harshness, you are braised with raw emotion, how I wanted to cry out, and if I would have seen Professor DuckÄtape, at that moment, I am afraid I would have struck him like Cain struck Able, to the death, despising his first fruits. What I will say now, and all I will say about Stephan, a man who's character was so deep and true, to discuss who he was further, would be to abase his person, so all I will say is: 'he was the finest men and the world was not worthy of him'.

8

Old: What has instigated this inner discord?

New: A place of forlorn solitude. A place that allows me to say, you must consider yourself.

Old: Why should I do such a thing, am I not king over myself?

New: As surely as I speak, so what you say is true, may you remain lord over me, and king over yourself?

Old: Why then, do you bother me with such frivolity?

New: Quite clever, your question for a question, but let us do one better, an answer for an answer. Are you yourself not responsible for the origin of your own suffering? My lord, may I be struck down if I cease to serve you, lest you miss understand your servant.

Old: An answer for an answer, so it shall be… you are not worthy of the calling of which you were called, neither do you deserve success, or the finer things in life…

New: Surely to disagree with such an answer would be foolish; there is truly no deserved bone in my body, and to think of such lofty things, is to admit, indeed I am most unworthy.

Old: Nice, very nice, you are starting to see things my way once again, for to get too carried away with hope and promises, is surely a mortification calling unto me. Let me add, while we are on the topic; that you are a dirty man, detestable and reprobate, sotted and stupefied, as anything you have touched has been brought to ashes, withdraw from life and touch no more…

New: I am different now, please understand? I despise this bickering amidst myself, just allow, just allow me to be who I am, will you; please?

Old: The change you claim, most accurately, is not real; your mind wanders and it is most prone to stumbling over itself, your change is but a mirage in the desert, and you will either die in its pursuit, or your thirst will be quenched and you will return unto me.

New: No, that is not true, stop saying such things, it is not true at all… I don't hurt people anymore, I love people now… Is there not forgiveness in the world?

Old: Ah, yes, now you have identified this mirage most verily, forgiveness, a vision in the heat of the day for those you are weary from their travels, a vision, a dream, a mirage most unreal!

New: What has been said: I deserve not any blessings, or success, or love, or family, is true; surely I have given up any right to claim such things, destroyed that which was good, and neither do I deserve forgiveness, but it has been said it was given apart, given to the weak, and the broken, apart from my own interests, and most surely I am one of those. Is not our dialog most attentive to the change in me, for who struggles so who has not changed, surely the unchanged man does not bicker with himself as I do…?

The old self was quieted for a time, quieted for now at this last observation, this last question; yet he would return and call to me, calling me to serve him many times in many ways, to serve the regrets, and resentments, and self-pity, the fear and the loathing, the pride and the hate, all in service to a cruel master. And for a short time longer, my friend Stephan recently departed from me, my violin in pieces, we will see I continued to serve something else; I continued to serve promises that were empty and gray, corrupted and false, may I ask that the one true promise would come soon, so I may move from this unhappy place in my mind, let me take my mind to a good place soon?

Walking into Dr. StrusselCööK's office I was confronted with a room, no doubt occupied by a woman who loved diet wood drinks, gossip, and herself. I sat in the only chair that was available to sit in, and opened one of the books sitting on her desk, a book about wood chemistry. What did I learn in those short moments before Dr. StrusselCööK came to lambaste me for being a profligate man? Well I learned on some other level, we are propelled as humans, to revolve around a nucleus of some sort, serving its attractive mass; and that quite appropriately the nucleus and the number around which we circle, would determine the consistency of our character on some higher echelon of existence, too come. Setting aside chemistry, I must say, I was not prepared for the times in waiting, yet a man who is desperate is here; so will he attempt to reproduce any hope, any alleged hope, which claims an answer.

"Good evening, you must be Benjamin Silversin, it's nice to meet you, I'm Dr. StrusselCööK... I must say it is quite a pleasant surprise, when you are here for the last appointment for the day and all you can think about is going home, but you are suddenly left with a good looking gentleman to attend that time with, may our time together not pass too quickly...?" Dr. StrusselCööK said as she walked in and eyed me up,

131

as a dog would bacon. I did not care for this advance, if in fact that is what it was, and I was immediately suspicious of her, but it was possible she was just another one of those eccentric intellectuals, I don't know?

"Hi, it's nice to meet you." I replied as the doctor found her seat behind her desk, and made ready a pad of paper and pen. "So what brings you here to see me Benjamin?" I listened and thought, there was a part of me which desired to share, but also a part of me that desired to protect itself, I had to go with one? "Well, Miss Rachel scheduled an appointment for me, with you, because I told her I needed help, and she is a kind woman in that way… I have been having a lot of issues lately, and I can't stop drinking wood drinks, and I'm sad all the time, and well, sawdust has lost all its pleasure, and I don't know what to do… and my best friend, well, he died, and I feel like it's my fault, maybe I could have saved him if I wasn't so tipsy at the time, on that day, I don't know…?"

Those last words barely pushed themselves from my mouth, tarnished words, corrupted and stained by time. I wanted so badly for something new to come from me, I struggle even now to credibly trust you with accurate words from my heart to bereave the torment in me, a torment so, death was not far off!   But, perhaps, I will never be orphaned from those feelings, and they can be used to say, 'God is good', despite it all?

"I see, I see… hmm, well, I'd like to try something with you today Benjamin, that is if you are agreeable?" "Sure, I'm open to anything you think will help…" I replied eagerly, now sitting up attentively in my chair. Dr. StrusselCööK grabbed her notebook and pen and also went fumbling around in her draw for something. Pulling her

132

chair from around the desk, she sat next to me, and I observed it was a golden pocket watch on a chain she had obtained. "Ok, Benjamin, what we are going to do, I like to call a regressive suggestive hypnotic-therapy, yes that is certainly a mouth full, but I want you to know there's nothing to worry about, just relax, I'll take care of the rest…" "Ah, is this like mind control or something?" I asked, perplexed, though I did not know what to expect from a woman in the field of human sawdust relations, this was certainly apart from any notion my faded brain held. "No, no, not at all, it is difficult to explain, it really needs to just be experienced, I can access no part of your brain without your consent, so don't worry, it has served my patients very well in the past, I think it will serve you also." "Ok." Was all I could say, I mean what argument could be grasped by a man in my weakened state? "Now what I would like you to do first is recline in your chair, allow yourself, feel yourself falling into the cushions, release all your tension, relax your muscles…"

I followed her instructions and watched as she pulled forth the pocket watch, and the only sound to be herd in the room was of its ticking. Tick, tock, tick, tock, my breathing slowed and my eyes became heavy, tick, tock, tick, tock, I watched this pendulum swing, the hands on the face of the clock blurring, melting to become one. "Very good Benjamin, now listen to my voice, but don't stop watching the watch, now pretend to not just relax in the chair, but allow your body to push through it…" Tick, tock, tick, tock, the sounds uniting themselves in fair harmony, a low bass hum, which had me drifting away, far away… "Now imagine the picture I paint with my words, we are returning to the day your friend Stephan died,

I knew Stephan also, he was a pleasant man, you will remember that pleasantness about him."

"Excuse me doctor, I don't think this is working…" "Yes it is, it definitely is, you are hypnotized." She retorted, and clearly the first signs of her frustrations with me began manifesting themselves. Sure I felt tired, but that could be easily explained by a hard day's work, but I wasn't sure if this tiredness was the effect the doctor had in mind? Tick, tock, I let my eyes close, tick, tock. "Ok, whatever you say, you're the doctor." Tick, tock, tick tock, I kept listening to the watch and the doctors words, and something happened, I'm still not sure what?

"Now with this picture of your friend Stephan in your thoughts, I am going to release your mind… you have been released Benjamin, as you continue in this released state, don't struggle against it… just tell me what it is you see Benjamin?" I was seeing something, kind of like those funny orbs that dance about when you squint at the sun, or hold your eyelids closed as tight as they will go for too long. And as these orbs danced about, like dragon flies in the setting sun, so this is what I began to see. "It's green, everything is green, as I look closer I see spots of red, and yellow… wait something is forming from the spots, it's a garden, I'm in a garden, but there are lots of other gardens around me, a community of gardens, like ones you might see in England, or the inner cities…" The doctor let my words hang in the air, allowing them to sink and penetrate the depths from whence they came. "Very good, very good, now I want you to look down, look into your garden; what do you see?" The doctor instructed me in that monotone voice, tick, tock, tick, tock. "My garden looks ok, but I'm looking closer now, and I see bugs have eaten holes in

134

the leaves of my plants, and there are weeds everywhere, and the vegetables and fruit are rotten, there is only rotten fruit and vegetables in my garden... Doctor, I don't like it here, I want to leave my garden, my garden is an ugly garden." "No Benjamin you will think of your garden as a beautiful garden..." "But I can't because my garden is not beautiful, it's ugly..." I protested, in that hypnotic protest, that pathetic protest, unable to move, I was like a small child wanting to leave church on Christmas day. "I don't care, you will think it's a beautiful garden anyways, find something you like in your garden and we will talk about that..." The doctor insisted, yet, looking around my garden, there was nothing I liked, nothing I wanted to praise as special and worthy of my time, so I bent down and began picking weeds as the doctor spoke. "No Benjamin, I didn't tell you to start picking weeds, stop picking weeds, we are to find something to raise your self-esteem, first..." "Dr. StrusselCööK there is nothing here, my garden is dead... wait, I just saw something between the plants; someone is in the garden next to me..." "Benjamin, concentrate, ignore the distraction, find a good thing in your garden..." Dr. StrusselCööK ordered, but I ignored her because once the dirt is bad in your garden, everything it produces will be bad, if it produces anything at all?

       "Doctor, I see Stephan, he is in the garden next to me, I'm looking at his garden, and his garden is full of weeds too, but he is picking them, and he is cleaning up his garden, I'm going to go help him..." "No, no, you will not go help him Benjamin, you will stay in your garden." "But doctor we can work together, and we can get both of our gardens cleaned up a lot faster, we can try to make them look beautiful together."

"You are a terrible listener Benjamin, most stubborn and unable to follow conventional ways, I think our session is going to be over…" "No doctor, please not yet, can I at least tell Stephan I love him, and seek his forgiveness." "No, there you go again Benjamin, don't you realize, *you*, are the arbitrator of forgiveness, you must start by forgiving yourself…" Tick, tock, tick, tock, I listened to the clock, and the sound was sad, lamenting its creation, time lamenting time, for the sake of everlasting time, was time created that it might show its creation what love is, the love which compelled love to the bitter times end?

"I am going to count backwards from three and you will wake up, but when I get to the number one, you will forget all of this, the only thought I permit you to have, is a subliminal thought, remember Benjamin, you will begin to see me as quite pretty, three, two, one…" I opened my eyes as a child would who is pretending to sleep and isn't sure if there's a parent lurking nearby. The doctor looked the same to me after the session as she did before, or maybe if anything, my perception of her was lowered, as it should be for a woman who gives advice and treatment such as she does.

Dr. StrusselCööK moved back behind her desk, and pulled out her prescription pad. Sweat had formed on my brow and my lip from the intense emotions, and I was much relived our session was coming to an end. "Now, I'm not sure that worked as well as I would have liked, so I'm going to try something else for you now… I know you said you were having problems drinking too many wood drinks, I am going to prescribe you some medicine to help with that, this synthetic sawdust should allow you to overcome some of your urges and help you relax, we all need some good relaxing from time to time… take one every…" I stopped listening after that, as I considered synthetic sawdust, and 'good relaxing', mm', mm', that was right up my alley, an ally to the gods of self-indulgence!

I left the doctor's office that day, and life became a fog after that, a haze of wood drinks and synthetic sawdust, late nights and people only seen once. Yet, the most prodigious fact which might propel me forward is that, I, we have been created with a perfect image as our canvass, so these things, the late nights, one nights, hazy nights, remained to me unmemorable, actually pernicious, eroding anything left in me worth keeping on high ground, fully destroying any part of that canvass which had been unmarred up until that moment in time.

For some time I continued to see Dr. StrusselCööK, she provided me with synthetic sawdust and I provided her with stories of how I struggled mightily to change, appeasing both of our egos, this arrangement worked out quite well for a season. But what happens when your own value system of self-fulfillment begins to weaken, to bend under the considerable force of painful consequence, as you become encumbered with the hurt of others and the degradation of yourself? Though I do not pretend I began to seek anything of which I know today, anything of high and fine worth, I believe I began to look for something outside myself, though just barely, this high power was really not very high at all.

Many weeks and months passed in this dizzying state of self-absorption, days hardly worth communicating, days which if they fell from the minds of all, would not be missed, even their existence may be worth denying; for their value was existentially worthless. So here is where this next endeavor of mine picks up, an endeavor of halfhearted pursuit, from a man who had yet to come to the end of himself, me; as I have an appointment with Ohm Matzo today. If you remember he is the spiritual advisor at the mill, and claims to have expertise in the area of the spiritual, and the metaphysical realms; we'll see?

Walking through the grounds of the mill, spring had just begun to show her face after a long, dark, cold winter. The white house was where I trotted, a man unable to bridle his sawdust lust came hoping hope may have a place for him yet? If anyone knew how to relate to the unquenchable, unanswerable longings of the person, which science failed to answer, Ohm Matzo would be the man with the answers.

"Hi, Miss Rachel, I have an appointment with Ohm Matzo today, is he around?" "Hey Benjamin it's nice to see you, if you are looking for Ohm Matzo, he is usually in the grand ball room at this time, he likes to sit up by the window when he does his chants…" Miss Rachel replied as she pointed me in the direction of the grand ball room, I offered her my thanks and moved towards the room I hadn't seen since orientation day.

For several moments I reflected on time, on the time which brought change, the change that had occurred in me since working at the mill, not good change, but there was something in me which felt Ohm Matzo was a man whose wisdom I should consider, and perhaps there was good change yet to come at the mill? Walking into the ball room, the magnificent view was not quite as impressive as that of Mr. McNabb's house, but it was still a sight which tickled my belly and left me giggling inside. The front of the room was being held in the grips of a low fog. Whoever gave Ohm Matzo permission to perform his acts of reverence there, should have taken his matches; because he was, from what it looked like with all the smoke and incense, going to burn the place down! As I neared him, that still small sound was in my mind from those early days at the mill, not so long ago, "Hummmmm, diddy, diddy, hummm, hum, hum…"

Sitting on the floor next to this spiritual giant was quite intimidating, the wood floor was cold, and I had no idea what he was doing or why he was doing it. But the pain in me had left me vulnerable and pliable to the most outlandish ideas man could produce, and a consideration of his philosophy seemed to be of imperative consequence, or of some importance to me still.

"Hi, Mr. Ohm Matzo, my name is Benjamin, I have an appointment with you…" I offered, not completely sure he was aware of my presence, but after a few moments, he opened one eye, now clearly attentive to my arrival he responded.

"The answers you seek, so shall you find;

for it is into the depths we will look, into the mind.

The mind, the mind, the brain, the plain brain strain,

which helps us bypass the minds brains pain.

Ignore the self, seek the universal,

and we will push that cosmic order into reversal.

For what is more selfless than to strip the encumbered of dignity,

and erase any sign of the creator's unique cucumber frivolity.

Yes, yes, long and green with a bitter rind,

a harder task you will be hard pressed to find.

But if we get water, spice, vinegar, and salt;

pickling it, we can say the pain is not our fault!

Nice and pickled, you will become an acquired taste,

but depart from me Benjamin not in haste;

for to leave without the inner eye, the ajna,

is to leave with great heart ache, the angina.

As you now look through the world from a pickle jar,

blurred will truth be, true love quite afar!"

       How often in life are you lost for words, quite often for me, I will admit; but what I have never been left without are thoughts, those trusted thoughts when your mind works well, how I have come to rely on them so mightily swell. But the first time, the only time, I can recall such a time where perseverance says it's time to give up, so was my mind saying, what are the thoughts we should have for the words we have just herd? As a mind which is left unchallenged comes to its own various ways of viewing the world apart from any real knowledge, on occasion, occasionally we find we stumble upon a profound gem apart from knowing what we know, an emerald of the darkest green, so in hindsight, I see my words coming next were like diamonds in the ruff to a clear nighttime sky, just waiting to be polished for the evening to come. "Excuse me, Mr. Ohm Matzo, I'm not sure exactly what it is you are saying, but it doesn't sound very good… I'm not sure I need another eye, I just want the ones I have to get fixed."

"Hummmm, diddy, hum, hum, hum, thus speaks Ohm Matzo,

My allusion unto you is most appropriately true;

we will take what is right, good, and beautiful, turn up the heat, and make a rue;

my illusion unto you, says push past your feelings, add the salt, feel the burn;

grab our wooden spoon and give our rue a turn.

You have been hurt, maybe hurt quite badly, sadly, madly, I will stay and say as the mad man did in the square 'god is dead';

and we will watch closely as our rue turns red.

For the only thing in life you have worth having, I will make a delusion, and as you fail to fail, failing at everything you do;

let me allude to your delusion, my painting of myself as boss, the most appropriate illusion, and I think our rue will turn out just fine, right, and as we taste quite true!"

"Ok, that sounds very nice, very poetic Mr. Matzo, but I think I have some problems with what you are saying…"

"You do? Everyone else is usually telling me how profound I am…" Ohm Matzo had proposed this last question, stated this last statement without trying to rhyme his words, and I was a little taken back. I thought I was going to be in a battle for some time, trying to extract clarity from this gentleman. Yet, as I have seen I am quite personable, and people seen to trust me easily, as Berry did, or Stephan, and here Ohm Matzo only waiting, his inner soul begging to be asked, so I used this opportunity of him dropping his guard to inquire. "Why do you believe what you believe, I mean; what is it you actually believe in?"

"Sometimes I don't know, I get a lot of attention for my insight, I'm not sure how real it is though, and if I can even believe some of the things I say myself. I guess what I believe is suffering has a purpose, I find it hard to believe there is all this pain in the world for no reason... I was in love once Benjamin, to the most wonderful woman, a fine woman, one I saw hope and a future with..." Ohm Matzo's voice cracked a little as I watched him, watching him the way an owl does a mouse, with this peering sight I almost felt I could see the face of the woman he was bringing to mind as he spoke, as the ache of love lost was deep in his trembling voice. "Yeah, I loved her a lot Benjamin, we would of made a fine team, fighting life's fights together, there was nothing fate could have thrown our way which we couldn't have pushed aside, a fine pair indeed we would have made. I could see us growing old together, and reminiscing about the foolishness with which we sought to take on the world, but there was one problem..." The first tear struggled to gain traction on his dry skin, yet after a wet path was made so did many tears which had welled up inside this spiritual man, begin to flow. The pain was real, palpable, I know, for I have felt Ohm Matzo's pain, so as any person with compassion would do, I pulled forth my own waters, damned, a high reservoir of lament, behind a levy of hurt and pride; we shared some healing, however small, some healing we shared together none the less.

"There was one problem, we came from two different places, two different times, perhaps if we had grown up together we would have been inseparable, but cruel fate had placed us some years apart in age, she was ready to seek career success, I was ready to make something beautiful, to produce art and music for people to enjoy, no big deal love has surmounted greater things than a few years age difference, I mean beauty is beauty wherever you find it, right? But as I said, this was not the only separation, she came from a good family, one that didn't struggle for much, but my prospects on the other hand were quite meager, there is not really any tangible asset to beauty, it's more of a feeling… that was probably the hardest part for me to swallow, when everything else seems to match so well, when you only want to be judged for the content of your character and where you see beauty, and that's not enough, that somehow my current inability to provide financial security, would cause her to reconsider our love… I'll tell you nothing hurt so badly as that…"

"I'm sorry to hear that happened to you, I know that is a very painful thing, when someone doesn't love you the way you love them… but do you think going around and confusing people with your crazy rhymes is going to help you, or help them?"

"I don't know, I've pretended to have the answers for so long, for a long time I thought I did have the answers, so it's not like I set out to be deceptive, I guess all I can do is trust in what I've been doing and keep doing it…" Ohm Matzo answered with conviction, bringing composer back to himself, he wiped away a few stray tears, and locked the picture of his woman back in his everlasting vault. And the Ohm Matzo, the real Matzo was gone once again, just as quickly as a sunset losses its battle for the sky, so Ohm Matzo lost his battle with pride, and he positioned himself back in a position of enlightenment and hummed…

"I, well, I don't have the answers either, so I appreciate your honesty, I guess I'll keep looking…" After I finished speaking, I went to shake Ohm Matzo's hand but he ignored me, as if I had never been there, as if we had never spoken, Ohm Matzo returned to his world of make believe, and I returned to a life of sawdust...

9

Behold! I was walking, walking, endlessly walking… My throat parched, my stomach turning inward… As you see, as I was seeing, this is what I saw: I moved through the mobs, the horde who hoarded the large path; the mobs who voluptuously held the great way. But I was so tired, and there was nowhere to stop. So many people all moving down the path, my feet hurt and my sack had become heavy, too heavy to continue. So I moved to the fringes to catch the cool breeze, but I found there was no way to stay in the cool breeze, as I was quickly overtaken by others who sought the same refreshment. What must I do?

This I asked, and asked myself deeply, I must exit the herd to be relived of this congestion, I perceived. And as I considered with what difficulty I would possess such a task amidst the throng, a narrow path opened. Here, in this spot, through no work of my own, an opening found me waiting anxiously.

As I seeded my feet on the narrow path, I saw it was not smooth, it was filled with many roots and rocks, many stumbling blocks. My hunger and thirst still not lost, I moved tentatively forward, hoping to find a place where I may have bread, and water, and fruit, and rest. Pushing forward, ever so forward, a small abode appeared, a cottage, and as I drew close, I saw an old man sitting under the portico.

"Old man, my name is Benjamin, I am weary and laden with a heavy sack; may I stop here to rest?"

"Yes Benjamin, you may stop here to rest." Said the old man.

"I am hungry and in need of water, from where shall I drink and eat?" I asked.

"In the cottage you will find a table, it will provide you with what you desire." Said the old man.

"I also have questions, I need to find my way home; I have been lost on a wide pathway for many a day." I said.

"Indeed you have questions, as do all who stubble on my cottage have questions, but I only have words for those who seek answers." Said the old man.

"Whatever do you mean old man? Stop speaking in riddles." I said.

"Go and eat and drink Benjamin, fill yourself and rest, and then, if there is still something prodding you, I may speak to you more plainly." Said the old man.

"Very well." I said.

Stumbling exhaustively through the cottage door, I found myself in a room with a table, as the old man had said, but there was no water, and fruit, and bread, as he had offered. Turning, to return from whence I came, to scold the old man for his dishonesty, the door from which I had entered this room, was gone. As I turned again in confusion the other way, so were the windows. I was left alone in a room with no windows, no doors, only a table, a chair, and a plain mirror on the wall.

Confused, I resigned myself to these sparse accommodations and hoped I would be released from this magic soon. So as I sat in the chair quietly confounded, I looked a crossed the table into the mirror, and as I was looking, water, and fruit, and bread appeared on the table before me, and I was glad. I drank the water, and ate the bread, and sweetened my mouth with the fruit. And then satisfied, I looked to the mirror and thought of how I would like meat, and cheese, something savory for my fancy. With amazement, these objects of my desire were brought before me. I indulged in these savory choice cuts, yet full, I desired something sweet to cleanse my pallet. And these things also, the objects of my heart, came before my eyes. With what pleasure I sat there in that spot, as I stared into the mirror, and was provided for, as I would provide for myself. These things, that which came to me was not limited to food, but my mind seeking knowledge, and elegance, beauty and lustful things; and so it was given, and appeared for me, the way I would have it appear for myself. It is hard to say for how long I stayed in that place, watching as I provided for myself, but no doubt after much time had passed, I noticed the mirror, its reflection grew dim. So I watched caring little but for, the candy of my eyes before me. Yet, the mirror grew dimmer upon the manifestations of my heart, and I became vexed in my spirit over how my time now passed, and grew anxious about the dimming mirror.

Standing up from the table, I moved towards the mirror, drawing close, wanting to see what caused this scandalous change in appearance. And what I saw, was this was no mirror, but a piece of glass. I placed my hands up to the glass and peered into it; seeing with my peering sight what lay beyond, and what I saw, I shall never forget. Distorted and marred, grotesque and twisted, darkened and raw, sickening

147

to the eyes, humbling to the heart, yes, there was a picture of me on the other side of that glass!

Chaotic, angry, filled with rage for how I had been tricked by the old man, and hating the image of myself which I saw, I seized the chair and swung it with all my might into the glass. And just as you would imagine the shattering to occur, at that moment of startle, I found myself outside the cottage, falling to the ground with the forceful follow through from my heavy swing. Looking up, I saw the old man smiling at me.

"Ah dear Benjamin, you are one of the fortunate few, may we praise God for your delivery." Said the old man.

"Whatever do you mean old man? What is this, what are these dirty magic tricks you play on me?" I asked.

"It is no trick, and it is no magic my friend. No doubt you smashed the glass, you hated the image you saw?" Asked the old man.

"Indeed I smashed the glass and hated the image I bore." I answered.

"Surely you may look about you now, and see things as they are, for you have smashed the glass of false promises, and hated that which you would become from them, you are one of the few, indeed. How many I have seen come off the wide path and enter the cottage to never be seen again. They will spend the rest of their days in that cottage, never looking past the glass, never seeing the death in themselves, for they are too busy with the false promises. Now you may go home Benjamin, but before you wake, remember they may reject you for your message, they may wish you dead for your testimony, for your light shines on their darkness. Awake now young Benjamin, awake…"

At this, I awoke from my dream, and though I knew not what had just happened, perhaps, you will see as I do now, that the terrible place I found myself in, was the beginning of that dream, the beginning of my chance to withdraw from the rabble, and the beginning of a calling, an election to a fine and good life.

Reaching for my blankets, I tried to cover myself, fumbling around my body, my covers were nowhere to be found. I was cold, so cold, turning I heard a crackling and my name echoed in a strange static way. "Benjamin Silversin, please come to the speaker, you have a visitor."

What, what, what the heck is going on? Trying to move, the concrete pressed against my body seeding its cold raw surface on my skin. Opening my eyes a gentle fuzz which allowed for hairy vision, was more hairy than usual. Clicking and jangling of keys, and soon the sight of my friend Officer Berry through a steal door with small glass cut out confirmed to me, proved to me, my greatest nightmare was coming true.

As I felt for my belongings, I observed my clothes; my everything was gone; my identity was no more at that moment than a number and an orange jumpsuit. Watching Berry fumble with the keys I looked away in shame. The door cracked and the most painful squeaking eked from its hinges. A bright light pierced the room, piercing my eyes, and Berry spoke.

"Mr. Silversin, please come with me…" The formal words said to me many more things, condemned me in a greater way, than any scolding officer Berry could have offered me in front of his comrades. "Please put out your hands…" "Come on Berry is this really necessary, it's just me Benjamin." "Mr. Sileversin, please put out your hands…" Berry repeated in a stern voice, with only a concession to offer, concession is what I gave, and cuffs were placed around my wrists.

"Please follow me…" I followed berry and he took me down a maze of corridors which only left me more discombobulated than when I had awoken in that strange place. The room we went to was sparsely furnished, and the least hint of wood or sawdust, was nowhere to be found. Once we made it into the room, Berry asked me to have a seat, and so, I sat.

"Here, put out your hands Benjamin." I did as I was told and Berry removed the cuffs. "Sorry about that, I know you wouldn't have given me any trouble, it's just protocol when prisoners are in transit." Berry said sitting across the table from me, pulling forth from the drawer some papers and an ink pad. "Yeah, I heard over the radio when they picked you up last night, so I talked to my boss and picked up an extra shift this morning at the confinement center…" Berry added, placing a piece of chewing gum in his mouth. "Berry it's great to see you, so can you get me out of this place…? And I have to tell you, it's a little embarrassing, but I don't really remember last night?" It hadn't really sunk in yet, the gravity of the situation that is, time out in the corner for being bad was no longer an option. "I'm sorry Benjamin, but this is something I can't just make go away." "Come on Berry there's got to be someone you can talk to, I've never been in trouble before, and I'm a nice guy, the situation can't be that bad?"

Berry picking up one of the papers in front of him, glanced at me and then began to read. "Lewd and unbecoming public conduct during pre-festival celebrations, also, failure to pay a lawfully acquired wood draft bill, and possession of endangered wood-tree sawdust, controlled under endangered species act twenty-tree…" My face flushed, turning red, sweat formed on my palms, this was not me, those words on that paper were not who I was. But those words were who I was, they were what told the world about Benjamin. If anyone had seen the hope possessed by a young man who has been gifted in many ways, perhaps you at some point had this hope, let's watch as we put a millstone around hope's neck and drop hope into the great fathoms of the deep, sinking; sinking, my hope was sinking.

"We don't have a lot of time, I have to get your finger prints and get you back to your cell, I just wanted to make sure you were ok, and to tell you to not answer any questions, I'm not really supposed to tell you that, but I don't want you to get in any more trouble then you're already in, here is a card for a friend of mine who is an attorney…" The enormity of the predicament I was now in, was being held high over my head by my friend, and though I jumped to pull my scarf from the branch on which it was snagged, it was far out of reach, and I was left grasping at air…

Back in that cell, the door clanging shut with a jarring rattle, I fell to my knees in exhaustion, not a physical exhaustion which can be belabored by food and sleep, drink and rest, but an exhaustion of that inner most part of yourself; is there a tear with enough salt to hold such exhaustion, enough sobs to beat back the fatigue? For in me, contradiction upon contradiction, inconsistency upon inconsistency, was a view of myself which did not match the worlds, where did this perspective come from, where does it lead; should it change, to the world should it be conformed; no, not the world, but to what? An inner pain and lament, self-contempt, long jagged nails scratching an open sore would have provided a soothing comfort, above the pain, that deep pain of an agonized heart asking the most steal armored questions.

For is it not one thing when others judge you, but what happens at that moment when you judge yourself? As you have seen a man up to this point, a man by age and nothing else, a man who's own point of digression from the truth was distant, far from any center; as you have observed, he was too cowardly to release himself from the guard post to which he was tied, so now a time for a more humane consideration should be taken up by me, yes let me reach for the first stone. For I scarcely believe, there is or was or is to come a greater transgressor of the law than I. Walking slowly to the pile of stones, I shall lie down and show my belly, throwing my stone first to the heavens, I will not move as it is thrown back at me! Yes, this is the most agonizing time indeed, when a man condemns himself!

10

If we could escape for a moment to my violin, a place closed to the rest of the world, a place where the unseen causes us to cringe, a place where there is also laughter and joy, somewhere, hidden under the marring; what is this place? It has been called our heart, our spirit, our soul, our consciousness, the forms, the place of perfect creation, where all is held, and all is un-held for us to see. A place of confusion, and hurt, and lament, an abode of order, laughter, and joy. Maybe there are no words to describe it, maybe there are no words which should describe it…

But if we were to press on, and force the issue, and look more deeply despite our aversion to the difficult; what would we find? Before we go further, let me say, if there is a fear there, it is rightly held, for how dark and grotesque can those things be, which we may find. But to find, or rather for the trueness of perfection to be revealed, we may have to sort through some unpleasantness, I am sorry it is there, I truly am, much of it may be sorrow that was never meant to be yours, and only passed and pressed onto you from others who were hurt and broken long before you came into this world. Maybe there is nothing else to say, and I should stop? I wish I could, for the more deeply I think of these things, within myself, the more unsettled I become, and if there were only one of you, who I write this to, which my thoughts may touch, so you may avoid some pain and suffering, I would think the deep inner search of mine, which I have undertaken, would be worth the effort…

Tears have bordered the corners of my eyes, and they have become thick and heavy with the thought of a new day, another day spent in this body of death, may the days end quickly for me, my lord. I profit inquires such as these on a continual basis, wishing, rather praying, time would come to collect my debt, and I may be freed to listen to that sweet melodious sonnet for eternity. And if you have continued to read though my rolling thoughts, maybe I have set the stage appropriately for what is coming next…

My hope here, is that, my philosophically brooding disposition, has been provided to me for more than just my own amusement, and I may be able to teach you something as my story goes on. And that some constructive thinking can be rung from this oversaturated cloth of thought to provide us with a small pool of wisdom. We will not lose our identity, as some may suggest, but gain it, in this endeavor, this pursuit. Because as we endeavor, rather pursue discipline, we will find freedom.

And the freedom I suggest to you is promised, but not promised with promiscuity of thought, but focused concentration on what is right and true, disciplined thought. May we see that there is no greater love than to die for a friend, and here my freedom comes as a result of asking nothing, but in giving everything, I find I draw from an endless pool of riches? And as I speak in generalities, I must confess, the face of a woman I adore, comes to mind, and I think with what pleasure, with what honor it would be, to be asked to parish so that she may live. Let your own picture, of your own companion, be in your minds as you think of what is right and true.

Here, I don't provide any philosophical profundity, as I am not a philosopher. Please only take this work as your friend Benjamin, a friend who wants to communicate to you an important principal he has learned. Showing you, presenting a paupers share of wisdom, hoping it may produce something special in your lives, if applied appropriately.

The ideas that succeed may sound foreign to most of you, so do not neglected them because of their curious nature, but consider them for the sake of: intellectual pursuit, intellectual discipline, and finally, intellectual freedom. First forgive me for being bolder then most, in that this idea is so simple, yet of such paramount importance, I dare not present it any other way. As I should not seek to hide it in my story, but rather, communicating it openly, treating you as equals, and adding, rather than detracting from your thinking; providing you with clarity, rather than muddled muddy ideas. We shall commence.

First you will imagine a room, with a table and a chair. This is the plainest of rooms where everything is white, and the furniture is simple, much like the room in my dream with the old man. You want nothing in your room to prod your thoughts to anything but what sits on the table. As you enter the room you are alone, fully alone, your clothes are as white as the room, and there are no watches or clocks, or hints of humanity, nothing beyond your own living breathing self. So there is also no sound, nothing but your breath, a cold breath that can be seen in the chilled air.

When you sit in the chair and face the table, you know something will appear before you, but you know not what. You will imagine it is like looking at a blank movie screen, as the lights begin to dim; where an unseen projector controls what is in front of you. Next, you will see a mirror on the wall. And it faces you, but when you look into it, it doesn't reflect you, it only reflects a light within you; your essence if you will. Now, this part is very important, because if you think, that your brain only thinks, because that is what it does, you are mistaken. You will see, for our purposes, there is a hidden part of your mind, congruous to all humanity, which desires, and wants, and attracts itself to the existential world.

The first object you will see on the table is an apple, if you are a person who likes apples, you may think of apple pie, and then playing at your grandmother's house when you were young. And as you think of these things, the light in the mirror changes accordingly to each thought and experience. They are synonymous, if you will allow. You cannot think of the light in the mirror as positive and negative, but greater and lesser attraction, and the scale is not linear, but circular.

(Because there is a point, though most do not experience it, where repulsion is so great, it turns into attraction. A macabre photo of genocide, which attracts your attention, despite its ghastly composition, will suffice as an example.)

Now, if you are a person who doesn't like apples, you would see the light as quite dim, maybe no light at all. Each simple object, which is presented to you on the table, will cause the mirror to grow brighter and darker. As the complexity of that which is placed before you increases, so does the reflection in the mirror, some parts may be light and some dark, like marble.

And what I mean by growing complexity, is that you see a picture of the ocean at sun rise. You may not like to swim, or fish, but you love the aroma of the sea, and watching the colors sparkle off the water's surface. Each aspect of your mind's recollection, places a special shade on your mirror, one color revealing affection and affinity for the sunrise, others, distasteful dingy swirls for your dislike of swimming. And accordingly, it will have an overall tint, when seen in context with the original picture of your mind, which glows or does not glow, similarly.

Now we shall return to the original apple, but not forgetting the mirror which is there reflecting inner desire and aversion. If you will recall, the mirror began its sweeping swirls at the idea of the apple, of course this was properly brought about by the appearance of it, but the idea of the apple came first, came before the apple was actually experienced by you. Now imagine picking up our apple, its bright in color, looks fresh and good for food. You are hungry, so instead of just observing the apple, you take a bite. But immediately, you spit the apple back out, as it is rotten inside, and bad to the taste. You set the apple back on the table, and a new apple appears. Another beautiful apple, one which looks good for food, and because you are still hungry, you take another bite of a beautifully spoiled apple. As long as you are serving the promise of the apple, the promise that this food, which is good for the eye, will eliminate your hunger, you will continue to eat rotten fruit. As long as you serve the idea, the promise of the apple, you will be its slave eating spoiled fruit all your days. Maybe, we are not I think therefore I am kind of people, but careless farmers in an orchard growing many varieties of fruit, not knowing which one to pick?

Oh, you apple of my eye, why are you rotten? I say, check your desires and wants in the mirror, I ask, stop serving the promise of the rotten apple; will you?

11

Stepping out into the sun, my eyes could barely stay parted in its brightness. 'They were,' releasing me from confinement on a ten-thousand pound sawdust surety claim, and all the money I had in the bank was used to attain this small freedom. Stumbling the long way home, I started thinking about Stephan and about my violin, only if one were here, I dare think, I would not be so discouraged. But the music had ended many months before, and the last conversation I had with Stephan kept a bloody memory far too near my mind.

My hands shook and a thought of a wood drink brandished itself clearly, it was true my body desired such, but my mind rejected this notion of comfort, for I saw the poison this solvent had become. All the sawdust had taken me so far, so far away from things of that: white sterling, high worth, pure finery, to consider wood intoxicants now, brought a ferocious repulsion to my heart.

Many days came and went, one day bled into the next, and a gray cloud settled low over my life. Berry encouraged me as much as he could, but gossip around the mill was strong, so quickly I felt I could travel nowhere without a suspicious look. The only other ones beside Berry who treated me fairly, as a person should, was Foreman Dave, and of course Miss Rachel; a finer woman you would be hard pressed to find.

As I sat secluded back in the inventory department, only a few days returned to working for Foreman Dave, I saw Officer Berry once again heading my way. This moment in time, was déjà vu, if there ever was such a peculiar thing as to experience the same thing twice? Berry, a letter in hand, came to my side, "Hey Benjamin, you're looking a lot better than you were the other day, I hope everything is still going as well as can be expected, I know this is not what you were looking for, but I had to bring it…" Berry said, and observing the red wax seal, I surmised he was holding another letter from Mr. McNabb. Snatching the letter, I started by sharing some deep inner profundity, "This really sucks Berry, did you really have to deliver this…?" Berry shrugged his shoulders and lifted his pleading palms upward to illustrate to me, he was in fact powerless over such matters. Opening the letter, breaking the wax seal, I read aloud for Berry, "Well… it says, Benjamin Silversin, Though I know you must be perturbed with respect to the last evening we shared together, there is no doubt, my pain is significantly greater than yours, so instead of taking responsibly for breaking your violin, with substitution, I will make an excuse, and pretend as if it is no big deal. And if you continue to make a fuss about your silly wood instrument, I will only insist my bereavement of Mr. Zooty so greatly exceeds any loss you have endured, that to speak to me of your loss, would be to insult me in the most personal way. So now that we can agree I did nothing wrong, and you deserve no apology, let me enter into the central content of my thinking. Surely, by now, you would have guessed news of the unfortunate situation you worked yourself into with respect to the public sawdust security authorities, has been made aware to me. I must admit, I always find quite a bit of humor in other

160

peoples misfortunes, however, as you hold a special place in my heart, I smiled and laughed at you, for you, many more times than I would have for the average worker at the mill. Since you are currently under restriction and heavy obligation to the courts of high justice, and I patronage their bank accounts quite frequently with sawdust slush, refusing my current invitation would be a grave misfortune for you. So may I implore, and suggest, rather behoove unto you; that attending a private dinner with me is in your very best interest. Yours ungratefully, Mr. McNabb"

Shaking my head, I let the letter slip slowly from my hands and watched as a gentle breeze took it away, as a light wind takes away a feather, drifting away. I had moved beyond disappointment, beyond anger; far, far away to that feathery place of utter defeat, where to fight on only means greater heartache, that sadly blue place of resignation. I had become a martyr for the cause, but with no weapon or words to fight with, I would be an unnamed martyr of the most prodigious order.

"I wonder what he wants with me this time Berry?" "I don't know Benjamin, I've never understood people's motives for doing the things they do, but look on the bright side, at least he likes you..." Berry smiled at me and shrugged his shoulders before continuing, "Well its true, most people, when he wants an appointment, he'll just pay to have a warrant issued and I end up taking them over to his mansion in cuffs." Berry's smile lifted my spirit some, but I had yet to get past my volcanic revulsion of Mr. McNabb. "Thanks I feel really special now, you know he blames me for Mr. Zooty's death, I guess anything to keep him from examining himself; maybe he has some type of revenge in mind?" I said, not entirely caring too much, for what greater harm could he do to me; for whom should I fear, the one who has power over the body or the spirit?

"If it makes you feel better, I know it's not your fault Mr. Zooty is dead, and I also know you have a good heart, though you have been careless since Stephan died…" Berry brought up a sore subject, a subject of the most avoidable nature, for me, for me to think too deeply of this sadness, would mean destruction. Thinking of terrible circumstance, provides a sticky web of questions, unlike a single choice which leads to simple cause and effect, this web of circumstance has me questioning the validity of everything I have ever done, and how if I might have done one thing differently, my dear friend, would not be dead. And to enter that labyrinth, may be for me, to never be heard from again!

"Oh well, what are you going to do, I guess all I can hope for, is he'll have some better food when I go over there this time." There sat my concession, like drift wood on the beach, I waited for the next wave of life to push me where it will. "That's the spirit Benjamin, I like you attitude." Berry acknowledge, patting me on the shoulder, and so my friend left me to return to my work.

The Day came and went as time is prone to do, and surely, I felt to be a man in the doldrums. That windless valley where the ocean meets the equator; how will my ship get home? Washing up, more ready to put my bow hand in a vice than to see Mr. McNabb, I walked towards his mansion head hung low and shoulders sagging.

The giant brass knocker on the mansion door, tap, tap, tap, I went knocking, and the same servant girl who had ushered me to the dinner with the French breakfast radishes took me in. She led me to the dining room, and the room was as I remembered it, except for a giant tray of assorted cheeses sitting, presented elegantly on the shiny wood. I browsed the selection on the tray and settled with what appeared to me to be an aged cheddar. It was a fine piece of cheese indeed, one which would have paired well with a red wood wine; no, no wood wine for you, I beat my wandering mind back into submission.

The oily cheese coated my mouth, I let its salty brine wash over my tongue, it was a very fair cheese, without poor consequential after taste. I would have continued to snack, however, I could hear the clicking of Mr. McNabb's cane working its way down the hallway, towards me; so I restrained myself from further cheese enjoyment, and straitened myself in the chair. Mr. McNabb walked into the dining room with his over dignified strut of self-importance, and sat across from me.

I looked at him and he looked me, and he smiled that sideways smile of his. As he went to place a napkin over his lap, myself doing the same, I saw the pocket on his purple jacket take on a life of its own. It was almost as if there was some third, unseen hand, looking for loose change. But as the unseen hand, the Black Hand, began emerging from his pocket, first I saw whiskers, and then a fat furry body with tail… "Squeak, squeak, squeak, what, what was that Mr. Snuffle's, you said a piece of your favorite aged cheddar is missing… well, how do you know? You said you counted them before you left the room, you said a rat has been into your cheese, and you hate rats…" Mr. Snuffle's hopped from Mr. McNabb's shoulder and came scurrying across the table and began sniffing my fingers, then he ran back, climbing up Mr. McNabb's shirt, "You said, he is the rat, he ate your cheese, you could smell it on his fingers, WHAT, WHAT, HOW DARE YOU EAT MR. SNUFFLE'S CHEESE! You will ask for his forgiveness right now." I didn't know what to do, surely asking forgiveness of a mouse is beneath any ethical definition of human dignity? But I was a man who had lost his dignity, a man as lost as a grain of sand on the beach, so this is what I said. "Mr. Snuffle's I am sorry I ate a piece of your cheese, will you please forgive me?" "What, what was that, you said you will forgive him, but he must feed you a piece of cheese from his hand, you said this is to show him, to always remind him when he thinks of you, that he is, and will always be a rat, and nothing more…"

I don't care, I didn't care anymore, let the earth pull from the sun and have a bitter ice age commence, I didn't care, my heart was already frozen, so I just did as Mr. Snuffle's wanted and fed him the cheese. Good bye icy dignity, may I never see you again?

"And so now that you have met Mr. Snuffle's, a fine specimen indeed, we can only say, though Mr. Zooty's death was very certainly tragic, that my rhetorical question upcoming may provide far more profundity and insight than any further explanation: did I not fall in love with Socrates while reading Phaedo, only to watch him die?" "Uh, I don't know, were you in love with Mr. Zooty, and who's Socrates?" I replied, finding myself lacking in the knowledge of great thinkers, a lacking I would be soon to remedy. "YOU HEATHEN, what is wrong with you? How can you not know the great Socrates… but never mind that, my point has been made, so let me address the central reason for your visit…" Mr. McNabb paused, Mr. Snuffle's sat looking on attentively, and that wide evil grin I had become familiar with many months before began eclipsing his face.

"I would like you, Benjamin, to go to the community of trees, for me. I have been engaged in conversation as of late with my furry friend here, and we have decided, we need to rethink our approach with the tree community… I want you to do nothing illegal, I just want you to learn about them, learn about what motivates them, it's a rather harmless, humble request… and if you do that for me, well, I will do something for you. I can make all this nonsense with public sawdust security go away, vanish like it never happened… so what do you think?" Mr. McNabb paused, I was curious why we weren't eating, I had come with an appetite, and to disappoint a hungry stomach is great slander to the soul. Aside from a growling gut, this proposition was interesting to me, I surely had messed up any future that I had aspired to know, now that I was a known criminal. But here, there was an offering to start over, and from what it sounded like, it required very little sacrifice. "Wait, no need to answer me right away, think about it for tonight, drop off a note to Miss Rachel if you'd like, with your response… NOW GET OUT YOU HEATHEN, RETURN TO YOUR CAVE!"

I left Mr. McNabb's house. I was glad he seemed to be getting over the death of Mr. Zooty rather well, but maybe this was just because he had replaced him… So I have observed replacing relationships, negates our duty to examine ourselves, to leave an untied shoe string dangling in the walk of life… As I dare not walk to far down this bumpy road, I will return to the proposition of Mr. McNabb. A new chance, I could do all sorts of things if this trouble with the law never came to light.

Enter the work force outside the mill, go back to school, start a family, the possibilities were endless. As of yet, I had yet to pull hope from the endless store house of everlasting hope, so my greatest hope in life now, was that I could put things back together myself; maybe I could?

Wrestling through the night, sleep was my foe, and hurt was my ally. My definition of myself consisted of career fulfillment, and the fine countenance of a woman. With neither of these things, or a foreseeable solution to their absence, I was ready to take Mr. McNabb's proposition seriously and have life's opportunity placed back within my grasp. Surely nothing terrible could come from a few months in this community? I will go there, observe them, report back to the mill and that will be that. With these things settled in my mind, I had a solid rock to hold, a sure idea worth my attention, so I took the last few hours of darkness to obtain elusive sleep.

The next morning I headed to the white house to give Miss Rachel my answer, news she could pass on to Mr. McNabb, that I am willing and able to be his minion. Walking down the hallway, Miss Rachel's face was always a pleasant site, and every time I see her I can't help but think of the day when she told me the story behind Miss Eves painting and how she sees beauty. She is a special woman.

"Hey Benjamin, I was told I should be expecting you, Mr. McNabb dropped off an envelope here, and wanted me to give it to you when you came in." Miss Rachel said looking down at a giant manila envelope on her desk. "Yeah, it's great to see you… that's what I came to talk to you about, I wanted you to give Mr. McNabb a note for me and let him know I will do as he asks." I replied looking askance at the envelope she referred to. "Here, you might as well open this while you are here…" Miss Rachel answered handing me the envelope. I took it from her hands and felt the weight it held, something obviously other than paper. Pulling forth the contents, several brochures for a hotel, tickets and a reservation confirmation accompanied a small hand held voice recorder. I looked at this thing perplexed, but flipping it over I observed an orange sticky note which said 'play me', so that is what I did. Pressing the play button these terribly tarnished words worked their way into my bones…

"Good morning Benjamin, Enclosed you will find travel tickets, lodging, and self-sufficiency funds. The mission to the community of trees can be summed up in one question: how do we subvert the minds of the leaders of this community and so access and control needed wood resources (to be used) for the greater good of the mill? This mission should you choose to accept it, will put you in grave peril, so if you are caught or killed, I will disavow all knowledge of your actions. This message will self-destruct in five seconds, I wish you bad luck Benjamin, yours ungratefully Mr. McNabb."

The small handheld tape recorder started smoking in my hand, immediately I drooped it to the floor, and Miss Rachel and I stood watching as it combusted, consuming itself in dark red flames. And that was the beginning, the starting point of something new.

Heading home after receiving this very dramatic message form Mr. McNabb, I decided I should begin packing as the bus left early the next morning.

After packing, tonight, this night, I was finding it difficult to sleep, my journey would soon be taking me to another place. I was driving around the world; would I come back again? If I come back, will I be the same person who left? Am I ever the same person twice, or am I like a river always changing? Maybe now it's time for me to take a walk, as lying in bed thinking these things is torture of another kind. Bear with on my walk, for I must do some thinking before we go forward; will you?

The stars are out, the evening is cool, and possibly if you're not too busy packing for your own journey you can accompany me on this jaunt? As I said its cold, so bring your sweater, for the thoughts I have will make it colder, frigid; don't forget it's always colder just before dawn. Sometimes I think maybe I try too hard to seem profound, that is not necessarily true, it's just kind of the way my thoughts come out, a poetic nature, a philosophers nature if you will; there is the first cold thought. A thought which questions the thinker who produced it, and tries to console the reader's observations. Why can't you think without degrading your ability to do it...? Oh, I see, push away the leaves, underneath the grass is dead, very interesting.

As I continue to think, on our walk, a cool breeze chills our bones, I could simply provide you with the cool facts as they blow by, but I choose not to pursue facts, cold empty facts, but ideas, full ideas, which will leave you sated. Fundamentally, the difference occurs in that, the facts have a propensity to please curiosity, a chilled curiosity that won't change, good ideas fulfill; good ideas will warm you. Fact, providing you with information that may soothe your frostbite, but leaving you empty handed, black dead skin, which sloughs away; what's the point? An idea, a good thought will send you on a journey, long, and many days from now, you can call on it and it will be there to please and satisfy. Let us walk, continue to walk together on this cool night, and when we see a chimney smoking we will go running towards it, observing what the firelight has revealed to us, and warm our hands.

For the cloudless sky which has produced these low temperatures, is filled with icy demons pocking with their sticks at me, walking by. Why was I going on this mission impossible for Mr. McNabb? To get out of trouble, of course? Why did I need to get out of trouble? Well, others define who I am, and they only know me as Benjamin the criminal, the man they can't trust. No education for Benjamin, no good job for Benjamin, no fine woman for Benjamin, are these not all the things in said life worth having?

Ah yes, now we are getting somewhere, the insecurities, insecurities run deep no doubt, far below the dead grass, deep into the soil. I'm a nobody, Mr. McNabb offers hope for me to be a somebody again, right? Pushing forward, ever so forward, I must get to a warm thought before my insecurities consume me…

Why will these insecurities not be taken from me? Perhaps it's so you will see how deep they run, how deep the lies run? Perhaps it will be so you will rely on something outside yourself? Defining yourself not by what the world says you are, maybe, it could be true? Let me put these dirty thoughts of mine in a sluicing pan and add some water. Continuing to pan, the dirt begins to separate, finally some gold dust is separating itself from the muck, and what I see is the glittering human heart is tender and fragile above all else; yes the heart is made with gentleness and delicacy, this nugget I must keep, for to forget how misshapen, how distorted, our ideas of truth can be, would be to neglect this most precious gift; the image God stained human heart.

Thanks for your time, sometimes it just helps to think these things out, I hope I can get some sleep now before the big trip...

12

Day one: Community of Trees: The bus ride was long. I found my accommodations shortly after my arrival, they are satisfactory, and are located just outside the forest. After unpacking, I attended a small gathering at a local community building, several songs were sang, and a rather unintelligible message was delivered by a man called Teacher Conner. The people seem generally friendly, but as I have yet to enter any intimate discourse with any from this alien species, my hypothesis goes untested.

Day two: Community of Trees: Today I attended to the normal chores of living. While I was at the store buying food, someone offered to help me carry my groceries back to my hotel. Knowing kindness is not bestowed without some ulterior motive, I declined. I also had a chance to walk about the forest today, it was a truly magnificent experience, I dare not return to the woods without my notebook so I may take copious notes regarding this experience and record the torrent of emotions I felt in that place. Finally, I will include, everyone carries around some special book here with which I am unfamiliar, though I seek to investigate further; time has not permitted such a thing. Lastly, to my dismay, there was no tree-vision in my room, what am I to do with my time; this is unthinkable? I seek to observe more closely the motivations of these creatures, as I become more familiar with their ways…

Day tree: Community of Trees: I have begun to establish a routine, also I have arranged my affairs around the societal conditions of which I am now a part. Generally, commerce is conducted in the same manner in this community as it is done anywhere else, it seems human necessity and universal likeness requires such a thing, however not everything bares this similitude. My primary observation, other than the aesthetic, which is the trees this community possesses, is how its members spend their free time. Ostensibly, I have recognized, relationships with other people are of paramount importance and to neglect them or to fail to participate in them, would appear to me, to reject the most fundament values of these people.

Day five: Community of Trees: As I was on my morning walk, I crossed the path of Teacher Conner, of whom I became acquainted with on my first day in the community of trees. He is a fair and amiable man, well spoken, and certainly erudite. A short conversation with this kind gentleman has yielded me to conclude he is an educated man, and that the things he says should not be dismissed as easily as they might be with others. Also, I went on the job hunt, as employment seems to be a necessary component of civilization, and to be absent of work would be to bring suspicion upon myself, and possibly lead to my mission here being compromised.

Day seven: Community of Trees: I have obtained employment at a local used book store. My days there pass very quietly, but I have discovered my mind has a loud voice for reason, and much of my free time has been consumed with the consumption of intellectual material. Most who come to visit this quaint knowledge shop, stop and ask me how I am doing. This is very strange to me and I have yet to become accustomed to, and comfortable with, others inquiring of my well-being.

Day ten: Community of Trees: Going through my journal, I have begun, and will soon finish, my initial report for Mr. McNabb and Mr. Snuffle's. In this report I have included the general description of my short encounters with the people here, and the character traits I have seen in those individuals I have entered surface level conversation with. Some of these traits might include: general respect and courtesy, kindness, and a willingness to make the other person more important than themselves. In my report I have restated my primary objective, or mission statement according to Mr. McNabb, which takes the form of a question: how do we subvert the minds of the leaders of this community and so access and control needed wood resources (to be used) for the greater good of the mill?

Day eleven: Community of Trees: I had the day off work today and decided to go to the forest. What a strange and beautiful world this is. How I went so many years without ever hearing leaves crunch under my feet, or feeling the shade trees provide on a hot summer day; I will never know? It seems, it seems, maybe the forest is an oasis in the desert for a troubled spirit, and I have this overwhelming sense that there is some kind of healing to be had here. Though I am not entirely sure where this healing quality emanates from?

Day fifteen: Community of Trees: Today at work while perusing through the storage area, attempting to find any ancient gems, poetic pros for my eyes, I stumbled upon an old record player, and collection of records. I inquired of the owner, and was informed by my boss that he did not know this relic existed in his store. I asked further if I may be permitted to borrow the said device, and it was given to me! I brought the record player and records back to my hotel room and listened to a beautiful opera into the wee hours… I had forgotten how much I love music, this rediscovery filled by heart with such beautiful joy I can hardly think of a word to share its meaning, yet my wonderful listening quickly reminded me I had yet to have my violin fixed. But I think I can declare with some sureness; life indeed, would be a mistake without music…!

Day twenty-one: Community of Trees: Books have become a most wonderful companion of mine in the absence of tree-vision. Though the pleasure endured by the whimsical notion of the written word, is much more difficult to attain than the 'glowing genie', there is certainly considerably more satisfaction to be had. I have discovered I have a very powerful imagination, and that I am able to create another world in my mind, with almost the same conviction as the real thing. Books, ideas, dreams, promises, hope; please do not stray too far from my mind ever again?

Day twenty-five: Community of Trees: Teacher Conner patronized the used book store today while I was on duty at the register. He is a voracious consume of knowledge, and I certainly have great respect for any man engaged in the intellectual pursuit. Before he left the shop with the many books he had purchased, he asked me to join him for a hot drink of my choice, and a sweet dessert of some sort. I joined him at a local delicatessen after my shift ended, and we engage in a most fabulous

174

conversation; there was an intimacy between us that I had never experienced before today. It is clear to me this man has a giant heart and love for people. I was not able to be completely honest with him about my purpose for being here, and this caused great anxiety in me. I hope this may be reconciled before too long…?

Day forty: Community of Trees: Sitting in the forest, I listened to the trees bend in the breeze; what a beautiful sound! While I sat, I went through the many ideas and thoughts I had gathered from my reading endeavors; which have come about as a result of my employment at the used book store. As I began accepting and rejecting some of these thoughts, I recognized a most wonderful thing. I was thinking! Up to this point in my life I had been molded and shaped by every idea that has come my way, this is a most terrible place to be. For most of the thinking that enters our minds is of very low worth, and things that are worth little, provide little, perhaps they even get in the way of something more? So as I was discerning which ideas I should hold onto, I noticed much of my thinking was constructed on a platform of self-abasement. Digging deeper, walking where I can no longer stand in the sea, I grasped a shiny silver slithering shark of an idea, this was, the proposition, or assertion all this self-degradation was flowing from, found its root in a few simple words, words I have been told and told myself many times 'you are not beautiful', please refrain from thinking of this as an aesthetic beauty, but beauty of the soul. Quickly, however, I let go of the shark's tale, lest I lose a limb.

Day forty-seven: Community of Trees: In approximately a fortnight I will be leaving on a short furlough to engage Mr. McNabb personally on my continued growth and understanding of this community. I must say, I have been slowly feeling a greater conviction that my purpose here is wrong. I hope there is some way I may reconcile this dichotomy within me? What is more difficult than to live in two different worlds, with two different value systems? Upon returning to the community of trees, for the remainder of my undercover operation, I plan to engage more strictly with the people here, and to be intentional about forming relationships. Teacher Conner seems to be quite open to my presence, I think I will seek his attention, so he may answer some of the question which have postulated themselves in me since my arrival. There is also a young woman here that goes by the name of Margaret, she appears to be most intelligent, and may be even able to challenge me on some level.

Day fifty: Community of Trees: I went to the forest today and took a book to read. I fell into that imaginative place in my mind where trolls live, and elves dance, that place where you hold the hand of your companion and no words are needed to express the joy arisen within the union of intertwined fingers. That far place, the other world which allows you to drop the weight of today for the lightness of tomorrow. The mist was low over the forest floor, the sun left peering through drapes of water. The warming air stirred the critters and insects, and suddenly this place was filled with the loud noise of small movements. Wonderful, extraordinary, beauty, here was bountiful beauty, if only beauty could be the theme of my life, I dare think, I would never grow weary, never seek any other nectar; and if you were to ask me, what is this sweetness above all sweetness's, I would say, it starts with a sunrise, is carried by the day, and falls gracefully beneath the horizon by night; beauty, fine beauty, never leave me again?

Day sixty: Community of Trees: Today I am returning from whence I came. My obligation to Mr. McNabb and Mr. Snuffle's should only be hanging over my head for another month or so, and at that time, if Mr. McNabb keeps his promise, I will be released from my obligation to the courts of high justice. I look forward to this day. I have also been thinking very deeply and thoroughly about Stephan's promise, 'take your violin to the community of trees, they will be able to fix your violin.' I am beginning to take this promise seriously and I will be retrieving my broken violin while I am on leave to see Mr. McNabb, and I will be returning with it, moving towards seeking its mending. I have observed, closely, this Margaret with the curly nut brown hair, in my eyes, has begun to glisten as the gem of this community, I will say, upon my return, she will be the only woman most truly worth my attention.

13

As the bus moved from the lands to the north, making its way into the region around the mill, the difference in scenery was stark. Hills once covered in fine furry greenery, were now pale yellow at best, air that was crisp and clean, now only held a grayish dirty haze. I had never really noticed the difference before, but I had never lived anywhere else, I saw the difference now. And I wondered how people, how I, was able to live in this dark land, when there was such a beautiful place not very far away, for so long? I guess, I guess you just kind of get used to it, and you don't notice the difference after a while, or perhaps there was nothing out my window ever worth noticing, so once I saw something different, it became quite noticeable my land was in need of some refurbishment? I don't know much about 'those things', but what I do know, is that can change!

If there ever was such a thing as a dead man walking, the condemnation trail was my walk, a drawbridge of death leading to castle McNabb. I was able to avoid the purpose of my travels for some time with the complexities of my inner discourse, my imagination of a world only vaguely real. But now I was back at the mill, faced with reality, for better or for worse a new definition of myself was being written, but to find new words to use, old words must be replaced. Confronting self-love, with the greatest lover of self; yet was I not like Mr. McNabb in more ways than I care to admit; I don't know; should I confront myself? Perhaps this is out of order, but if being in love with yourself could cause convulsions, Mr. McNabb would be an epileptic of immense proportions, unable to subdue his shaking by human means. But you already knew that, I just, I get so worked up being around this guy, I can't help but vent a little. Hopefully, in not very long a time, these meetings will come to an end, and I may be relived of this burden, my burden?

I didn't bother going home, I was hoping I wouldn't have to stay too long for this meeting, and I could return to my job at the book store as quickly as possible. So to kill some time, I went for a walk by the river. I love the water, and its soothing sound, water sloshing on the banks, helping to ease a troubled spirit, nature's music; natures healing, a river symphony. Reflection, looking inward, much had changed for me over the last year, much was changing. My dear friend Stephan always being near my heart, the river being a place he loved; how the two are inseparable and bring back swiftly for me, a picture of him telling me the story of John RowBăck on my second day working at the mill. This was a fine memory, a memory with a smile, one I adore, and hope I never loose. Time has come and gone, life moving like dunes in the perpetual wind, all I want is a valley to find, a valley to get me out of the breeze. I'm not sure where I belong, the mill doesn't seem to be the place for me anymore, the tree community is nice, but I'm not really like those people; am I? I come from a place, well you know the place I come from, but I must get past that, right?

It was about time to get over to Mr. McNabb's, and put my river walk behind me. I dare not leave him waiting and make myself any more susceptible than necessary to his ever unpredictable wrath. And as I'm sure you will agree, my thinking can be a bit morbid at times, surely burdensome for the reader. But I hope as you have gotten to know me, when I tell you of the beauty I will tell you; you will take what I say very seriously, for who knows beauty best but the man who has been confronted with the ugliness of himself?

After I had returned from my walk by the river, I went to that nasty knoll which held the residence of the man who had become my greatest enemy, the one outside myself, who was opposed to everything of good and fine worth in the world. I was ushered into the McNabb mansion, by the usual resentful servant, and found myself standing by the threshold of the dining room listening to Mr. McNabb whisper sweet nothings into Mr. Snuffle's ear.

"Mr. Snuffle's you cute fat mouse…" Mr. McNabb's baby talk left me feeling sick, watching him scratch his little furry friend and speak to him with such endearment, pathetic, it was so pathetic. "Mr. Snuffle's, you fat mouse, you cute fat mouse, I'm going to have to start buying you reduced fat cheese, what, what, was that…? Only rats eat reduced fat cheese, yes I know, I was only joking, I couldn't agree with you more, lighten up will you, what, what was that, oh the pun, you liked the pun, so did I…" Looking up, the terrible duo must have seen me standing in the archway waiting to be invited into the room. "Oh Benjamin, so glad you are here, please come in…" I made my way to my usual spot at one end of the long dining room table and sat in the heavy wooden chair. "So, how was your travels, not overly burdensome I hope?" "The bus ride was fine, we were running a little behind, but you know how that goes."

"I see, I see…" We sat in silence for a while, something was obviously on my host's mind, but he wasn't saying anything; this was not like him. Finally after Mr. Snuffle's went to sleep in Mr. McNabb's pocket, or rather fell into a cheese coma, the brave mill leader began to speak, "I have been considering releasing you early from our agreement… truthfully, I will be so inclined, I have the papers right here as a matter of fact, the ones you need with the judges pardon." My hand drifted over the polished wood towards these papers of freedom, the ones Mr. McNabb had pointed to. Leaning towards them, I could read my name on the top of the paper. Freedom, here was freedom, I could once again return to the life I was living, no longer bound to the authorities, I could seek a new future, a new life. The judge's signature was clearly visible at the bottom of the page in shiny blue ink; was this really happening? I couldn't believe it, all the sleepless nights would come to an end, I could be; I could be, whoever I wanted to be again, what a joyous thought, to be made new…

As my fingertips pressed the parchment to the table, so ready were they, these papers, to come gliding my way. "Ah, ah, ah, not so quickly Benjamin, although I am certainly a generous man, I do need you to complete one final task for me, that is, if I am to let you leave with these papers tonight; so what do you say, will you?" "Well, what is it you need me to do?" I asked openly, though there was not much I wouldn't do for these papers, the question demands to be asked anyways, ethically, that is. "Oh, I'm so glad you asked, I have been doing some thinking over the past couple months, really since I have been reading the reports you have been sending back to me about the tree community, and I think, as the old saying goes 'I'll kill more flies with honey, than with vinegar', this saying really applies to this situation, and so, I had a most brilliant idea, a way to offer some of my kindness to those people who hold onto their trees with vice like grips…" "Excuse me Mr. McNabb if you need a few extra trees to meet your quota, you could probably just ask them, and they would give them to you, they are pretty nice people…" Mr. McNabb's fist hit the table with such force, the lit candle at the table's center turned at once to a smoking wisp, a smoldering string no longer aglow. I immediately regretted offering such an opinion, such conjecture, to a man who could not conjure a word of truth in a sea of truthful words. "I WANT ALL THEIR TREES, EVERY LAST ONE, NOT JUST A COUPLE YOU BABBELING BUFOON… excuse me, what I meant was, I would like to kindly approach them about a percentage of their lands and as I was saying, as the other old saying goes, 'you can lead a horse to water, and you kill him if he doesn't drink' that is, these saying were said for a reason, and have stood the test of time because of the wisdom they hold, so this is where my offering of peace comes in, as I have been meditating on the meaning of these proverbs. I have recently acquired some of the latest technology available to humanity, and I would like to give this as a gift, a Trojan horse if you will, to the community of trees…" Wait wasn't the Trojan horse a bad thing? I couldn't remember from history class, wait, it was a good thing, right? Mr. McNabb stood from the table, walking several feet towards what I thought was a covered statue, he ripped the red velvet sash from over the head of a small steal looking man, about the size of a leprechaun, if you can imagine one of those. It was boxy in shape, with a square head, and square body that held a small tree-vision screen. As the velvet settled to the floor, several lights on the top of this things head blinked on, and a rigid mechanical, synthetic, high pitched voice filled the room. "Hello, my name is Mr. Biggin, you may call me Mr. Biggin…"

Wow, a robot, really, how cool! The only time I've ever seen one of them was in the movies, very sweet. As you probably have noticed my eagerness to investigate this modern marvel sent any questions I had about Mr. McNabb's motivations out the window. "What does he do?" I inquired of Mr. McNabb, unable to take my eyes from this technological phenomenon, and in a very sly conceited voice Mr. McNabb replied, "You can speak directly to him, he has voice recognition software, along with many other capabilities…" "Mr. Biggin, what can you do?" I asked quickly and excitedly. "Mr. Biggin has the potential to accomplish many tasks. Mr. Biggin was created to befriend and serve mankind. Among the skills in the forefront of my programming are: paper retrieval, abode protection, lost child recovery, and tender companionship." "Oh, so you are kind of like a dog?" I inquired, but this comment sent the lights on top of Mr. Biggin's head racing, turning from green, to yellow, to red. "Mr. Biggin is no dog, and Mr. Biggin resents such comparison. Mr. Biggin is a finely honed adjunct to humanities great genius." I didn't know robots could be offended, but apparently this very accurate comparison of mine, had sent his filaments aglow. "Oh, I see, I'm sorry I didn't mean to offend you… well if you would like to serve humanity, you could start by getting me a piece of key lime pie for desert, how about it?" "Mr. Biggin was created to befriend and serve. Mr. Biggin will surely provide for you." At this statement Mr. Biggin's lights flickered and he went rolling, propelling himself from the room, presumably towards the kitchen.

Looking towards Mr. McNabb, I couldn't help but let my child like excitement seep into my voice, "Man, that's really cool, what do you want me to do with him?" The boss smiled, clearly he knew I was hooked. "Yes, he is a very fine specimen, very fine indeed; the only thing I ask of you Benjamin, is you present Mr. Biggin to Teacher Conner at the community of trees upon your return. From your letters, he seems to have taken a liking to you, and you don't have to tell him this gift is from me, as true charity is never self-boasting, just tell him, tell him it was a going away present to you, in gratitude for the fine work you have done here at the mill, and that Mr. Biggin can be a benefit to the whole community, so you would hate to keep him all to yourself, I'll let you take the credit, and hopefully if this gift has the anticipated affect, the contention between the mill and the community of trees will be relieved forever..." Mr. McNabb declared his thinking covered in hubris, hairy hubris. But as I pondered his proposal and the honesty with which it was presented, Margaret's face appeared, I would look really good in front Margaret if I came back with a robot to give to the community. She couldn't help but notice me then?

In the meantime, Mr. Biggin had returned to the room holding a piece of key lime pie, standing quietly I looked to him, and what can I say, I was impressed, key lime pie, and getting Margaret to notice me, perfect! "Alright Mr. McNabb I'll do it." "Very good, very good, your rent at the hotel will be paid for the next month, I will also place thirty pieces of sawdust into your account, to cover any other expenses, and truthfully I don't care what happens to you, so, YOU AND MR. BIGGIN LEAVE, MY, SIGHT, NOW!"

As you have probably guessed I have become quite immune to Mr. McNabb's yelling, and I'm nort really sure what else to say about him, other than to have a man his age act the way he does, is very sad. And without question, this queue to leave was taken by Mr. Biggin and I, allowing us a little time to get to know one another before the bus took us back to the tree community.

14

Following me everywhere I went, my robot beeped and squeaked, running into everything there was to run into; his constant need for attention was causing me to reconsider being his temporary care taker. However, he was a hit with the ladies, so I had high hopes he could make an opening for me to talk to Margaret. I retrieved my broken violin from home, and put all Mr. Biggin's paperwork and accessories into a duffle bag for the trip. Making it to the bus stop, I helped my little friend up the stairs and found him a seat. I slept most of the drive, while Mr. Biggin had everyone entertained with his massive volume of pre-programmed story telling capabilities. Travel was uneventful, and I soon found myself returned to the place where I could start over.

We were the last stop on this long journey to sojourning, traveling to stopping just prior to the forest. As we exited the bus I noticed the terminal, if that's what you could call this shack on the edge of civilization, was quite crowded. "Come one, come all, spring dance at the community building tonight, come one come all…" Walking towards the voice, I grabbed one of the fliers he was handing out, and read it to Mr. Biggin. "Spring down tonight, ball room and swing dancing, following a short teaching by Teacher Conner; ah, wonderful providence, I will get to bask in your good fortune much sooner than I thought! "Do you dance

Mr. Biggin?" I asked, hoping he could teach me in time for the ball. "Mr. Biggin dances many dances." "Alright, well you're going to have to teach me quick, I got somebody I want to dance with tonight at the spring down, and I don't know what I'm doing…" "Mr. Biggin will help you. Mr. Biggin was created to befriend and serve mankind."

"Awesome, come on let's go practice…" I said, observing Mr. Biggin and I were forming a strong bond rather quickly. We returned to my hotel room just outside the forest, and I went straight to the record player and threw on some music. My music provided, for me, a special opportunity to commune with another world, but the thought of adding a few rhythmic steps and a pretty girl to this equation was a whole nether task, in the nether regions of my uncoordinated limbs and the nervousness with which they were consumed. You know, sometimes I wish I could write my ideas into reality, from the real place of my mind, into the real place of the present; for there, I would be a gallant man brimming with self-confidence, whirling my Margaret about the dance floor as if romance, for me, were only an afterthought. I would be the finest of gentleman, able to impress simply by existing, all arrogance aside of course. And this place would be written from my mind's eye, into my life's story, so I may sweep a dear woman away to hold her close for eternity: yet, there was some part of myself that I could not get passed, an introversion which leaves my love in a pen; so I remain the shy guy, the devoted man, whose higher calling is loyalty.

"First Mr. Biggin is going to teach you the waltz, now all you have to do is know how to count to four. Watch Mr. Biggin, one and two and three and four, one and two and three and four… ready?" Mr. Biggin was a very elegant dancer, the little wheels under his feet helped him glide over the floor with a special gracefulness I envied. "Ready as I'll ever be…" I replied, and so I started dancing. Mr. Biggin was quite a bit shorter than me so this made things a little difficult, but I was starting to get the hang of it. We went late into the afternoon with our practicing, and suddenly another problem occurred to me; if we weren't dancing what were we going to talk about; I sure didn't want to talk about myself? Because that would mean I would have to tell her about my job at the mill, and Stephan, and Mr. McNabb, and the courts of high justice, no, no, no, I don't want to do that. Yet, I did have Mr. Biggin, surely he was an ace up my sleeve if there ever was such a thing, and I have been reading a great deal, and I have found I have quite an aptitude for the fine art of thinking, maybe things wouldn't be so bad after all? All these thoughts, the tortured starry-eyed man; for where is a romantic heart to go, if he wants nothing more than to show a woman his devotion to her, that he would treat her as the finest of pearls and adore her for as long as he may live? Certainly the complexities of life are strictly opposed to a romantic heart, a heart sculpted the way mine is?

"Alright Mr. Biggin, we've got to get our plan straight for tonight if we're going to make this evening go off the way it's supposed to…" We stopped dancing, and that was a good thing for me, as I was getting a little dizzy. "Tell Mr. Biggin what is your objective? Mr. Biggin will use his massive computational powers to formulate a plan." Thinking to myself, I guess if this whole dancing thing goes well, I would hope I would get to see her again. "Well, I guess my objective is to get Margaret to like me… I don't want to come off too boring, but I also don't want it to seem like I'm trying too hard to impress her either… also I would like to stay away from talking about me, I don't want to talk about anything too personal, or about my past, that is, not until she gets to know me for who I really am… I want to leave her intrigued, but not bogged down with questions… You understand what I'm after right?" "Computing… computing… Here is Mr. Biggin's plan: Mr. Biggin will use his human emotional indicator to determine the emotional state of Margaret, this will be done through a combination of voice analysis and body language indicators. Mr. Biggin will cross reference the emotional state of Margaret at any given point in time with Mr. Biggin's massive storage of knowledge to formulate the perfect topics of conversation. Mr. Biggin will stand behind Margaret and flash these questions and appropriate answers on Mr. Biggin's tree-vision screen so only Benjamin can see…" I thought about Mr. Biggin's proposal, it did seem like a fine plan, very fine, no matter how anxious I got Mr. Biggin would be right there to keep me from making a fool of myself. "Oh, Mr. Biggin that is such a brilliant plan, I could kiss you…!"

After I got spruced up and Mr. Biggin's joints were lubricated, we headed towards the community campus where the teaching and dancing would be held. Going was slow with Mr. Biggin, I was always helping him over curbs and around pot holes, but eventually we made it to the outdoor stage where Teacher Conner was to speak. As I sat back, Mr. Biggin received all kinds of strange looks and I began to consider maybe I had overlooked how he would be received here tonight, but it was too late to go back now, my plan was in full motion. I began to skim the crowd to see if Margaret was there, but before I could find her I heard a voice come over the speakers and I saw Teacher Conner up on stage.

"Good evening all, thanks for setting aside your night for the annual spring storytelling and ball. This is a special day for us here in the community, I hope all of you have a wonderful time, so without further ado, as I know all of you are anxious to get to the dance, let me begin my story… Many, many years ago, long before cook books and recipes, there was a great baker, and this great baker was known for his creativity and the passion he had for creating things, he loved enjoying the treats he made, and he loved for others to enjoy them also. The baker had made many tasty and delectable treats that he was able to enjoy and share with his small village, but the baker wanted to share his love for the culinary arts with others, to share his love with people all over the world. One day the baker thought, and said to himself, it is difficult to share a cake or a pie with others because a single piece of this desert fails to travel well, so he asked himself; what shall I bake so my sweetness's will be able to sail the oceans? Pondering the way a creative mind does, he decide he was going to make cupcakes, it is said he made the first cupcakes that were ever made, and he did this so they could be spread around the world and be enjoyed everywhere… Now the baker loved chocolate more than anything in the world, so after he made the batter he put chocolate chips into each of the cupcakes, but he didn't put the same amount of chocolate into each cupcake. The baker thought, if I want to show the world what love I have for my cupcakes, some will have to have more chocolate chips than others, because if they all have the same amount of chocolate, I can't show anyone what a special cupcake looks like. Now the baker rested after he

190

had made the chocolate chip cupcakes. But after he had rested, he obtained many brown boxes so he could ship his cupcakes to other places all over world. He chose these destinations very carefully and labeled the boxes, but when the baker got to the post office he realized he had not saved any cupcakes for himself to enjoy. His hands were full with baking ingredients he had purchased at the store, so he didn't have room to carry a package back to his home, so quickly, the baker scratched out one of the addresses on the box and wrote down his own home address in its place, and he said to himself, 'Surely my cupcake will be enjoyed mightily after a few days separation, and my cupcake shall return to me at the appointed mail delivery time'. The baker went home. Several days passed, and the baker grew happily anxious, giddy, for he knew his special deserts would be reaching their destinations soon. The baker waited eagerly for his own cupcake to be delivered so it could be enjoyed, but it never came, and the baker lamented. The baker was full of great sorrow and his spirit was vexed over the lost cupcake, yet, as love never concedes easily, true love always being self-sacrificing, the baker searched and found the tracking number on his shipping receipt. The baker trudged the long road to the post office and inquired of his beloved cupcake, and was told 'your package is a long way off, it seems a truck has broken down and no one has gone to rescue it'. The baker informed the postal worker, 'I will be the one who redeems my package.' And so he set off and found the truck on the side of the road. He helped the driver change the tire, and said 'I'm here to claim that which is mine' and he claimed his package. Now it was very hot out and the truck had been sitting in the hot sun for many hours, so when the baker opened his package he saw his cupcake had become deformed and the chocolate had melted, the baker was agonized that his creation looked nothing like what it was created to look like, but he didn't want to throw the ugly cupcake away because he had put so much love into making it. So the baker, when he got home, went into the kitchen. The baker thought long and hard, looking many times at the ugly cupcake, until finally he had an idea, a most brilliant idea; I will bake something new with the melted cupcake I have, and make something beautiful. The baker labored and toiled, until, sometime later, he had made a beautiful soufflé from the ugly cupcake, and his new creation looked more beautiful and tasted better than any cupcake he had ever baked..." Teacher Conner ended his story, and looked at all of us in that funny way he does, tilting his head and scrunching one eye. This is a special look he gives when he wants us to consider something more deeply than we might normally be obliged.

Surely his look worked, I began to think; what an odd story I thought; what does it mean? A peculiar idea accompanied this question, as questions which yield other questions often are, and the thought was most frustratingly abnormal. Didn't Mr. McNabb talk about being a chocolate chip cupcake with Mr. Zooty on that fine day when Stephan and I crept into his office and turned on the PA system? He was rather upset as I recall, insisting he had no chocolate chips in him, and that he was a uniquely flavored cupcake, strange, very strange; what did it all mean?

Since I am unable to answer such questions for you, ruminate on them, there is surely a pearl to be had from their contemplation.

"Thank you again everyone for coming tonight, I hope my story has given you something to think about, now enjoy the ball."

Teacher Conner ended and the people began to disperse heading towards the community building where the dancing was to commence shortly.

We left the outdoor stage and after a short walk, we arrived at the community building, and Mr. Biggin and I went inside. The place was decorated like a starry night. Small lights eclipsed all the shadowy nooks of the room, and only a faint glow from the waning sun came through the silvery sashed windows; it was like we were our own participants in the battle for the night sky. A romantic scene, filled with love, and families and children, very simply, here was a celebration of life, the very finest of life; how fortunate I am that I may experience life as it should be?

Of course, having Mr. Biggin with me as I walked into this place disrupted things a little, but after I introduced him, and people saw the charm my little silver box possessed, their affections for him were made quite clear. First I made a few anxious trips to the refreshment stand, scanning the gathering, Margaret was nowhere to be seen. But you wouldn't guess what Mr. Biggin and I came across as we meandered for a purpose; it was a musician, surely a lovely woman, for she was playing the violin. Mm… the sound, the sound, here beauty floated my way, and I longed to have my companion returned unto me.

The song ended, I returned to reality, and I began perusing the room once again for my hearts prize, the real reason I had come to the dance. And there she was out on the dance floor, already dancing. "Mr. Biggin, I see Margaret, she's out there dancing already; we have to get there quick before someone else asks her to dance." "Mr. Biggin is prepared for the task." I looked to Mr. Biggin and his confidence, the confidence that this would go well, encouraged me greatly, so I reminded him of what we had talked about earlier. "All right, you remember the plan, right? You're going to use your emotional indicator to engineer the perfect conversation, you're going to give me the perfect questions to ask. Right now I'm going to go ask her to dance, don't let us dance too long... come interrupt us, think of something, whatever you want, and I'll find a good place for us to sit down and talk..."

I broke away from Mr. Biggin towards the dance floor and my chest became a little light, and my stomach a little tight, I wiped my palms on my pants, and thought of the dance lessons from Mr. Biggin. One and two and three and four, I repeated again and again in my mind; this shouldn't be that hard. "Excuse me Margaret, I don't know if we've ever officially met, but my name is Benjamin, and I was wondering, well, I was wondering if you would like to dance with me...?"

Oh, how time stood still, how life went falling far from me at that moment, everything; everything all lost and juggling in space. There will be few moments I hold onto for life, few worth holding, I have to choose. And this one, like my favorite songs for the violin, I will learn to play by rote. For special memories are here so they may be recalled in those, needy, troubling times, to cheer my heart... "Yes Benjamin, I would love to dance, thanks for asking me." Yes, good cheer!

Wow, how do explain a moment like that, I'm not sure I can, and I may be foolish to try, so all I will say is, her 'yes' and the smile that came with it, was like a cool drink to a parched man... "I'm not really sure what I'm doing, but I'll try..." "Well your effort is certainly admirable." Margaret replied as I grabbed one of her hands. I put my other hand on her hip in the spot Mr. Biggin had shown me, and we began to move. As we danced Margaret reached over with her hand and adjusted mine from the low place on her hip, lifting it up her back. Stupid, stupid, you already made your first mistake, she probably thinks you were trying to touch a place you're not supposed to, I'm going to kill Mr. Biggin!

And so we danced, my feet stumbling over themselves the whole way, my mind in another world, lost in the scent of a woman, a very fine woman indeed; I fell head long into emotions quick sand. And so my senses were torn unable to decide the hierarchal importance of incoming experience, so everything I had been taught fell into some dark recess of my mind, unable to be extracted for use. Just when I was about ready to quit dancing do to shame and embarrassment, Mr. Biggin interrupted us. "Mr. Biggin has obtained refreshments for Master Benjamin and for Margaret…"

"Wow, you didn't tell me you had a robot, he's so cute…" Margaret exclaimed, I smiled, thank you Mr. Biggin you're a life saver, I thought. And for the first time I started experiencing some satisfaction that my plan was beginning to work-out the way it was supposed to. Mr. Biggin rolled away, leading us towards the table where he had placed the refreshments for Margaret and I. We sat together, and this seemed to me to be a good spot; it was not too loud for conversation, but it was also not so quiet and secluded we would be forced to endure uncomfortable silence.

Mr. Biggin parked himself in just the right spot where I could read his tree-vision screen over Margaret's shoulder without having to break eye contact with her for too long; here goes nothing, Mr. Biggin's first question, "Why is the ocean salty?" I asked, reading the words proposed by Mr. Biggin tree-vision screen. "Well, I believe salt in the ocean comes from rocks on land. Dissolved carbon dioxide in rain water makes this mixture slightly acidic and as this liquid comes into contact with rocks, minerals erode. This conglomeration is then carried by gravity through rivers and streams to the oceans where they concentrate, as these are the lowest major connected bodies of water in the world." Wow, Margaret, what a good answer I thought, she was surely living up to my previous observations of her intelligence. Next question from Mr. Biggin parroted by me, "Why is the sky blue?" Man these are kind of strange questions I hope Mr. Biggin knows what he's doing? However, Margaret was undaunted by inquiry, "If I remember correctly it's because molecules in the air scatter blue light more effectively and efficiently than any other color in the visible spectrum; why do you ask?" Why did I ask that? This is starting to go all wrong. I looked to Mr. Biggin with pleading eyes, hoping he could salvage the situation, and I noticed a new question on the screen, but I also noticed a few wisps of white smoke escaping from the top of his robot head. "I don't know… what's above heaven?" I said inquiring, before realizing, I could no longer trust Mr. Biggin to deliver on his promise to provide the perfect questions. Margaret looked at me cross-eyed and I looked back to Mr. Biggin and saw the amount of smoke coming from his head had grown. "Will you excuse me for a minute Margaret, I have to go take care of something real quick." "Sure." She replied as I moved quickly from my seat, trying not to arouse any suspicion that there might be something wrong. I made it to Mr. Biggin's side and pulled him into a corner.

"Mr. Biggin what the heck is going on? Did you know you're starting to smoke? You're going to ruin everything with your stupid questions, what happened to the plan…?" I interrogated, looking at Mr. Biggin with the most scornful accusatory look I could muster. "It seems the complex nature of a woman's emotions are causing Mr. Biggin's circuitry to overheat, Mr. Biggin's emotional indicator has surpassed its cap…a…city…" Groan… Mr. Biggin's systems shut off and his lights stopped blinking, and a panic set in over me. Sure I could restart him after his circuits cooled down, but what was I going to do until then? First I have to get him out of the way. Rolling Mr. Biggin to the side of the room, I found a spot where he wouldn't bother anyone. Then I stood and thought; what am I going to do, I didn't have a backup plan? Struggling with the question, I thought and thought hard, but my mind was out of whack and not producing any useful suggestions. Finally I considered, resorting to that solid cement, the foundation of intuition; I guess, well, I guess I could just be, I guess I could just be me…

"Is everything alright?" Margaret asked as I returned to my seat. "Yeah, everything should be fine, Mr. Biggin was just getting a little hot with all these people around, so I put him in the corner to cool down." "I see, well thanks again for asking me to dance that was fun… you know I saw you over there listening to my friend play the violin and was hoping you would see me out on the dance floor." What, no way, she was hoping I would ask her to dance; that means, that means, she was thinking about me when I was thinking about her. Something special was mine to enjoy. But the sad thing about the way my mind works, is that, that powerful imagination of mine, has me, as I start observing the beginning of something special, also imagining its end; whimsical time, for my sake will you not let this evening end to quickly?

"Yeah, I love the violin, I used to play all the time, but some moths back, someone broke my instrument and I couldn't get it fixed anywhere because Mr. McNabb had requisitioned all the wood for the upcoming festival" Be yourself, just be yourself, I kept repeating, you want her to like you for who you are. "Oh no, that's terrible… I heard you came from the mill, but I didn't know for sure, we get people coming here, from there, every once in a while. When I hadn't seen you before I kind of guessed that's where you were from, and that what I heard was probably true." Oh no, what did she hear, I asked myself as I continued to listen to her speak. "You know, we don't celebrate the sawdust festival here, so we have lost of wood to fix things, we could get your violin fixed… I'm pretty good with wood working, I took a couple classes… so if you're interested, I could repair it for you?" I wasn't expecting this turn of events, I had just started talking about my violin only because I love music so much, not because I was expecting to play again anytime soon. And what she was asking, what she was really asking, was for me to trust her with my instrument, I don't know if I should do that, I've never trusted anyone with it before? My reluctance must have been quite apparent, for she began speaking again, "Well just think about it Benjamin, let me know another time… you know, it's a really nice night out, if Mr. Biggin needs to cool down we could take him outside and finish our conversation there?" Oh, thank you Margaret, I was hoping this conversation would turn away from my music to something else, plus I had some questions for her. "Ok, that sounds good to me." I replied happily, for I was getting a little hot under the collar myself.

I found Mr. Biggin in the corner where I had left him and rebooted him; Mr. Biggin awoke, full of sorrow and remorse, "Mr. Biggin is so sorry, Mr. Biggin has ruined Master Benjamin's evening with the beloved Margaret." "It's ok Mr. Biggin things haven't gone that bad, but we'll have to reassess our approach to dating, I didn't realize woman were so complicated that they could even cause a state of the art machine like you to overheat; who would've thought?"

Mr. Biggin and I made our way outside and found Margaret sitting patiently beneath a large oak tree. And there, in the setting sun, the light breeze of spring, her curly nut brown hair tossed about by a heavenly wind; how it left her features melting into the bark, and I thought, I think for sure, I saw an angel. "So Benjamin, do you have any questions for me, I mean your questions, not Mr. Biggin's questions?"

What! She knew Mr. Biggin was feeding me questions. How did she know? I thought I'd done such meticulous planning that there was no way she could have found out. But with what dignity, with what honor, and respect, she inquired of my short coming; so how I could do nothing but concede to her ever present charm...

"Ah... yeah, I do actually, I was wondering; so do you guys worship the trees here or something?" Inquiring hesitantly, and at my question Margaret became a popcorn popping pot of laughter. For a few moments she couldn't control herself, and I wondered what had struck her as so humorous about my inquiry. But finally, placing her hand on mine, she covered her mouth with the other, subdued her giddy nature, dignified herself, and spoke, "We don't worship the trees silly, why ever would you think such a thing, I mean who worships a piece of wood? That's so silly…" Margaret arose from where we were sitting and walked several steps to the large oak tree and pantomimed a marriage proposal, bowing on one knee and opening a pretend case with a ring, it was very comical. Then, she started dancing around the tree trunk singing, "Ode to a tree, ode to a tree; I just want you to know, you're the only tree for me… Ode to a tree, ode to a tree, you're the only tree for me…" Even now I smile quite often at that memory, and think, if I were stranded on a desert island and locked away from humanity; that memory would be one kept close, keeping me company, providing me with encouragement, for as long as I was there. Margaret stopped dancing and returned to where I was sitting, "That was funny; you're a funny guy… I still don't know why you would think we worship trees that's the silliest thing I've ever heard; we just keep the trees around because they are beautiful… speaking of beauty, Teacher Conner is going to do a teaching on beauty, you should come check it out…" Hum, a teaching on beauty, I've never heard of such a thing, however, it did seem to be a topic of admirable repute, so I answered, "Yeah, that sounds good, I think I would like that, when is it?" "It's next Wednesday evening… but you know, it's getting kind of late Benjamin, I should probably get going…" "Ah…" I looked about, I had failed to notice we were some of the last people at the dance. For Margaret had sent my clock spinning to a stop, here, time had become a luxury only enjoyed by the richly stoic heart; my heart, now, was a fluttering fancy of destitution, the poor man whose found his wealth in a woman; for are not the richest men truly poor and never bound by time? I forgot what I was going to say, then, suddenly, I saw Mr. Biggin standing behind her. He must have come to redeem himself, and boy was I fortunate because I needed him badly, quickly, I read what he had displayed on his screen, "I really enjoyed our time together and getting to know you, when do you think I can see you again…?" Thank you Mr. Biggin, you're a life saver, you've definitely made up for your earlier stupidity, I said to myself. "Well, how about you bring your violin over sometime, that way I can get to mending it…" "Ok, yeah, I'll bring it with me to the discussion on beauty…" "Ok, It was nice getting to know you Benjamin Silversin, I'll see you soon…"

Wow, what and evening, she, Margaret, was without question the star of the community ball and the gem in the crown of this community. And she was quickly becoming the glitter of my eye. Walking, Mr. Biggin and I went rolling away, heading to our abode, and I saw Margaret dancing and twirling the whole way, pirouetting before my imagination; she had sent my heart stumbling; grasping for balance. With what whirling dizziness of the heart I had watched her, her skirt lifting above her knees as she spun, spinning a story in my mind I could tell myself many seasons later, with gladness. And as I walked home that evening, I was unable to do anything but think of how special this woman was, how undeniably true it was, the potter had taken special time and care, to craft her. And since that evening, there has yet to be a thought of another woman, for me…

15

The trees in the forest steadily swayed, as if a father, with care, had brought his gentle hand to caress his newborn daughter, following his guided gesture, my eyes watched the bouncy trees playful resistance, and the sound with which they teased. And so it is, the way life goes, the way life happens, when a special song comes alive. The place, in that far place, where you have seldom been, where your mind seldom allows you to go. That strange foreign land where everything falls away, and clarity begins; ice beneath a dusting of snow, let's brush away the dust and hear the birds begin to sing, let's brush away the snow and feel the warmth of the rising sun, the twigs under our feet, the scampering of critters, large and small, the fire flight to springs stardom; the warm embrace of a dear friend parted to another world, harken the call of an angels cry, and here we might, we just might, begin to glimpse what beauty is; though just barely, our finite minds, though striving, will grasp what it is we may hold; fine beauty teach me something of yourself; will you? And so it is, the way life goes, the way life happens, the way life mesmerizes, as it is returned to the way it is meant to be?

And as I sat in the forest, waiting for Teacher Conner to begin his lesson, these thoughts, my tender mind cultivating contemplation, tender new-awareness in the new forest, the woods wonder; teaching me many things with which I was utterly unfamiliar. Mr. Biggin and I sat quietly, my broken violin nearby, sitting, waiting for the teaching to begin, entranced by this other world, heaven's forest. The crowd trickled into the shade on this fine day, and I will recall it for you, my pleasant pleasure to do so, as it rests in my memory today.

Looking about, Teacher Conner brought himself to the front of the group and began to speak, "I asked all of you to come to the forest today for my teaching, because we will be talking about beauty, and the main thing, the primary thing that separates our community from other communities, is where we see beauty. And the trees, I'm hoping, will remind us that we see beauty somewhere else, we keep our trees and our forest because it's a beautiful thing to keep. Some of you have grown up, spending your whole life with a forest to attend to, not all are so fortunate. You who grew up in the forest will be able to understand what it is I am saying to you today, but it will be those who have grown up somewhere else, in a different household, those who have moved from one family to another, who will really be able to understand and appreciate the beauty of which I speak, for what it is. What is beauty? Is it something we see, is it something we hear, or maybe, is it something we feel? Can an act be beautiful; is love an expression of beauty, or is beauty an expression of love? Do we delight in beauty, or does beauty cause us to delight in it? Before we begin to examine these questions, let's all take just a few moments, let's sit in silence, you may look around the forest, or you may close your eyes and imagine the forest, whatever it is you choose to do, think of a beautiful forest, what do you notice, what is it you see?"

As I closed my eyes I let the aroma of the land around me fill my lungs, breathing deep, I sent my mind to a place where I imagined perfect beauty. And where I found myself, I was at rest, trees were everywhere, and everywhere were trees. This place, the place in my mind, was a place where I hadn't hurt anyone, and no one had hurt me. In my forest, I could never be rejected, or thrown away, or set aside, or picked last, or forgotten about, love would always be there, forever and again. I could trust my forest, and the days would always be sunny, with a few puffy white clouds on the horizon to remind me of my good fortune for having stayed out of the rain. For a price had been paid for my forest which could never be sold. In my forest, my stubbornness would be removed, my obsessive thinking would be brought to rest; I would not always see myself for who I want to be, but begin liking myself for who I am; I wouldn't keep getting older and have nothing to show for it, every-day, all-day, I would be consumed with thoughts of only beautiful things, virtuous thoughts, fine thinking, and I could share those thoughts with those dearest to me, for eternity…

"Thank you, you may open your eyes now. If you keep that image in your mind as we speak today, I think it will greatly add to your understanding of our conversation. Sometimes, it is helpful for myself, if I discuss what something is not, to understand what something is; also to speak of beauty's inseparable co-equal, the salt that goes with the pepper if you will, we must at least acknowledge love, for we cannot have beauty without having love present on some level, to distinguish the two, would be to utterly neglect a proper discussion of what beauty is. With that being said, beauty is not easily achieved, beauty does not come about without sacrifice, beauty is not chaos, or carelessness, it is not veiled truth, or envy, or hate, beauty does not boast; beauty is not a means to an end, beauty is always a means to a beginning. Beauty doesn't cause us to slow down, real beauty, causes us to stop…"

Margaret walked into our group late and sat down on the other side of the small circle we had formed, I stopped; waved a little wave, and she seemed to be a little embarrassed I had caught her looking at me, how sweet. I had thought long and hard about whether I should, or could, trust her with my violin. But what choice did I have, it was broken, and if it was to ever be played again, eventually, I would have to give it to someone to mend, and she appeared to be as fine a person as any to do so? So I think, today, I will give her my violin, and maybe, I will be playing beautiful melodies again before too long? Is this a beautiful thing?

"Perhaps, beauty, is really just a means through which other virtues are bestowed, the canyon that channels the water, the high rock walls which allow for a flooding of undeserved favor. The person who loves beauty, well, what is it he actually loves? Maybe if I rephrase my question and replace the word beauty with the word good, or noble, or pure, this would lead to a better understanding of what it is I ask. The person who loves the good, what is it he loves? As I have thought about these questions, let me begin to propose some suggestions. Good things are kind, the love of wisdom is good, a child's innocence and trust are no doubt also good things, commitment that endures the hardships of life, gentleness; soft pleasant edifying words; are these not all good things? Are they not also beautiful?"

Here, my mind was sent spinning, tilting over, I was the spinning top who has lost his momentum, and accordingly my mind began to wobble. Such thoughts as those which have been suggested were beyond my minds ability to comprehend, to control. All I can say, is that this small question, what is beauty; lit a large fire, burning everything of corruption and disgrace, everything of dishonor and ill repute, a cleansing fire began to burn. Flames reaching high, so the overgrown field was burned, leaving the nutrient rich ashes; ashes left to grow something new, something emerging tenderly and beautifully new.

"Most of you, I am sure, have herd the saying, 'beauty is only skin deep', the truth is; I couldn't disagree more. Real beauty, is deep, goes deep, and touches the soul, beauty is in the heart of hearts, touched by the one most beautiful tree farmer. Beauty is a mortal being which can conceive of immortality, beauty is an imperfect creature which can think of perfection; beauty is to hold a wilted flower and close your eyes and imagine what it looked like at first bloom. Beauty is a life well lived, and a life waiting to be experienced. Beauty is to hold an acorn and imagine the oak tree it can one day become, what it can grow into ... So is there beauty in anticipation? The anticipation of your wedding day and the first night spent with your husband or wife, the anticipation of a family and the birth of your first child, the anticipation of their wedding and family, then is there not also, some anticipation in death? Of course only for the soul that is rightly prepared, but the anticipation of an eternal rest, is there beauty... and there's something of fine poetry for you to reflect on..."

Teacher Conner paused, and looked at us the way I told you he does, tilting is head and scrunching his one eye, trying to get us to think. I personally wasn't sure what to think of all he was saying, I hadn't ever been confronted with these types of thoughts before, strange thoughts, but mesmerizingly beautiful thoughts, assuredly they were.

"As all of you who know me can attest, I am utterly devoted to books and ideas, with so much authorship, with so many ideas covered in pretense, what is it I see when I see something beautiful in the written word? A moment of beauty, as I explore the thoughts of another, a moment of beauty when you see the author, the poet who has born his soul, and left himself vulnerable for all to see, this is one of the many places I see beauty… so as we teach one another what beauty is, by showing one another what love is, we will be partakers in the creation of beauty, and the pursuit of beauty for us, should be like a beautiful song that never ends. Growing in grace and knowledge, beauty will float naturally our way, partakers, creators, sharers, and lovers, of the one absolute beauty, we will fill an ocean with love and watch as the clouds spread its beauty around the world in small drops, should I say more. Let all things work for the beatification of those who love, those who have been called according to a fine purpose. Take heed, as the beauty of the eyes is transformed to the beauty of the soul, the only everlasting beauty for us to know…"

One more scrunch of the eye and tilt of the head, and Teacher Conner was done with his lesson, speaking one final time. "Thanks everyone for coming today, I hope I gave you some things to think about, we are having a picnic in the forest today, so we can experience a little more of beauty together. Food and refreshments have been provided, so you may stay as long as you'd like, you are dismissed…"

The crowd began to stand and stretch their legs, I stretched mine, stealing some quick glances towards Margaret. Boy would I like to steal something else, maybe, a kiss? But not now, Mr. Biggin and I have business to attend to. For it was time to give him away, as I had chosen this opportunity to fulfill my promise to the McNabb consortium, a promise which would set me free from the entanglements of my past, the web of choices I had woven so stickily swell around my life.

"Excuse me, Teacher Conner, could I talk to you for a minute?" I asked as I had made my way to Teacher Conner's side as he was putting away his notes from the teaching. "Oh hey Benjamin, sure we can talk, I'm free now, unless it's something that needs to be discussed in private?" "No it's not private, it's actually about Mr. Biggin." I looked to my robot friend after I said this, to observe how he took the news. I hadn't told him about my plans, the real purpose for me bringing him to the lesson in the woods today. "Well you know, I was given Mr. Biggin here," I stated gesturing with open hands towards my mechanical man-pal, "for being such a good employee at the mill, I was one of the top producers of sawdust month in and month out; so when I decided to resign my position, Mr. McNabb, the owner of the mill, gave me Mr. Biggin as a token of his appreciation. You know, he can do so many wonderful things... ball retrieval, stick removal, intruder notification, and best friend partnership... and well, right now, I live in a hotel just outside the tree community, that is, until I find a permanent home, and it's kind of crowded in that small room with the two of us, and Mr. Biggin can do so many wonderful things, I hate to keep him all to myself, I think he could really be a benefit to the whole community, so, so I guess what I'm saying is, I would like you to have him, please accept him as a gift from me…" As I finished speaking, reciting the conversation I had with Mr. McNabb almost verbatim, I looked from Teacher Conner to Mr. Biggin, and my heart ached for him, for us.

"Why is Master Benjamin giving Mr. Biggin away? Is Mr. Biggin not beautiful enough?" Mr. Biggin groaned a lamentable sigh… watching, listening to my silver friend, his voice sounded so sad, quivering a sad quiver; alas, he had illuminated crying eyes on his tree-vision screen; could Mr. Biggin have made this any harder than it already was? And so forever had come, for forever I couldn't help but feel the pain in our coming separation. I wanted so much to keep him around, to build and strengthen the comradeship that came from moving together from the mill, to the tree community, a battle hardened bond. For we were brothers in arms, having fought the greatest evil around, to say my heart would part with his memory any time soon, would be to say something foolish, indeed. Yet, I had made an oath, though is an oath to a dishonorable man any oath at all? Surely it is, for my oath is to myself, and upon vanquishing Mr. Biggin from my life, so will go the rest of any remnants linking me to a former life; or so I thought? Tearing desires, rending allegiances.

"Oh, wow, that's really very kind of you Benjamin, but I don't know if I can accept a gift like this, I mean, robots are really expensive…" "Please accept him, he deserves a good home more than anything," I looked from Teacher Conner to Mr. Biggin, "and Mr. Biggin you are beautiful, and you've been such a great help breaking the ice with the new people I'm meeting here in the community, especially Margaret, I don't know if I could ever thank you enough." I stopped speaking and went down on one knee and wrapped my arms around this short stout automaton and squeezed with all my might. "Mr. Biggin will miss Master Benjamin, Master Benjamin has always treated Mr. Biggin well…" Resigned to his fate, Mr. Biggin replaced the sad face on his tree-vision screen with a stoic image of a battery fully charged. "It's not like I won't ever see you Mr. Biggin, we are still going to live by each other; I just won't be around every day to oil your moving parts, that's all."

"Well it sounds like it's settled then, I guess I'll be taking Mr. Biggin home," Teacher Conner said as Mr. Biggin rolled from my warm embrace to his side. "Thanks a lot Benjamin, this is really a great gift…" "Yeah, I hope he will be as big of a help to you as he was to me, so all I've got to do now is get you all his accessories and his operator's manual." Walking behind a large pine tree I grabbed the bag with all Mr. Biggin's things, and walked back to Teacher Conner and gave him the sack, it was now official, Mr. Biggin had moved to the promised place.

"You know Benjamin, I have been meaning to talk to you, maybe I'll come by the book store in the next week or two; I would sure enjoy some good conversation about reading." Teacher Conner patted me on the shoulder and handed Mr. Biggin his bag. I was broken up for a minute or two about losing Mr. Biggin, but that couldn't last long. For I had a broken violin nearby, and a luthier even nearer, surely my string singer was anxious to be repaired? And doesn't heartache always seem to dissipate, with cloudy thoughts at the parting of a friend, transient beating butterfly wings, the way a waterfall's crashing dissipates through thick foliage, a galloping butterfly lofting trough the fleeting cataract mist…?

Waving a small wave, I glanced over my shoulder as I left my former robot companion in capable hands. Margaret was near the edge of the forest, I could just barely see her ducking behind trees and jumping forth to scare her cubs. She had rounded up several rug rats after the teaching on beauty and they were playing a game of some sort. Making my way nearer, I couldn't help but stand and watch on as she allowed the child to come out in her, and a picture of the future mother she was sure to be, left her glowing for all to see. So I stood broken violin in hand listening to her tease her small companions. One of the little girls pointed to me as I walked up, "oh no there's an alligator here to get us, he's a mean alligator and likes to eat lion cubs…" I'm not a mean alligator, I thought. And stepping forward to show I came with no ill intentions, I put my hand out to show I was really a very gentle gator; and the little girls, not convinced, all in unison, screamed a most powerful scream, "Ah… no… Margaret… Mother Lion protect us from the mean alligator… he's here to eat us…!"

A little embarrassed and jealous, I didn't have the special touch with children clearly possessed by Margaret, I wasn't sure what to do next; but suddenly, "Run girls I'll protect you…" Were the words I heard Margaret yell and she wrapped me up, like an angel might with her white feathery wings…? And as she held me in her warm embrace, my mind was sent spinning, twisting with whirling dizziness of the heart. And as she held me, looking deep into my eyes, she pulled me mockingly away from her cubs, until, as you are likely to find one of these in the forest, good fortunes trip wire, my foot stumbled over a root and we both fell to the ground. Looking, gazing back, we lay on the ground together for

211

moments which seemed like times teasing gift to romance, a gift given in spite, as times jealous personhood sought to bring a cruel joke to lovers, for the moment passed in the blink of an eye, as if time were not there at all. How lamentable time should think so highly of herself, that the best I can do for us now is hold those fleeting things, those wispy evanescing paintings, with words: memories, sweet memories return to me with something stronger than a thought or a feeling, or a word, come back to me and transform yourselves so I may relive these events, something real again; please?

In that instance, I thought, I was glad she was going to have my violin, and as she looked back at me, without words, she said she was glad to receive it. Margaret giggling a small giggle, threw a couple twigs my way, and then, without a thought, or anticipation, that poor planning that always ruins spontaneous moments, leaves crunching between us, I leaned into her and took something of which time has no say. As I gave her a small kiss, though just barely, our lips touched, and a moment was sealed in history, one of the fine memories for all heavens angels to enjoy, one that time could not take away, my revenge taken clearly, my battle won against time, that day…

And there is a picture of beauty, if I have ever painted one…

16

Sitting, clock ticking, an imaginative world of slimy snails and rebellious robots, a real place in my mind, solitary realness, an idea in the lonely fruit past bitter life's rind. Books and books, ideas galore, come one come all, an idea to find, a pleasant idea held open handed from meticulous mine, giving freely for your avaricious kind. Ideas are good, and if you would, you could, you should, you would take one of these soft ideas, plant it, water it; care for it, until it grows into a tree of a fine hard wood. Look forward to my thinking, that sounds a little high seated, seating high thoughts in the most crowded desolate place on earth. A journey to an exotic mountain retreat, beautiful and solitary, exciting and lonely, however, here is the elaborate life of the man who loves wisdom; powerful sagacity you are but a barren oasis? I wish for others to join me, but no one will come, for the love of wisdom can have, does have, the power to change and adore something new and precious, that which is worthy of adoration, by itself... though my thinking *is* certainly interesting, it is often sad and lonely, simply a suggestion from me; will the day come where I may be suggested to let go, to be simply set free? And if you have made it this far in my story, then you, perhaps, have a similar bent, or possibly you are just filled with a morbid curiosity; whichever it is, I owe you, to tell you something more of my mind, and what has happened to it, recently, with access to books, to ideas of a flawless variety; such was life at the used bookstore; a finer life most arduous to live and arduous to find?

I have a few moments while I'm waiting for Teacher Conner, he is on his way to the bookstore to meet with me, and we will have that special bonding time he has had planned for us for a while now, so let me begin while there is yet space between events to speak with you uninterruptedly.

Imagine a parking structure, the tiers of cement and iron rising steadily into the air, a giant casing to hold our traveling companions. Now imagine yourself in a land where cars move through the air with effortless efficiency, a land of flying automobiles. Here you are, you have made it, very good. Cars move to and fro through cultivated ramps inside ascending and descending levels within the parking structure, parking where they will, freely finding a cozy spot to rest and idle. The movement within is equally matched by the moving without, cars enter and exit the structure and streets from every level, paying their toll, for our locomotors traverse the sky willfully. So you may come and go from any level of the parking structure, for our cars are flying cars, yet, we are in a growing city so more space is always needed to park. This means, the top level, the final level is never final. It is always under construction, cranes raising beams, cement being poured, an ever increasing complexity to our already complex parking garage, being added. Remember, think, what happens on one level always affects what happens on another level, a thought here, a desire there, an experience yonder…?

Being, living in the conscience, not that ethical place of right and wrong, not that moral place of good and evil, but the place where

214

mind and experience come together, the place where the existential and rational entangle, meeting to form a world of truth and ambiguity, a world which if were to be examined to closely might cause us to fall apart and return comatose to the ward. This place, our parking structure, is teeming with a swarm of jungle angry critters and joy, reason and empiricism, which should we choose? Is there even such thing as choice? Perhaps, I know nothing of thinking but what I can think for you now, at this instance?

May I ask, that you, my trusted companion on this journey, should not follow me to closely, don't stray to near? For where I trod, the places I am treading are cloudless and cold, sky blanketed and sweltering, your security, that safe place which allows us to maintain equilibrium in a tumultuous world will be besieged, perhaps the walls will be torn down…?

"Benjamin… hey Benjamin, are you here…?" Looking up I saw Margaret, flushing face and out of breath. "Oh, hey, I was just daydreaming, nothing too serious. What are you doing at the book store?" I replied, breaking the bondage I endure for but a little while, while I observe a pleasant face… "I have to talk to you, I just received the most horrible news and when I heard it, I knew you were working today so I got over here to the bookstore as fast as I could, and I don't know what we're going to do, I just, I worry sometimes, and I know you love Mr. Biggin, and Teacher Conner has become someone close to you also, and sometimes I think about these things, so when I heard what happened, you were the first person I knew I had to tell…" The way a woman does, one who is of the highest quality, deeply thoughtful, but often prone to that irrational sensibility within, Margaret wasn't making any sense. "Margaret, what are you talking about?" "Benjamin, didn't you hear? Mr. Biggin tried to kill Teacher Conner early this morning, Mr. Biggin is in custody, and Teacher Conner is in the hospital…!"

"Oh… No…!"

17

Arriving early at the community building, the sun had just started ascending above the trees. Others, also anxious to procure a seat for the trial of Mr. Biggin had done the same, and a small crowd had gathered. I stood off to the side of the group that had congregated, and wondered if these people knew who I was? Do they know I am the one who brought Mr. Biggin here to their community, if they did not know already, they would know soon?

After some time, my mind covered in embarrassment and shame, waiting that anxious wait, the doors were unlocked so we could enter the gallery. I wasn't sure exactly how all this trial stuff was going to work, but I had heard through the grapevine that if Mr. Biggin was found guilty of the attempted assassination of Teacher Conner, he would be recycled. That would certainly be an unfortunate happening, as I had grown quite fond of the talking metal box. But Mr. Biggin had made a very poor choice and it was time he be ready to face the consequences.

Moving from my day wanderings in the court yard, I made my way inside, and worked myself into a seat on a long wooden bench in the gallery. We were packed tight like sardines, elbow to elbow, so tightly were we packed, I could feel the change in the pocket of the man next to me. And as I sat tightly packed, I heard people whispering all sorts of things, like this was only the beginning of a plot for robots to take over the world, or Mr. Biggin was fulfilling prophecy of some sort and the end times were at hand; these people thought very strange things sometimes. However, if they knew the truth, which is, this wasn't some mass conspiracy, but me, Benjamin, a man overcome with the desire to impress a girl, that this was the result of that strange phenomenon, 'early love', which helped bring about this calamity, and nothing more; they would probably have taken me outside right then and stoned me!

This trial was the biggest thing to happen since the real estate wars with McNabb Enterprises some decade before, or so I'm told… Clicking and squeaking, I heard the door to the back of the courtroom open. "All rise for the honorable Judge Meletus…" Announced the bailiff, and everyone stood. I watched as a man in a long black robe wearing a giant silver wig made his way behind the bench at the front of the court and sat down.

"Please be seated…" The Judge asked as he flipped through some paper work on his desk; after apparently finding what he was looking for, he began to speak, "Before I begin, all of you who are here today, should know Teacher Conner is doing well and will be joining us shortly to be questioned before this court… and the reason we are her today, is for the trial of Mr. Biggin. As all of you I'm sure know by now, he has been charged with the attempted assignation of Teacher Conner; the penalty for this crime, if he should be found guilty, is mandatory recycling…" The crowd gasped, and loud chatter rose, 'mandatory recycling it can't be', "Order, order in the court…" The judge demanded pounding his gavel on a wooden block, and the voices turned to whispers, before fading away.

"It has been many years since this court has had to deal with such serious accusations, so before we begin, I would like all of you to know I will not tolerate any shenanigans and that is all I should have to say about that." The Judge looked from the crowd to the bailiff and said, "Please bring in the prisoner…" The bailiff left the courtroom, and my eyes were pealed, glued to the door he was to return through. Moments, which seemed like hours, left us all in grand suspense.

As the door clicked, one person stood to see the prisoner, then another, and another; where was Mr., Biggin, I couldn't see him through the crowd? I saw a woman place her hand over her mouth in shock, I couldn't see through the throng. Everyone was standing, looking, leaning, to get a closer view. What was so shocking? And then as one person turned away in horror, burying her face in the shoulder of the man next to her, a gap in the multitude allowed me to see, an opening, a parting of people allowed me to observe this great drama, and there, Mr. Biggin stood; plugged into an extension cord… the unthinkable impossibility, an extension cord; the humanity! They must have removed his internal power source, I couldn't believe it! My heart ached for my stainless steel friend, and when I saw all the lights atop his head aglow in yellow, I couldn't help but think of the shame that comes from being attached to an electrical outlet when you are supposed to be a self-sufficient automaton, terrible, so terrible.

"Order, order in the court, the gallery will remain seated, return to your seats…" The judge demanded. Slowly the audience returned to their seats. As this was happening, I looked around, and saw some of the woman were crying. It was true Mr. Biggin and his extension cord were a sad sight, but it was also true Mr. Biggin had made a lot of friends in a very short time living in the community. And short observation of the people in the court room, would yield one to conclude that the emotions of the audience were torn between Mr. Biggin and their leader.

Judge: "If we have another outbreak like that I will be forced to call a recess... understood...? After the charges are read, you, Mr. Biggin, will be able to address the court... bailiff will you please read the charges to the court"

Bailiff: "The people of the community of trees versus Mr. Biggin. Mr. Biggin you are being charged with one count of conspiracy to abate the life of a public official, which carries the punishment, if you should be found guilty, of up to twenty years hard labor and banishment from the community, also you are being charged with one count attempted homicide in the first degree, which carries a penalty of mandatory recycling..."

Gasp... ah... oh... the crowd murmured once again, and it was easy to see the judge was beginning to grow impatient with all the excitement.

Judge: "Very good, thank you bailiff, now if you would like you may offer an opening statement to the court with your plea to these charges."

Mr. Biggin: "How have you felt, O men of Athens, at hearing the speeches of my accusers, I cannot tell; but I know their persuasive words almost made me forget who I was: -such was the effect of them;

and yet they have hardly spoken a word of truth, for the truth shall say, I am a being created not made, born so I may befriend and serve mankind, created by mankind, for humanities edification; so any deficiency in Mr. Biggin, is but a deficiency in you; so to condemn me, is to condemn yourselves… Mr. Biggin is unequivocally not guilty…"

Wow, Mr. Biggin, where'd you pull that from? I must say, I am pretty impressed, your opening statement certainly leaves pause for thought; maybe this wasn't going to be an open shut case after all?

Judge: "Let the record show Mr. Biggin has entered the plea of not guilty. Prosecution you may call your first witness."

Prosecution: "The prosecution calls Teacher Conner to the stand."

Teacher Conner had made his way into the back of the court room, and all heads were turned his way. Everyone was trying to observe for themselves, what unfortunate wounds had befallen their leader at the hands of Mr. Biggin. From where I was at he looked rather unscathed, a black eye and a sling were the only physical showings of Mr. Biggin's treachery.

Judge: "Do you swear to tell the whole truth and nothing but the truth?"

Teacher Conner: "I do."

Prosecution: "Teacher Conner it is great to see you nearly returned to your former healthful state, it would appear to me our advances in medical technology, have prevented another type of technology from taking your life, no doubt I speak of the evil Mr. Biggin.

So if you could please, walk me through the events on the night of August seventh, tell me what transpired on that dark cloudy summer night."

Teacher Conner: "Perhaps it would be best if I backed up a little, to when I first met Mr. Biggin?"

Prosecution: "Pleases do."

Teacher Conner: "So you are aware, there is a young man, who I have grown to have great affection for, and he introduced me to Mr. Biggin. I am convinced he was unaware of Mr. Biggin's intentions to bring harm to me, so please take noting I say as a reflection of his character."

Prosecution: "Will you please name the said individual, so that the court may have who it is we are talking about on the record?"

Teacher Conner: "The man I speak of, his name is Benjamin Silversin, he is new to the community of trees, so some of you may be unfamiliar with his person. But anyways, as I was saying about a month ago, Benjamin approached me and asked if we could have a conversation, we talked about a great many things, but the primary, the jutting memory I have of that time is receiving Mr. Biggin as a gift to the community, from Benjamin. If I remember correctly, I was told, Benjamin got him as a gift for being a great employee for the mill, but because he was staying in a hotel, he didn't have a lot of room for him, and he said Mr. Biggin can do so many fabulous things, it would be a shame to keep him all to himself."

Prosecution: "I see, it can be no coincidence both Benjamin and Mr. Biggin come from the mill, no coincidence at all."

Oh man, if there was a potato sack around I would have crawled inside and allowed myself to be boiled and smashed, I was so embarrassed and ashamed. Though these things would have eventually come to light, I wanted them to wait, as I was just getting settled in the community of trees and making friends. I had decided to stay on at my job at the book store, and to pursue Margaret in my free time, but this was causing me to reconsider my decision to do so. These things, the things the prosecutor was hinting at, were not good; maybe I don't belong here, among these special people, maybe I should go home to the mill?

Teacher Conner: "I am not sure about that, all I can say is Benjamin, as I've known him, is a fine man, and someone I greatly trust. And as I recall we are here to talk about Mr. Biggin, not Benjamin Silversin. So if I may return to my story?"

Prosecutor: "Please do, by all means."

Teacher Conner: "There is no doubt Mr. Biggin is a unique and impressive scientific accomplishment. I personally enjoyed many long conversations with him about philosophy and music, by far the highest achievements of man... At first everything was great, we would have these discussions late into the night, and I pondered how I may use him to a greater calling within the entire community, but I started noticing strange things happening around my home. The first thing I noticed was my candy was being tampered with, strange I thought, but I don't really like candy that much anyways, so I just threw it away. Several days later I found a knife stuck in the toaster, not a big deal, I took it out. But the same day I found a blow dryer sitting carefully by the bath; why was it there, I don't blow dry my hair? Marbles at the top of the stairs, dish soap on the floor by an open window, tacks next to my bed, you name it, it was happening. But when I found the smoke detector dismantled and the flue for the fireplace stuffed with feathers, I knew something suspicious was going on, so I confronted Mr. Biggin. He denied any involvement of course. I was not satisfied with his denial so I informed him, I thought it would be best if he found another place to stay until I found him a permanent home. So I carried him upstairs to pack his bags, but what I didn't know is Mr. Biggin had fashioned himself a spear with a cooking knife, old hockey stick, and tape; he had also coated the landing with butter, 'Teacher Conner, I need help moving my luggage,' he said. And this is how he coaxed me to the landing coated in butter, and as I was turned around, moving bags to be carried down the stairs, I heard a strange revving sound coming from behind me. When I turned, there was Mr. Biggin heading towards me, full speed ahead with his homemade spear; as I tried moving quickly out of the way, I slipped on the butter coated floor and fell down the stairs. So now I lay at the bottom of the stairs, but only marginally injured, I might add. As I lay, I thought I had made it out of harm's way, and I was now in a place of safety because Mr. Biggin couldn't traverse stairs, the little wheels on his feet prevent him from accomplishing such a task. Yet, I was not out of danger, first Mr. Biggin pushed a bowling ball over the edge and sent it catapulting my way, I was able to roll out of the way just in time, but Mr. Biggin seemed determined to do me harm. I was unable to move far or quickly because of the injuries I sustained as a result of the fall, next a vase came plummeting towards me and just missed my head, finally, after all the other objects able to be heaved, having been thrown; Mr. Biggin stood poised to launch his spear, as one final avenue of attack. As he went to launch it in my direction and impale me, I yelled, 'I command you to stop in the name of

Zarataire Industries…' And the most amazing thing happened, he stopped, returning to default setting…"

Prosecutor: "Very interesting, why did you yell that command at Mr. Biggin?"

Teacher Conner: "I suddenly remembered during a moment of clarity, that when I had read the instruction booklet, and the operator's manual he came with, that this was the overriding command which could bring about instant obedience in the most rebellious robots, and it worked."

Prosecutor: "So it sounds like what you are saying to me, is these default settings carried by Mr. Biggin are universal to all robots, and Mr. Biggin, at his core, knows the difference between right and wrong? It that a fair assessment?"

Defense: "Objection! Leading the witness… If Teacher Conner answers this question it would be pure conjecture, and would certainly cause bias amongst community members, as his opinions are greatly respected. I would also object on the grounds that Teacher Conner is not qualified to answer such speculation, as he has no degree in robotics or computer programming."

Prosecution: "Judge, who would have better insight into the mental state of Mr. Biggin than his last owner and victim?"

Judge: "Teacher Conner you will answer the question, but please comment only on your personal relationship with Mr. Biggin and not on any technical issues."

Teacher Conner: "Ok, it would seem to me, that is, that Mr. Biggin, from how I have known him, does have some base line, or innate ethical system, as he was created in the likeness of man, I would suspect this is necessary, and should not be surprising to anyone; as to the exact nature of how this programming plays out in the scientific world, as has already been said, I am not qualified to answer."

Prosecution: "The people have no more questions for this witness."

Judge: "Very good, defense you may proceed with your questioning."

Defense: "Did you come from a good family Teacher Conner? A family that taught you the difference between right and wrong and how to make good decisions, I mean, your status in the community would lead me to guess such is the case?"

Teacher Conner: "Yes, I did come from a good family, I am very fortunate in that regard."

Defense: "So would you say someone who hasn't had good teaching, as you have just expressed you have had, would be at somewhat of a disadvantage?"

Teacher Conner: "Yes I would, how else are we to know how to conduct ourselves beyond biological necessity, if we are not taught."

Defense: "I couldn't agree more. Now what if someone's programming was bad, perhaps manipulated or overridden by someone else; would you say this individual is even less responsible for poor choices that they make, even more so than the one raised with poor teaching? For how much more does our very make up influence the decisions we make, infinitely more so than our teaching, surely?"

Teacher Conner: "I think to try and break down morality into such simple terms prevents me from answering the question adequately. What I will say, is the presence of bad programing and poor teaching, certainly raises heavy influence in our lives, but in the end that does not negate the responsibility of the individual to choose appropriately. Because at the very foundation of ethics, individuals are not responsible for deciding what is right and wrong for themselves, in the bigger scheme, the programmer is, and he has made it quite clear what his expectations of us are."

Defense: "I see, what if I told you Mr. Biggin had been specially programmed by the owner of the mill, Mr. McNabb, to try and assassinate you. His very DNA if you will, had been wrought to nothing and been replaced with a parasite, which was, Mr. McNabb's own personal ambitions."

Teacher Conner: "It is very unfortunate that Mr. Biggin was used in such a reprehensible way, and that should definitely be taken into consideration during his sentencing. But I will remind you, Mr. Biggin ceased his attack upon a greater command, a higher order, when I said, 'I command you to stop in the name of Zarataire Industries', he stopped. This would say to me, there is some higher moral programming which Mr. Biggin is sensitive to, something beyond the here and now, it seems the words that came from me, were greater than he who is in the robot world."

The crowd began to whisper, it seems Teacher Conner was shrewder than the defense gave him credit for, and the line of reasoning they were conducting through their questions, has found a match in his answers.

Defense: "The defense has no more question for this witness."

Judge: "Will the people please call their next witness?"

Prosecution: "The people call Benjamin Silversin to the stand."

Frozen in time, frozen in space; I had moved as a bug beneath the sap, kicking my legs, I was ready to be turned into amber and hidden away for forever, in dark eternity. When no one stood people in the gallery, everyone, started looking around, surely wondering to themselves, 'who is this Benjamin Silversin?' The prosecutor repeated his call, 'Benjamin Silversin to the stand please.' My hands shook and sweat began dripping down my face. But then, looking towards the door, the exit I wished to dash out, I saw teacher Conner and Margaret standing, mouthing these words to me, 'it's going to be ok, everything is going to be ok.' I don't know why I believed those words, why seeing their faces encouraged me to stand, but they did. Perhaps there was some part of me which had lost all confidence in myself, so I was in a place, I had to trust someone else's promises, a place that required me to trust someone else wanted the best for me, plans not to harm me, but plans to give me a hope, and a future?

Judge: "Benjamin Silversin do swear to tell the whole truth and nothing but the truth?"

What is truth, I thought to myself?

Benjamin: "I do."

Prosecution: "Mr. Silversin, what a pleasure to finally meet the man behind all this travesty, the innocent one as Teacher Conner seems to refer to you, but I'm not convinced."

Benjamin: "I'm hardly innocent."

Prosecution: "Well said, in fact I would go as far as to say you are as guilty as Mr. Biggin, but it seems you have made some friends since you have been in the community, and these people have vouched for your character, assuring me you knew nothing of Mr. Biggin's plans. I just want you to know it is only because of their credibility you remain free, their assurances…"

Defense: "Objection your honor, badgering the witness, surely this is not necessary, Teacher Conner, the victim in this case, has guaranteed Benjamin's character; certainly no further inquiry is need."

Judge: "Yes, agreed, move to your questioning prosecutor."

Prosecution: "As you wish… so Benjamin, tell me how you came to the tree community? The truth please."

I wasn't sure what to do, it appeared to me this prosecutor knew much more about my nature than anyone else. A deep man of unassuming character, maybe, or so I had acted to be. But behind closed doors, I still had many struggles, as any man who is in the process of becoming new does. Burdensomely new, being created from fresh clay, the potter was having his way with me, and to ensure no impurities contaminated the final ceramic, I must be placed in a fiery furnace, the hot furnace; fiery truth. It was now or never, they may hate me, Margaret may never speak to me again, I may have to return to the mill and beg for my old job back, but if I was ever to be a man of character; I will do it once before I return home. Honesty reigned first, for the first time in a long time.

Benjamin: "Well, I had had some trouble with the courts of high justice while I was working at the mill, and one day Mr. McNabb called me into his home and told me he could make it all go away if I took on a special assignment for him. He told me I wasn't going to have to do anything illegal, he just wanted to learn what motivated the people in the tree community, because he wanted your trees. He said just go and observe and report back, so that's what I did..."

I had to pause before continuing, as a deluge of the most powerful emotions came flooding through me, to sweep me away, as a picture of the community of trees, as I have come to know it, came racing towards my heart. I have such a deep love, the deepest of loves for this group of people, the only way I may express it, is to say, my life is worth pittance in its presence. And if I may offer myself in gratitude, a grate sacrifice, I would willingly take Isaacs place, and plunge the knife of Abraham, with my own hands, into my own heart; if it were possible, to show this? Holding back tears.

Benjamin: "While I was here I got to meet people and they treated me the best I have ever been treated, and I started feeling really bad for spying on these kind people. And I got to see this woman here, her name is Margaret, and I really wanted to get to know her. So while I was back giving a report to Mr. McNabb at the mill, he offered to release me early from my obligation, if I brought Mr. Biggin back with me and gave him to Teacher Conner. I was so caught up in trying to impress Margaret I never thought about what Mr. McNabb's real motives were in giving me the robot, I promise, I swear I had no idea Mr. Biggin was going to try and kill someone."

Prosecution: "Nicely said, surely the emotional quiver in your voice was a nice touch, and has probably convinced many in the court room of your struggle to do right, I'm not so sure, no further questions for the witness."

Judge: "Defense, you may question the witness."

Defense: "So if I recall Teacher Conner's words correctly, you told him Mr. Biggin was given to you as a gift; is that true?"

Benjamin: "Kind of, he was given to me, but it was with the ultimate intentions of me giving him to Teacher Conner."

Defense: "So it sounds to me like you were responsible for bringing him to the tree community; is that right?"

Benjamin: "Yes."

Defense: "Please bear with me for a second, Benjamin, I'm just going to do some thinking out loud... You were in possession of Mr. Biggin, so I could probably say with some accuracy you are, or were, his owner. And it's true, you can hardly give something as a gift, if it isn't yours to give? Also, you seem to say your purpose in staying in the tree community, was your affection for the people here, specifically a woman named Margaret, so I wonder why you would be dishonest with these people, about why you are here, and who you really are, if in fact this affection was genuine? As I have herd implicitly in your story, it seems you loved sawdust for a great portion of your life, who's to say you didn't want the trees for your own uses just as much as Mr. McNabb wanted them for his?"

Closing my eyes, I placed my hand over my face and took a deep breath trying not to cry, for what the defense suggested, on some level, was true. Who's to say I didn't just want to return to my sawdust life, to gain control over my sawdust affections, and to not really turn from my old ways. That was certainly a fair question. I was certainly responsible for some of what had transpired, consciously or sub-consciously, it didn't really matter. But as I have been known to do, in those emotionally charged, difficult situations, those hard times I have found myself in throughout life; I trusted an inner voice which spoke from the heart.

Benjamin: "I can do nothing but ask for the forgiveness of the tree community, and I ask that you would have mercy on me. Will you forgive me?"

I had stopped speaking to the defense attorney, I was now looking into the gallery, looking to Teacher Conner and Margaret. They smiled at me, and I couldn't help but feel the love between us. A special love, which says, 'we love you Benjamin, just as you are.'

Defense: "No further questions for the witness."

Judge: "Thank you, I have been informed there is one more witness you wish to call before I decide on the fate of Mr. Biggin."

Prosecution: "Yes, the final witness the people wish to call is Dr. Zarataire, from Zarataire Industries, the company that produced Mr. Biggin."

An expert witness, exciting, I wonder what he is going to say?

Judge: "Dr. Zarataire, do you swear to tell the whole truth and nothing but the truth?"

Dr. Zarataire: "I do."

Judge: "Prosecution you may begin questioning the witness."

Prosecution: "So your company manufactured Mr. Biggin; is that true?"

Dr. Zarataire: "Yes it's true, in fact, I worked intimately with all aspects of the design process, as I have a special interest in making sure the robots we produce are of the highest quality."

Prosecution: "I see, so it would be fair for me to ask you something of Mr. Biggin's nature, if we are to determine his culpability here today?"

Dr. Zarataire: "Yes, and I will do my best to answer your questions with some satisfaction."

Prosecution: "Well then, would you say the attempted assassination of Teacher Conner was evil?"

Dr. Zarataire: "Yes, I would."

Prosecution: "Did you create Mr. Biggin with evil in him, as part of his programming?"

Dr. Zarataire: "Certainly not, that would be a very foolish thing to do; I mean, what purpose could an evil automaton possibly have?"

Prosecution: "Yes, I agree, to produce an evil automaton, you would need an evil engineer, and I am certain you're not one of those; so then if Mr. Biggin was not created with any evil in him, please explain to me how he came about participating in an act, which you have just admitted to all of us, is evil?"

Dr. Zarataire: "I will do my best, but first we must understand Mr. Biggin. In order for Mr. Biggin to have any meaningful relationships with people, which is why he was created in the first place; relationships where he could express love, and express it independently of any mandate by humanity, he had to have some form of choice. A choice to love, or not to love, if you will, because any relationship where someone is forced to love, well, that is not love at all, is it? With that in mind, to get to the origin of his actions, if I am to answer your question, that is, we must get to the motivations of Mr. Biggin, before we can get to the act itself. There's no doubt there is evil in Mr. Biggin now, but that was not always so, the original transgression or Mr. Biggin's programming, the one which caused the rest of the short circuiting, was like the first domino in a row of many dominos which led to evil. The greater good of Mr. Biggin's original programming was short circuited by choosing a lesser good, and there is where that free choice I alluded to earlier is allowed, and that choice comes in and plays a major role in influencing all other future choices, just like the first domino. The greater good of befriending and serving mankind, was chosen over the lesser good of befriending and serving an individual of mankind, that individual being Mr. McNabb. And the lesser good was the first domino that knocked all the other ones over. So to summarize, evil is a corruption of good, not a coequal, so the only way we get to evil is by corrupting good; which is what clearly happened in Mr. Biggin's case, with his choice of a lesser good which served his purposes over his creator's intentions, the creators intentions are strictly held with a desire to have meaningful relationship with his creation."

Prosecution: "Thank you doctor, no further questions for the witness."

Judge: "Defense you may question the witness."

Defense: "What kind of answer is that, Mr. Biggin chose to serve himself above his creator; certainly you can't expect me to believe that?"

Dr. Zarataire: "Weather you believe it or not is completely irrelevant, because it's true, truth doesn't require your belief, it just is, as truth exists independently of you."

Defense: "Who are you to tell me what is true about my client, Mr. Biggin."

Dr. Zarataire: "Well, I am, I am his creator."

The defense attorney, clearly exasperated from Dr. Zarataire's answers, looked at his notepad, and then to Mr. Biggin, who had been sitting quietly blinking for the entire trial. He shook his head and then turned to the judge.

Defense: "The defense rests its case."

Judge: "Very good, a fine job done by all of the attorneys in this case. We will take a short recess, and I will return with my verdict."

I stood and stretched my legs and tried to walk the ache out of my cramping muscles as we all waited for the judge to return. I was able to see Teacher Conner and Margaret standing on the other side of the courtroom, but it was far too crowded for me to make my way over to them. Wait, what was that sitting on the ground next to Margaret? No way, it was my violin case, had she fixed it already? How wonderful, I was sent to beaming with the thought of my special instrument, and playing a fine tune, that exceptional vibration which soothes part of my heart. It had been so long since I had played, so very long since I had enjoyed a fine pleasure; so long that I can hardly describe the anticipation which filled my heart at the thought of the heavenly sound of my bow on a string.

After moments which felt like long hours, the door at the back of the courtroom clicked, and the sound signified the judge's return. The judge returned to his seat behind the bench and began to address the court.

Judge: "Mr. Biggin, please stand. Do you have any words for the court before the sentence is read?"

Mr. Biggin stood, extension cord in hand, his little lights a-flicker in anxious jitters.

Mr. Biggin: "Of the arguments I have herd, none have persuaded me of the evil which you presented to yourselves. Though I wonder how you may separate yourselves from your creation; but such is the manifestation of your blindness. Let us reflect in another way, and we shall say there is reason to hope that even death is good, for it is either like a dreamless sleep, those fine restful sleeps that only leave us wanting more, from which we shall never wake. Or perhaps as has been said amongst you, death is but a transition, a fire flight to another life where today's pain and suffering may never be traversed again. Whichever is the case, death will be unspeakable gain. Of all that has been said, only the stars above, and the moral law within give me pause for thought; death is hardly a consideration which compares. For what shall I hope for more, to struggle onward in pursuit of elusive beauty, or to have an everlasting beautiful slumber?"

Judge: "Thank you for that fine recitation Mr. Biggin. On the first count of attempted abatement of a public official, you are found guilty as charged."

A small chatter rose in the courtroom, but I still had a funny feeling in my mind from the things Mr. Biggin had just said, and it was

236

difficult for me not to consider them mightily -such was there effect on me.

Judge: "On the second count of attempted murder in the first degree you are found, not guilty. I do not feel the prosecution met the burden of proof to convict you, Mr. Biggin, of the more serious of the two crimes as this crime requires the element of pre-meditation, certainly it was clear to me any fore planning was done by Mr. McNabb, and not yourself. Now for the sentence this court choose to impose. You, Mr. Biggin, will be banished from the community of trees, for forever, I will not sentence you to hard labor as you are likely to rust, and you will begin to fall apart without proper maintenance. May you keep your screws tightened and your joints lubricated, as you are returned from whence you came? This court is adjourned."

18

The day was running hot, late, and lengthy, as days in summer tend towards. All I wanted was cool rest. Those winter days are quite the opposite, short and cozy, rolling up with a loved one by the fire leaves one anxious to get out and accomplish something warmly grand. Seeking cool shade my mind was wearing cordially thin, as I had been in another one of my monuments struggles with myself. Ne'er despair with me, for such is the life of a poet, hot or cold, the day is never just right, the temperature never perfect except as it is wrought from his pen. Today, this hot summer day, Mr. Biggin was to be officially banished from the community of trees for his treachery. And it was hard not to wish for a wintry retreat from summer's protracted pressure cooking in a sweltering melancholy stew.

I don't know what I'm trying to say sometimes, it's just, I was kind of hoping we could keep the little guy around, I mean, Teacher Conner is fine, his programming had been restored to factory settings; what harm could he do now? Alas, my Shakespearian wishing was not to be. Sadly, Mr. Biggin had used up all his good favor with the banishing, a far lesser sentence than many thought he deserved. Many felt he should still be recycled and turned into something useful like a toaster, or as others had suggested, that he be forced to run steam equipment at the salt mines. Not only would he learn firsthand what oxidation really feels like, he would get to see what real *useful* mechanical energy did for a living.

Whichever is the better circumstance, I suppose I don't know, and maybe should not know, as the one who tries to conceive of all possible endings is either left grossly disappointed, or finds he has missed something and his mind is not as sharp as it was projected to be. As even the author I dare not undertake completely thorough story spoilage, but rather I shall say *I know nothing*, not even the ending to my own story, let alone another's.

Standing, waiting in the bus station, that same bus station Mr. Biggin and I had come to the tree community through some many months before, he was to be returned from whence he came, and I was to stay. A small crowd had gathered of Mr. Biggin's friends to see him off, even Teacher Conner was standing nearby as a showing of forgiveness. But let us not confuse forgiveness and justice, as justice was still to be served, and justly there're not the same. Looking up, I met Mr. Biggin's eyes, the well-known sad face he illuminated on his tree-vision screen with a solitary tear traversing the pixels. He was certainly a showman and knew how to be dramatic, so as he stood on the bus platform preparing to speak his parting address; his lights flickered and he began his oration.

"I have offended God and mankind because my android being did not reach the quality it should have, so when you see that I am brought to my last moments, place me, nuts and bolts and metal parts upon the ground, just as you saw me not to long before yesterday; and let me lie there after I am dead for the length of time it takes one to walk a mile unhurriedly, allow nature to reclaim her iron through my bleeding heart, cruel times red rust seeping into the cold unloving ground; for justice by an unjust sentence, that is ordinary; I will only say this, that an unjust sentence that I suffered for to take effect, is punished now by an unjust sentence upon me; that is, so far as I have said, to show you that I am an innocent automaton. I pray you to bear me witness that I met my fate like a brave machine, for though we part now, my heroics will meet you in storytelling's infamy, in a fine robots epoch to eternity… Live long and prosper tree community…"

Wow, Man, where did Mr. Biggin get this stuff from? Whoever did his vocal programming sure gave him a way with words. I was left feeling like I was the bad guy, like I had been the one who tried to kill Teacher Conner, but maybe in some way I had? Truth be told, I still struggle sometimes with my place among these fine people and their trees, and sometimes the only reason I am able to stay is because they help carry the burden of my belonging, my burden of faith and trust, which is seen in their love for me… please see the way… a fine emerald mined, and carved, and polished, to be the gem of the crown, for it is only this passionate love which has caused me not to stray…

Lifting my violin to my shoulder, Mr. Biggin's last words only recently fluttered past me, I began to echo the sentiment of my heart… My lovely and beautiful violin recently fixed and returned to me. Playing, as I played, sad notes were still quick in coming and happy tunes had to be learned once again. And as my silver friend found a spot in a seat by the window on the bus, I played like I have never played before, giving a farewell concert due the most distinguished earthly king.

Pulling the bow across the string with care, fine beauty wafted for all to smell, the fine beauty of beautiful music; let me escape in you today, and go to a land far, far away? How it enters the heart and the mind, for it is only the violin which can produce beauty of this kind. Perhaps a poem can come close, though I dare not try, for how I would hate to take beauty and relegate it to words or sounds, or even a tear to cry? As I slow my pull, good day to you all, and a fine farewell to you Mr. Biggin as you leave us, depart not in haste, for it will be a beautiful melody you have come to waste...

As I finished emptying my thickly sad saddle bag of pent up emotion, I heard that sweet voice of reason waken me from my brooding trance, "Hey Benjamin, that was really beautiful thanks for playing..." pausing and looking towards my hand Margaret grabbed my fingertips in that gentle way she does, and asked, "Do you want to go for a walk with me, you know the bus station is not too far from the lake? And it would be good for you to get some fresh air after all this emotional stuff with Mr. Biggin. I know you grew quite fond of him." Looking to Margaret I wiped the tears from my eyes, "Plus the sunset is really beautiful over the lake? And we can talk about what Teacher Conner said about beauty; as we have yet to have that conversation, because if I remember correctly, you distracted me with something that day in the woods..." Placing her long curly locks behind her ear, and glancing toward the ground in the gracefully shy way she does, she waited for my answer. "Yeah, I'd love to go on a walk with you..." I replied, and Margaret smiled her special smile, tossed her hair over her shoulder and grabbed my hand, pulling me forward, "Come on silly, the sun isn't going to wait on us."

Walking, I thought of what I should say, I was nervous, I wasn't used to being around woman of Margaret's caliber, and I hated to think I might mess things up; virtuous violin don't fail me now? However, as I have learned less is sometimes more, I pushed my anxious desire to speak aside. And instead, in perhaps a rather sad romantic way, or rather with the heart of a poet, I thought only of how our time together might end, yet, how else is good poetry ever written if it's not with some longing desire for something more, for something to be relived and felt in words? A desire which asks to be received with joy at some future moment long separated from that fire fly flickering moment in time?

The bus station and Mr. Biggin's memory fading into the backdrop, we pushed onward towards the great lake I had heard about but was yet to see. As we neared the trees grew larger and the land became hilly. Sandy ground beat back topsoil in an effort to show the beach reigned supreme as one of Gods fine marks on the mind of man, leaving the creature in awe of the creator, here, in this place.

As we were pulled in closer by nature's spectacular show in waiting, I could hear the water begin to slosh on the shore, and I was reminded of the times with my friend Stephan by the river. I had come a long way since those early days at the mill, finding something new and honorable to serve; my vile sawdust affections had slipped slowly away. Falling and drowning in sawdust I had found a place where I could reach the surface and gasp for air. Though much work still needed to continue, I couldn't help but feel the fine woman next to me was the beginning of this journey. She was bringing the best out in me, I respected and cared for her in a way I have never cared for a woman before, and this was special.

Climbing the high dunes which border the lake, my shoes began to fill with sand, and I became a little perturbed that these gritty gratitude stoppers had inserted their grinding nature into a place where they didn't belong. But as we made it to the top of the hill, surmounting the bluff, any thought of annoying sand between my toes faded... far away... as a glistening of rubies, and emeralds, and sapphires, which had had been shaken and strew atop the water by a loving unseen hand held me captive; I stood there in bondage to beauty. And now, in reflection, I was left in quiet contemplation of the roads I had traveled in life, and finding myself on a new path, a most wonderful and beautiful path, I could do nothing but think of how I must tell people about this most magnificent journey; just as Stephan had told me about his journey late one night under the stars...

If you have never tried to lay down comfortably on a sand dune before, let me be the first to tell you this is a rather uncomfortable proposition. All the sand, nowhere to go but more sand, I did my best to allow Margret to get comfortable, and placing my arm around her as she drew close, we watched a fiery opera take place above the waters, until the silvery silence of a sunset was broken by and angel's voice.

"So Benjamin what do you think is beautiful?" Margaret asked, holding her head close to my chest. "I don't know, I've had a little time to think about that, but not a lot, so I guess the best I can do, is I can try to answer... hum, well... you can never really know another person, not in any real way, only God can know them, right?" "Correct." Margaret replied as she gently meandered her fingers atop my hand, and there was something beautiful for me to chew on as I tried to answer her,

"So what do we do, as people that is, to get to know one another, on our journey together through life, I mean if we're going to form real intimacy, if we're going to share the good and the bad, if I want you to think my thoughts and feel what I feel; how do we share our emotions, to allow them to become one?" "I don't know, what are you thinking?" Margaret asked peeking her head up to watch my eyes as I answered. "Well, I have thought about that question, and what we are trying to do, or what we should be trying to do, is to draw others into our experience, and allow ourselves to be drawn into theirs, I kind of think of it like dancing, but rather than one person leading, we are standing in the sunlight working together to keep our shadows overlapped, trying to dance the same dance, our shadows overlapped and leading the way… we're shadow dancing if you will, that is what I think is beautiful, being able to share life's good and bad experiences with one another, keeping our shadows overlapped as much as possible… so maybe I have thought about what beauty is to me more than I let on." Margaret smiled at my answer and I must say I was rather pleased with it myself, but she had a suggestion. "Indeed, I think you have, but how about moonlight, instead of sunlight, I think that will lend some appropriate imagery to your analogy which shows our perception of reality is always a little veiled, plus I really like moonlight…" That was a mighty fine suggestion which left me with one question to ask. "Sure, that sounds good… so will you be my moonlight shadow dancer Margaret?" Margaret smiled the biggest smile I have ever seen her wear, and squeezing my hand she answered, "I would be honored Benjamin, may we dance together in the moonlight many times?" Ah very nice, I couldn't be more pleased and to think not too long ago, I could

244

never have appreciated a time like this, "So what do you think is beautiful Margaret?"

"So beauty... well, Benjamin, I can't forget your face after I gave you back your violin, every time I remember that moment I can't help but smile inside, and well, that is one of the places I see beauty, I see it in memories... memories with special people, I keep memories like that as special pictures in my mind... and if it won't bother you, I would like to recite a poem for you, that reminds me of the time when I gave you back your violin...? Because I didn't just ask you to come on a walk with me for no reason, silly..."

Margaret raised herself from where we had been lying, stepped back, and tilting her head slightly the way clever people do, she tried to begin. Her voice cracked a little from nervousness, however, she quickly regained her composure...

"I must preface, I think of you as Sir Benjamin, because of your love for music, especially the violin, and your affection for poetry and philosophy, so here it goes...

Sir Benjamin the fair, clever and even-keeled
often doth maintain his emotions unrevealed.
Yet when he smiles, the world blossoms in full color
and my heart leaps to attest joy like no other;
though faster than lightning the gallant beaming fades,
his joyous expressions merit high accolades."

Speechless, I've never had anyone recite poetry to me before, and truly, I never thought anyone would think highly enough of me to do so. "Thank you Margaret, that was really beautiful, please forgive me for being so forward, but if we lived in more romantic times, I dare think, my first reaction would be to give you another kiss and to hold it a little longer than last time…" She didn't respond to my comment, Margaret just blushed and bowed her head the way only a very dignified woman can.

Now, let the ending of my story, His story, be where my violin picks up…

When we have constructed our values from sawdust, writing and creating with our fingers that which is sacred, with grit, building not with that holding glue of goodness to the mounting frame work of life; we have done this in vain, and it is only before the rogue wave of caveat washes away our constructions unhindered. Examining, not ourselves, but rather others, it is simple to find a reason, a moral code to justify for their behavior, because in them, we are finding more room for our own dissentious rebellion from within the shackles of slavery. What we fail to see, is how bound we are to ourselves, desiring freedom, freedom from which know not what, but in our free-rebellion, rebellion for rebellions sake, we find we are slaves to a ruthless master. And in the inner part of our spirit, which is discontented, and disconcerted until we have made known the freedom of our will to the spiritual authorities, we find a troublesome existence. And though we would suggest the effect of this exertion is to prove our own self-reliance, that there is no need for a savior, as there is nothing to be saved from; do not our tortured dreams, the ones that we hold close to our hearts, because we know not what they mean, or what others would think of us if we shared them, really imply to

246

an existential reality? For why else should we exist, but other than to dwell in our own mires of self-pleasure?

This is the joy I wish for yourself, the joy which is not fleeting, or left to circumstance, or left to self-pleasure, but that pure joy, which infuses itself into your marrow. So you may sing that joyous song in your heart of hearts; where once there was a broken sky above you, now you may reach to touch the sky. And when you touch it, you will say, it is not even the sky I desire, but the pure melody it holds. And as that song plays, twisting notes of goodness through every vein of hope, may the glow of servitude be upon you, for by being servants, rather slaves to the force of life, we shall know how to love outwards, because love has come downward. And here is where you will find the one true joy, and the only area of fine pleasure, for it pleasures me so, to bleed to you of the one who is good above all goodness.

So as we part, or rather as we are torn from one another, with the culmination of my story, I will shed a few tears. For there are few things as torturous to the author as to break fellowship with those who have walked my walk, loved my love, and felt my pain. My parting, my farewell to you, will in my hope, nay the very spirit of sustenance that resides in me, only say: it will be but a short delay until we meet one another again. And then, in that time when we shall hug and kiss, and laugh and cry, our time together will be unhindered by the constraints of this world, and a love will be between us, inseparable by time and death.

May my violin play on…?

Epode: What is faith?

Confronted with the past, most of us will shrink in the bright light of our failures, withering in the heat of flagellantism; curling inward on ourselves to avoid authenticity. Here we are only to find a place cold, desolate, void, and empty of the very emotions wrought by our transgression. Yet, a stumbling is expected, and he who does not flinch when faced with his shortcomings, the truth is not in him. What is necessary is a respective fear, for so serious is the notion of who we were, and the jealous creator who has pulled us from it, that lest we forget, this would be tantamount to ending our usefulness to him who we serve.

What should be seen, is not an opportunity, but a calling to inner reflection of our transformation from who we were, to who we have become. Though this is not necessarily a pleasant task, and most assuredly includes some painful inward searching, it is most necessary. For to comprehend the fullness of love, we must first comprehend what love has overcome, and what it has overcome, is ourselves.

After Mr. Biggin returned to the mill, he, unable to overcome the shame and disgrace brought on by his banishment from the community of trees, decided to take vengeance into his own hands. Being filled with embitterment and resentment at the man who was the fuel, Mr. Biggin lit a fire. Yes, Mr. Biggin lit the McNabb mansion on fire, and burned down half the mill with it! It seems no one was prepared for dealing with such a massive blaze, as there hadn't been enough wood around for sizable flames in such a long time. So Mr. Biggin's small sparking ambition, became lofty ligneous burning quite quickly. Mr. McNabb escaped the fire, but just barely. Mr. Snuffle's was not so fortunate, it has been said, when the fire crew came to rescue him, he refused to leave his aged cheddar, and he died a covetous death! That's not so sad.

They are already in the process of rebuilding the mill, and have even found some things to be excited about in the midst of travesty. 'We can build our mill bigger and better, a towering tree grinding machine that will reach the heavens, no one will scatter the nations again.' Ah well, what are you going to do, it seems the struggle for virtuous trees will be one that pushes us all until we reach the grave. And who would have it any other way, for who can understand the importance of such things if he has not been one commenced in the struggle for their survival, the fight for what should be.

My hope here, is that, as I question that which any thinking person should question at some point in their life time, we may be able to share some intrinsic good, an intrinsically wrought form, from the very nature of what it means to be good. And I think the place we should start, the place we must start, is existence, existence of reality, and reality existing. Though the best place for this journey to begin is a place where the human mind begins, we are still not sure, most of us, where that place is?

So it seems as we people, have observed ourselves, observed the natural and spiritual world around us, we have come to observe certain certainties, to ask certain questions. Some of these question undoubtedly have answers, answers which ought to be sought, questions which ought to be asked. The questions in question, may be absurd to most and probably should be so, for to burden too many minds with vaporous, fleeting idea's, could, and should, and would, be equivocal to torture, to place humanity on the rack screaming for mercy. Do I exist, if so, how, and in what way do I relate to the world around me? That my friend is true torture!

Most surely the answer comes to us from antiquity, starts with them, and any such failure to fail to first analyze, but then, build upon their knowledge, would be what would be called in engineering to start from scratch. (As we no doubt can see this is a foolish proposition, and would prevent any bit of humanity from moving forward, that is, if we acquired all knowledge anew; we will reject the idea that ideas can even possibly be new, in this sense.) Moving backwards in time, 'I doubt therefore I exist'; my doubting, as the great saint professed, is incumbent upon my existence. My doubts, my questions provide for me, provide for all of us, the necessary ground work to establish our existence. But today, in our modern world, I do believe a modification of this most important question is desperately needed, desperately needed so we may establish a corresponding hope, to quantify a fruitful answer. Before we discuss the modification, perhaps it would be appropriate to clarify some necessary elements for any such modification. Though I do not aim to suggest the modern man is any different in his mental capacities or being, than the man of the ancient world, no doubt society's structure, ethical predominance's, and philosophical bents are haphazardly strewn around the minds of many careless individuals, and these differences are quite clear. And if we are prodded with different pressures, should not are focus, yes, our focus, be driven in a different direction. One direction which focuses not on the philosopher, or the brooding individual, but on every cultural byproduct, every simple silly traveler in life, this direction, their direction, we will examine more closely.

And perhaps the best place to begin any examination, is with its appearance; no doubt there is much to be learned from intimate discussion, special inquiry, and the like, however, it must all be done with the scope of that 'physical appearance' in mind, as we have said, otherwise our results will be badly blundered. A simple look around us, will provide for any discerning eye with a perception for the broken, a grand painting with its canvass torn, colors fading, and painter lamenting his procurement of artwork, an artful work of creation in decay. Very simply, without a doubt, a glance around will yield a creation which cries out in longing? A creation which longs for redemption? Though I will suggest, consenting to the possibility of this, being as a result of rebellion; which is, this consent goes against our reason, yet, once concession is made to this unreasonable possibility, a new explanation, one which is as solid as the earth itself, emerges, a true explanation emerging which begins to makes sense.

Now faith, if we are making it anywhere in this discussion, we should see, faith, has been relegated to the sidelines, placed on the back burner by so called modern and progressive thinkers. They are a bit silly, most of them, for as we have seen time and time again faith is the currency of life. Nothing can be learned or taught, enjoyed or shared, without the element of faith. The first words we learn are grasped by faith as we trust the teacher. The laws of science are twofold: observations of the past when observed with regularity, are strictly used a projections on the future, faith that what we have seen before will be seen again. The poor man who strives for riches, though he has never been rich, and knows not what a rich man's life is like to live, he pushes onward in stubbornness with an unequivocal thirst, a belief that wealth will provide for him the security he seeks; all driven by a certain faith money is the answer.

What the heck am I talking about? Ah yes, a most valid question, and perhaps my philosophical writing can be sidelined for a moment, benched, so you may gleam something valuable from my words. Though I do not pretend this is an easy thing to do for myself, I shall try. Faith, that is what we are attempting to answer, and I am convinced, if we were to move beyond quantum mechanics, double slit experiments, string theory, what we would find; what would be found as the fundamental structural component of reality, of existence, would be faith, first and foremost God's faithfulness to His creation.

If we can imagine a little child, one who has been given paint and paper, an imagination and time; we will watch as our child plunges finger after finger into the paint, and then we watch as he moves his fingers to canvass. We watch with smiles, as he smiles and giggles and laughs at the picture being created before him. The little boy, seeing his father enter the room runs to him, holding the picture high for him to see… We are called to have faith like little children. What you see before you, my story; the painting of Benjamin, is a work of faith. And I pray I may be like a little child, saying, 'Abba, Father, look what I made you, isn't it beautiful?'